DEATH BY VIOLIN

ALSO BY J.T. LEDBETTER

POETRY
Plum Creek Odyssey
Gethsemani Poems
Voyages
Voices and Echoes
Concordia
Blue Galaxy Iris (with E. John Solem)
Underlying Premises
Old and Lost Rivers

NONFICTION
Mark Van Doren

DEATH BY VIOLIN

STORIES BY

J.T. LEDBETTER

STEPHEN F. AUSTIN STATE UNIVERSITY PRESS
NACOGDOCHES ★ TEXAS

This is a work of fiction. All characters, organizations, and events portrayed in these stories are either products of the author's imagination or used fictitiously.

Death by Violin. Copyright © 2014

All rights reserved. Printed in the United States of America. No part of this book may be used or reproduced in any manner whatsoever without written permission except in the case of brief quotations embodied in critical articles or reviews. For information, address:

Stephen F. Austin State University Press PO Box
13007 SFA Station Nacogdoches, Texas 75962

Design by: Laura Davis
Copy Editor: Brittany O'Sullivan
Author Photo: Brian Stethem

ISBN: 978-1-936205-99-8

First Edition: September 2012

ACKNOWLEDGEMENTS

BATEAU
"Roots"

BITTER OLEANDER
"Dreamer"

HAWAI ' I REVIEW
"The Swan"

HELIX
"The Mysterious and Probably Inevitable
Rise of Verias Toggs III,"

KNOCK
"Fesque of Willoughby"
"Bob From Accounting"

LAKE EFFECT
"Apes"
"Under the Chicago River"

READ THIS
"On the Job"

ROSEBUD
"The Dreams of Claire Harding"
"Black Walnuts"

STEAM TICKET
"Zoo Story"

for Dolores,
whose heart and words are true

CONTENTS

"In the life of each of us, I said to myself, there is a place remote and islanded, and given to endless regret or secret happiness; we are each the uncompanied hermit and recluse of an hour or a day; we understand our fellows of the cell to whatever age of history they may belong."

Sarah Orne Jewett, *The Country of the Pointed Firs*

He watched her sitting quietly in a canvas chair, half in shadow, studying the Istrian Marble of the Palazzo Ducale. Pigeons fell like confetti into the piazza. He waited for a chair so he could watch her swan-like movements: her long graceful neck, her arms, white, like the Marble of the Palazzo. That night his wife asked him why he sat so long in front of that old building. "It's peeling." But he could not tell her about the beautiful young woman studying the delicate shadings in the marble, so he listened as she talked about the dirty water eroding the lower floors of buildings, letting his mind wander to the cafe where he sat long with the old men drinking coffee under the green awning, lulled by water lapping against the stones.

If she pressed him, he might say, I'm in love with a young woman studying the Marble. He knew it was dangerous and foolish to fall in love with a girl less than half his age, a lovely, thin quiet girl reading from a pamphlet she held on her lap, adjusting the sun glasses on her olive face. She would laugh at him, and he would have to walk away, slowly, and tell the Gondolier to steer for some place quiet, a place he loved as a young man when he watched a girl studying the Istrian Marbles, a girl with long arms and tapering fingers, who looked at him and took his hand and went with him and became the joy of his life for many years before she died, leaving him long days poling his gondola through the canals, and longer nights, dreaming of her framed by the setting sun, lifting her skirt as she stepped into the gondola as if she were stepping into a life neither of them had imagined, yet understood and accepted as if it were ordained. He might have said all this. He could have.

He adjusted the shutters so he could watch the little waves lap against the steps of their apartment. A light rain was falling. A man carrying a loaf of bread under his arm tucked it under his coat. "They really should fix these buildings," she said. "It's all so old." He watched the man stop to pull up the collar of his coat and pass on. There were several arched stone bridges as far as he could see from his window. The man crossed over one and disappeared. The water was flat and dark. The tide must be out, he thought.

"I want to go home," she said. "We know who we are there."

"Yes, we know who we are there."

He looked at her reflection in the window, her face segmented from the blinds. Across the canal a woman opened her window and threw something into the canal, saying something to someone inside. A man laughed, and she shut the window as the rain came harder, pocking the water, hiding the bridges.

Home proved nothing. He worked at his office and brought it home and worked some more. His wife took up micro-gardening. They slept separately and ate in shifts. Mail was open on the table when he came home. All of it. He sighed internally, drank two stiff ones, and went to bed. The moon was full, reminding him of moonlight on the canals as lovers floated in and out of the ancient city, their arms "round the grief of the ages". He wondered who said that.

"I'm going to retire after next year," he said one morning over oatmeal. The silence lasted until his second cup of tea, then: "What?"

"I said I'm going to retire after next year." She ran water in the sink and swiped at something.

"Then what will you do? What will we do? Have you thought of that, or are you still dreaming of bumming around Venice and drinking that wretched coffee with other men on the dole? Have you forgotten what things matter?"

He knew she did not expect an answer, nor did he have one. Nor did she know he was packed, his single one-way ticket in his coat pocket. I'm a coward for not telling her the truth, he thought, but it's the best way. She has her mini-gardening and her crusades against other people's happiness. It had been too long for him to dwell on it or try to talk about solutions. When he hailed a cab, he felt a sudden pain, and crumpled to the street, half-aware of people hurrying past, and a dog licking blood on his hands--sirens--a policeman with his ear to his lips--cars, angry voices--darkness sliding down the tall buildings to the street covering him...*but he was already in a chair in the Piazza San Marco, the long-legged, olive-skinned young woman at his side. He drank coffee. She, a tall drink with bubbles. Both wore sunglasses and held guidebooks. An accordion player strolled past them, pausing, moving on. When the Venetian sun became unbearable, they stepped into a gondola, hands together, the sounds of the Piazza, fading, the gondola floating beneath the Ponte dei Sospiri where women had their pictures taken, crying, and into shadows where windows opened and closed -- until he felt the gondola lift on a ripple, at which point the gondolier stepped off at one of the summer palaces and handed the pole over, waving his hat as the gondola leaned against the tide and into the current that circled the Island where he nosed the gondola away from the city until the ocean took over, sweeping them out past the Garda Buoy and through the breakers ...the long wake of moonlight narrowing to a point of light on the dark water...*

Anhydras Smollet watched her husband's pickup through the black walnut trees the moon had frozen to the window, lost it as it passed behind the ruined barn, then followed the points of red tail lights around the white-rock road to the highway. She watched the truck as he made the sharp curve at Union Grove Cemetery before dropping behind the hill to town, the frozen landscape disappearing as her breath fogged up the window where she stood wrapping and unwrapping her hands in her apron.

At first it wasn't so bad, she told her mother. But her mother wanted to know if it was ever good. Not being so bad was not what marriage was supposed to be, she told her. "Maybe if you had married Arnold Havilke when he wanted you, instead of Jurl Smollet, things would be different," she said, pouring herself a cup of tea. She glanced at her daughter. "Surely, there have been some good times, Annie."

"He never calls me Annie," she said, still pressed against the cold window. "He calls me Anhydras. I've asked him to call me Annie, but he just smirks. I think he's making fun of me by calling me Anhydras." The old dog whined on her gunnysack behind the stove, and thumped its tail when she looked at her. "I think he loves that old dog more than he does me, except he kicks it if it gets in his way. He hasn't kicked me yet. I guess that's something. I'm going to check for eggs now."

She made her way through the barnlot, lifting her slender legs in and out of the snow that blew against fences and covered the cellar where glass jars and eggs lined the shelves. She knew her mother watched her go, and would tell her one more time that no man in his right mind would expect his wife to go out in a blizzard for eggs that he could just as well get for himself. There was little she felt she could say at such times, and she feared his reaction if he came home and found her crying. One time he told her mother she was not welcome in their house anymore, and if she didn't like it she could take her useless daughter and her pretty clothes she kept in the trunk in the attic and go on back to where he found her working in the Blue Lantern Café out on the Interstate.

She walked the long row of nests, feeling for eggs, sometimes lifting one to the light from the bare bulb hanging in the center of the barn, holding it warm against her face. The hens watched her with their black- button eyes, clucking warning as she made her way from nest to nest, turning the eggs, sometimes jabbing at the back of her hand as she felt beneath the silky feathers, furiously scratching the straw and fluffing out their feathers before settling over their eggs. She often lingered in the barn, enjoying the heavy milk-breath of cows that filled the darkness. Once, after he hit the big Guernsey with the milk stool for knocking off his hat while he milked her, she leaned her head against its side as he stomped through the barn, cursing. The barn was always warm and quiet for her. A safe place.

It has not always been so bad, she thought. When he courted her at the dances in Springfield, she thought him the most handsome man she had ever seen. Her mother told her that her father, had he lived, would not have approved of him at all. "He has a meanness just under his skin that will find its way out," she told her. "I don't think he would have left you the farm if he had known who would have it now." But their first months on the farm in New Salem were wonderful and full of talk on their walks through the woods searching for mushrooms. But when the crops failed, he swore and said luck was not with him. And when the tractor broke down he smashed his axe against it and went to town where he drank with his friends. She watched from the window beneath the eaves for his truck to turn into their lane, and when she heard him bang through the screen door, unsteady on the stairs, she pretended to be asleep, but he put his hard hand at the back of her neck and pulled her to him, his breath raw against her breast. When she tried to pull away he slapped her and said she was not a real woman, and would go back down the stairs to the kitchen, and she would hear the sudden bark as he kicked at the dog. Sometimes she found him sleeping at the table, the bottle he kept in the cupboard on the floor.

But it was something she could work on, she told her mother. She would make it better. Maybe work harder around the farm and save him the trouble of working at the steel mill then coming home to work the farm at night, so she harnessed the one mule and wrapped the reins around her waist and plowed the upper garden by moonlight, and cut the tall horse weeds he hated. But when he said he was going to cut down the black walnut orchard, she cried and begged him to leave them alone, that her father had planted them, but he laughed at her and said to get used to the idea, that her father was long dead and the farm was his now anyway.

It was well into winter when he brought two men from town with crosscut saws and told them to start on the orchard. She ran through the snow and tried to make him listen to her, that she could not bear losing the trees. The two men blew on their hands and waited. But when he pulled out a bottle from beneath his heavy coat and tried to make her drink, she pushed him away and ran back to the house and watched from the kitchen as they tried to saw through a tree, laughing and falling in the snow, until they finally gave it up and got back in his truck while he pushed through the snow to the house.

"Anhydras! Anhydras! where are you. You're goin to get it now. Come on over here and see what this strap will do for that temper of yours. The boys are waitin or I'd give you a taste right now. You can just wait up if you want, or go to sleep. Don't make a damn to me. I'll get you up anyway and show you what happens to a woman who won't stand behind her husband." She listened from the landing outside their room, curling her toes away from the cold wood as he banged against the table and cursed the dog before slamming out the door.

She did go to sleep, though it was fitful and full of dreams of following her father through the black walnut orchard, showing her how to finger away the hard skin to taste the nut, filling her apron with them. And later, when the moon filled her window, she pressed herself against the cold glass and let her nightdress fall to the floor so she could feel the cold and watch the black walnut branches weave shadows against the snow.

It was well past midnight when she heard him come in. She held herself stiffly between the sheets and waited, but when he did not come up, she pulled on a thin dress and went to the landing and looked down into the blue mist swirling in the rooms from the open door. She came down the stairs slowly, stopping to hold her breath and listen to what sounded like heavy breathing from the parlor. She paused at the open door, then put her head in a little and saw them on the floor. She stood, frozen, listening to his harsh breath coming in little gasps, and then the woman turned and looked at her, but there was nothing in the black girl's eyes, no emotion, no sign of fear or wonder or anything. Just her dark eyes staring at her.

She couldn't remember what happened next, her husband screaming at her from the floor…saying he would finish here then kill her…
that she better run and hide because he would tend to her for good
and all…never was a help to him…she could watch him cut the orchard tomorrow…but she was running, skipping over the old dog who
cracked bones on the kitchen floor, feeling the cold on her bare feet
as she found the way to the orchard, moving quickly among the shadows of branches etched in awkward angles on the snow, to the place
where the woods began, picking up a single walnut before taking the
path she made as a girl when she went with her father to bring up the
great horses from the fields, their sweating backs glistening like jewels
in the winter sun, then down a steep gully into thick tangle of ruined
stumps and chokecherry vines beside a frozen ribbon of water. "I will
walk until I'm tired," she said aloud, "and then I'll sit down and rest,"
and she followed her white plume of breath in the darkness, pressing
the black walnut tightly against her, feeling the hardness through her
dress.

First Mesa Bank and Trust

When Marvin Small arrived at First Mesa Bank and Trust, he had no idea how he would rob it. He had read accounts of bank robberies, he had watched speed chases of the police after bank robbers, and he had seen footage of actual robbers in a bank, walking up to a teller. Some had sweatshirt hoods over their heads; some wore sunglasses, others in T shirts and shorts. What to wear?

He rose earlier than usual, looked at things in his closet, and for the first time he understood how his wife could look in her closet and say, "No, not this. No, that won't work." When she came home from the mall she would say, "They didn't have anything." Or, "I couldn't find anything." He always wondered what that meant. He knew there was a huge inventory of women's clothes in those stores. Now he stood in the closet and wondered what a bank robber would wear. What might make him stand out when the cameras caught him in the act.

The First Mesa Bank and Trust was busy. He picked this bank because he didn't have any money in it. As good a reason as any, he thought. Besides it was in a neighboring town, which somehow made it safer and less a crime. He did not work that out, but he thought it.

He went to the little table in the middle where blank checks and other kinds of material were kept in neat little rows. He liked neatness in a bank. He wished his children kept their rooms as neat. He finally gave up after his wife told him to leave them alone, that he would scar them for life with nagging at them. "Their rooms are their castles," she said. "Maybe if we had a bigger house you wouldn't have to notice their rooms. Maybe if we had..." he knew the litany.

He was third in line and watched the young woman behind the counter. She couldn't have been much older than his daughter, only dressed nicer. Her hair was long and came forward over one shoulder. He had not seen that since Lauren Bacall wore it that way in a Humphrey Bogart movie, and it pleased him. He noticed the brooch on her suit jacket. It looked like the U.S. flag, but a beefy man was in front of him and blocked his getting a good look at it. There were a lot of things he couldn't see clearly since he lost his job at the University. "Financial exigency" they said. He had heard the word exigency before, but thought it was something a surgeon had to remove when it became enflamed. Now nothing was the same: his wife, his children,-- even the family dog seemed distant, as if he sensed the new attitude in the house and resented it. Animals can do that, he thought. They can tell if an earthquake is coming, or someone dies. That was what he heard.

Now he was second. His hands began to perspire so he rubbed them up and down on his pants. He looked around to see if a bank guard was watching him, but there was no guard. Don't banks have guards anymore? He supposed they were the first to go in the present economy. He remembered going into the bank in his home town with his father and seeing the bank guard standing by the door. He liked to look at the big gun he carried on his hip. A bank without a guard was not a real bank, he reasoned, and he felt better.

He suddenly thought of his son who left home and how his wife blamed him for it. "If you had just encouraged him instead of always criticizing him he might have found himself." He wondered how a person found himself. What happened to the time when you grew up, left home, got a job, got married. What was finding oneself? Where could you be that you needed finding? But his wife told him that between his hounding the boy to get a job, and nagging their daughter to clean her room, he was driving her to distraction. He wondered if he should say, "Marge, if you'll pick out where you would rather be, I'll drive you there." Maybe there's a Distraction, New Mexico, he muttered to himself.

He looked at the teller and wondered if he should say, "Good morning." or just, "I'm here to rob your bank." His feet felt heavy and his tongue was thick. He brushed back his straggling hair and coughed: "Good morning, I am robbing your bank and I would like you to put your money into this paper bag." He disliked that particular bag. All the stores were using them. They were thin. He told his wife that they would break before they got home from the market, but they never did. She told him there were any number of things that he should be worried about of more importance than a paper bag. He wanted to explain to her that they were not really paper, rather some kind of synthetic thing or other, and that he could not fight the gods or City Hall or the University, but she was already behind the wheel. She drove more now since he lost his job. Why was that? "I've got to have the car, I'm working you know." She always stared at him after saying this, making sure it went in, did its job. It did, but he could not tell her the kind of job it did.

"Sir. If this is a joke, it's a bad joke. Haven't you read about people coming into a bank and just kidding around like this? The cops never think it's funny, and I don't either. So just tell me what kind of transaction you wish this morning." He looked into her hazel eyes and wondered how many people had hazel eyes. You never see them anymore. All browns and blues. What happened to hazel? When he courted his wife he was always looking into her eyes trying to determine their color. They looked black, but he knew that was wrong. But they always looked black. And this morning, when she told him she was leaving him and taking the dog, they looked big and black. There was no light coming out of them. Her red mouth twitched when she told him, and kept twitching as she went over the ways he had failed everyone.

"Sir?" He stared into her hazel eyes and sighed, "Miss, I would like the money in your drawer. Just put it into this thin ugly little bag. You can put the change in too , because it won't break. My wife says so. Said so." It occurred to him that he didn't know what color his daughter's eyes were. It would come back to him, he thought. He had heard of people not being able to see their spouse's face after they died. He couldn't see his Marge's face now. He saw her mouth twitching and her deep black holes of eyes. "Just put what you have in the bag, "he told the teller softly, "I'm holding up the line."

The next day's paper carried a picture of Marvin Small lying dead on the floor of First Mesa Bank and Trust. The article was abruptly brief, he might have said. There was nothing he would have found interesting, nothing about his former life, his former work,-- or his former love-life; nothing about how his kids stopped calling him Dad, or how the dog he raised and fed avoided him--after eating the food he put down. The plain clothes Bank Guard's name was listed, with a list of community awards he had won. It even mentioned the names of his wife and family. He liked to help people, the paper said, and had worked steadily since high school. "What kind of man who doesn't work just decides to rob a bank?" he asked, turning sideways to show the big gun on his hip.

Marge Small saw the paper and wondered what he was thinking, wearing brown pants and that awful blue shirt. She put the paper down and boarded the bus to Albuquerque and did not see the woman pick it up and look at Marvin sprawled on the cold granite floor. "Horace," she said to her husband, "there's entirely too much of this kind of thing today...not in our neighborhood, of course. Be careful, you're dripping your ice cream down the front of your vest. God will certainly deal with him now!" Horace looked at the blood around Marvin Small's head, staining the floor of First Mesa Bank and Trust, and thought of pointing out to his wife that Marvin Small had robbed *their* bank. Instead, he carefully tore the photograph out of the paper and put it in his pocket. He thought he might take out an ad in their paper: "Have you seen this man? Did you talk to him? Did he do business at your bank?" He knew he would do no such thing. But what he would do is take the man's picture out of his pocket and insert it in the scrapbook his wife kept, labeled, " People to Think About." He didn't know about God, but he was not going to leave Marvin Small on the floor of the First Mesa Bank and Trust. Not today.

I

Nebulizer Smith was a preacher. At six, his father found him standing on the top board of the hog pen, shouting to the rooting hogs. "Oh, ye swilling pigs and grunting hogs, pulling at the swollen teats of that great brood-sow, Satan!"

"That boy is strange," his father mumbled through his biscuits and gravy. "I caught him preaching to the hogs. His eyes had an odd glaze over them, and he just kept giving it to them, right and left, making up proof-texts for the little pigs still nursing. He's more from your side of the family."

"Leave him alone," his wife said, laying out the rabbits on a clean towel. "He's different. He has the calling."

" He's different all right. And he'll get called! Next time he yells at the animals instead of doing his chores he'll get called. From the same strap my father called me with."

"Leave him alone, Horace. He has something else to do with his life. I can feel it. He's special, somehow. I don't know just how. I know he's heading for something special. He has the calling." She looked out at the clothesline drooping into the mud. "I just hope he has better luck."

" I don't know what he's heading for that's so special. He won't be any help to me on the farm. But I suppose if we had another one it would turn out to be a girl." He picked up his plate and licked the gravy from it, and pushed his chair away from the table. "Why couldn't you produce normal boys? It would make my life a lot easier around here."

She watched him from the kitchen window, picking his way carefully through the cow pies to the barn where he would milk the two cows they kept on the forty acres they rented. She wondered at "producing" babies. That was not how he talked on those hot nights when they sat in the swing under the huge maples on her father's farm in Greenville. He talked nice and smelled nice. Her mother told her he wasn't the one, but she didn't listen. There was not a constant stream of boys coming down their lane, she said. Horace knows farming and wants me. Her mother wrapped and unwrapped her hands in her apron and sighed, and it wasn't long before she died and was buried beside her father in the upper garden.

She felt a pang in her heart as she thought of another child, a girl. Horace would not want a girl. He made that clear enough when they rolled against each other in the terror of their dreams at night in their room beneath the eaves, his body hot and smelling of chaff, his hard hand at the back of her head, until he fell asleep, one hairy leg thrown over her, while she held herself stiffly on top of the hot sheets and listened to the rain sluice through the rain gutters, wondering if this was all there was ever going to be.

When he was twelve he sat with the other children in the one-room farm school and watched the boy across the aisle sneak a paper from his pocket and begin copying. "I denounce you, Bub Henry, in the name of the Six-Winged Seraph of Jehovah and the Brass Bull of Zion, for a sneak and a cheat!" The teacher was used to his sudden tirades and motioned for him to sit down and be quiet. The rest of the class giggled. But Bub Henry took exception to being caught cheating and glared at Nebulizer Smith, and doubled up his fist. "Just wait!" he said. But Nebulizer Smith smiled his beatific smile, confident of the conviction in his heart and the power of his words that he, Nebulizer Smith, was called to root out evil in the world, wherever he found it.

That night his mother made the neat cut at the back of the rabbits' heads and peeled the warm skin down their pink bodies while her son sat in the shadow in the corner of the kitchen, an old handkerchief wrapped around some ice against his face.

"If you didn't take it upon yourself to speak out about things that don't concern you, Neb, you wouldn't have that black eye and bruised jaw right now, would you?" He watched her cut up the rabbits and wash them, then lay them on the clean towel to dry. He moved closer as she ran clean water, sluicing the bright blood around the white porcelain sink, a pale moon floating in the thin film of blood at the bottom.

At fifteen he resented his father's temper and the hard leather strap. In the winter he cleaned the barn and dug up the frozen cow pies, and when he forgot, he heard his father's heavy step on the stairs and pretended to sleep, knowing he stood there in the dark, his breath a blue mist in the cold air before he brought the strap down on his back and legs until the sheets were soaked with his sweat and sometimes blood while he cursed his father in the name of the Following Flame and the Sword which, he said, would cleave his father in twain until only a shadow remained that would have to walk the earth, friendless, unloved, cursed by mankind. But the more he screamed the harder the strap fell, until his mother banged on the door, crying.

At nineteen, he listened to his parents argue in the kitchen, and when he heard his mother scream, he went out on the landing, curling his toes away from the cold wood, and heard his father slamming doors and knocking over chairs. When he saw him coming up the stairs, carrying the strap, he braced himself against the banister, and when he lifted the strap over his head to strike, Nebulizer Smith hit him in the face, hard, and felt the spurt of blood on his face as his father flew backward, landing in a heap at the bottom of the stairs.

He left the southern Illinois farm that very night and found an open boxcar on the Southern Illinois Line and rode it until the sun came up over the Tennessee mountains; and when it slowed outside Memphis he jumped out into the mists rising off the Mississippi where fishing boats bobbed at anchor, and he cocked his head at the deep-belling of a channel buoy where large boats moved in the darkness past Memphis heading for the Gulf. He breathed in the heavy smell of rotting vegetation and strange growing things. I need to be heading for something, he thought.

It was not long before he found and enrolled at The True Light Rose of Sharon Seminary outside of Dog Fouling, Tennessee, where for awhile he relaxed along the banks of the Loosahatchie River, watching students stroll hand-in-hand on Sundays as the band played from the white gazebo in the city park. Nebulizer Smith watched and counted up the ways in which Satan was working in Dog Fouling, Tennessee, and took note of the liberal ways in which the Bible was explained to the eager Seminary students. But he was quiet. Biding his time.

"Mr. Smith," said the kindly New Testament professor, "would you come up here and tell us all how you feel about John 3:16. I've noticed your papers are powerful witnesses to the faith, and I think the class would benefit from your thinking on this beautiful passage." The professor sat back and listened to a bird chittering in the maple brushing against the window. "He's an odd one, Gert," he said to the librarian. "Mark my word. But he has a fire in his belly that he can't put out. It will consume him one day." He watched her climb the ladder to bring down the book he requested for his class, standing on one leg, the other bent at the knee, causing her skirt to slide up her leg.

Nebulizer Smith rose slowly from his desk, straightened his shoulders, and walked to the front of the room, followed by curious glances, smiles. One boy in the back laughed out loud. They knew Nebulizer Smith. They had heard him preaching in the woods on the far side of the river as they searched for mushrooms, or lay on blankets. Once he had come on a couple in fervent embrace, and instead of withdrawing quietly, he stepped up on a stump and said "O ye vipers of the polluted earth! O ye musky whores and damned Jack Mules that ye fornicate beside this river flowing from the mouth of the Almighty. Beware the Seven Trumpets for they wake the demons, and you will be eaten, body and soul, and there will be gnashing of teeth in hell as you approach the Satan who watches you rolling against each other, touching that which should not be touched, your mouths sucking at the font of beauty while lusting for that which is holy and cannot be defiled. For shame! For shame!"

When word got around, students avoided him at lunch and rarely spoke to him. He seemed pleased with that and carried his black Bible close to his heart, "a mighty shield against the wicked, "he said.

"Mr. Smith," the professor continued, "please tell us your understanding of this passage from St. John. Isn't it true, Mr. Smith, that if one follows this passage one will certainly be saved?"

Nebulizer Smith glared at the professor and began, slowly, quietly, bringing up proof texts from some dark well of memory and imagination, gradually growing louder, until he suddenly thundered: "All in this room have fornicated and come nigh to the evil one. Hezikiah 3:12 tells us sin is everywhere and that fornicators will burn in hell. What the professor wants me to say cannot be said because we do not deserve forgiveness for the secret sins in our hearts and minds. Why, even Professor Goetsch here has sinned! He wouldn't want you to know it, but there's a librarian in the Old Testament stacks that he talks to during his lunch hour. And when she reaches for a book from a top shelf I have seen him slide his hands under her skirt and..."

"Stop! I think you have said enough. I don't know where you get such notions, but you can't spread lies in my class. You may leave, Sir, and do not return. I will talk to the Dean, directly!"

So it came as no surprise when they found his room empty the next morning, a note on his pillow addressed to the President of the

Seminary saying he was heading for something better, something cleaner. What the rest of the note contained was never revealed, but some said an old understanding between Professor Goetsch and the Dean made explanations unnecessary, and the quiet school on the banks of the Loosahatchie continued without fire and brimstone or any kind of controversy as students walked solemnly into the chapel on graduation day to detail their private conversions, those who managed tears much loved by the faculty who sat stiffly in their pews, or dozed by open windows, safe from Hezikiah 3:12 and the condemnations therein, and glad to be rid of one who saw them and knew them.

Nebulizer Smith took it as the hand of Providence when he was picked up by an eighteen wheeler carrying a load of prime manure bound for Bakersfield, California, where, the driver told him, you could still buy a nice house if you knew which alderman or town supervisor had been paid off, allowing the good rich land to disappear into ugly houses and asphalt. "This here is the great California desert," Oliver Moon said, a match flaring against his cheek. "Smoke? No? No weaknesses, Neb? Drink, neither, I suppose. I got something in the glove box will set you free, if you've a mind. Pass it on over here." He took the brown paper bag and blew at its top, found the bottle and tipped it with his right hand.

Nebulizer Smith looked at his face staring back from cactus and black rock. "Surely this is the work of Satan!" he said. "This blight on the landscape, this devil's liquid you swallow to your damnation, this cigarette smoke you take into your lungs, the temple of the holy ghost. What you do is dirty, dry, black like the rocks in this evil place."

Oliver Moon hit the brakes, sending Nebulizer Smith hurtling into the dash. "Get your sorry ass out of my truck, you shriveled up little bastard. Now!"

Nebulizer Smith watched the last glow of taillights fade into the inky darkness of the California desert. "O Lord, of Hosts," he intoned into the night. "Strike down that serpent and bring him to the Judgment Seat. O viper, O..." He broke off and swallowed hard. A tear formed in one eye, but he choked it back, picked up his suitcase, and humming a hymn his mother sang, followed the broken white line into the night.

II

Myra Skaggs loved a poodle. The kind of dog that always wins the best of show in N.Y., but the kind of dog most people can't stand. But when she finally left Harold, she took the dog with her. Had to take it because Harold said to get the hell out and take the dog. Just get the hell out!

So good by Cedar City, hello Bakersfield, where she and the dog were seen at odd times in the city park where she watched Dewey & Sons Funeral Home play the B.P.O.E. while her dog crapped on the dichondra next to the soft drink stand. But Saturday night, when a lone man walked into the truck stop, Myra Skaggs was working behind the pass-through, watching him eat his cheeseburger, and noticed he only used one napkin. That with a cheeseburger!

When he asked for change to play the jukebox, he saw her holding up holding a bowl of steaming chili, her hair damp and straggling out beneath the white cap they told her she had to wear, or else they could get somebody else to work the counter and she could just go on back to Cedar City, Utah where they all wore white shirts and ties anyway. She wore the white cap, and worked the night shift while her dog slept on a little mat behind the kitchen and ate scraps. But when the big rigs pulled out, leaving Nebulizer Smith studying the jukebox, she knew her plans were about to change.

"Say, Missy," he said in his best Seminary voice, "where in this flea and sin-infested world are the gospel songs. All you got here is honky-tonk and other such trash, unfit for ears used to praise and harmony. This all you got?"

Myra Skaggs admired his spunk. No one ever criticized the selections on their jukebox before, and she noticed the owner watching from the corner. She looked him up and down and wondered what store he bought his clothes at. His pants were too tight and too short. But he was cute, she thought.

"Mister, these tunes is what the truckers like, and I'm sorry we ain't got any gospel songs for you to listen to. But if you whistle a bar I'll be happy to try to sing it for you. I was raised a Methodist, and until I got dropped off in the west I was always singing. Want to hear one?"

Nebulizer Smith stared at her. "Sister, are you telling me you are among the saved, the six thousand, the angelic tribe of Benjamin born to wear the silver wings bequeathed by Daniel and Bathsheba? I have walked a far piece since being dismissed from an eighteen wheeler bound for a place called Bakersfield in California, and I have a terrible thirst to hear the gospel."

"Mister, you have come to the promised land. This here is Bakersfield! You are in it, right up to your…" But his head was on the table, and his eyes were closed, so when she turned off the neon sign and locked the door she took him home with her to her rooms over the hardware store in downtown Bakersfield, a town she told him, Merle Haggard loved to sing about, a town of heat, wind and dust. A town sorely in need of salvation, he thought, and Nebulizer Smith knew he was the man for the job, and set himself up on a prominent corner where he waved his Bible at passing cars and shouted: "O, ye, vipers in your sinful automobiles, O ye theological-misfits, begotten of the Whore of Babylon, offspring of Astarte and the Seven-Teated Vestal Virgins of Thebes. Woe, I say woe to you and yours! May you hear my words and renounce filthy lucre, the strong drink and evil wads of tobacco between your cheek and gum! Woe, I say again, Woe!"

Myra Skaggs stood in the shadow of the drug store and watched for awhile until she caught the spirit and began singing, more-or-less to herself, then louder, until Nebulizer Smith turned, smiling, and said, "Sister Myra, your voice is the voice of angels gathered at the golden throne where Michael the Archangel and Athanasius the Just lead the heavenly choir. Come up here on this corner and sing your songs, and we will save this sinful town and baptize all comers in this pitiful stream you call a river, though it be mostly silt and poison oak. We will strip them of clothing and sin and show them the underside of their lives as they plunge backward into the water and open their eyes to the Truth and the Way!"

People quickly took notice of the pair, and after two unsuccessful attempts by the city council to evict them from the corner, they became part of the town-lore, something for people to honk at, tourists to take pictures of, and so they let them alone, not knowing, or caring of their secret wedding performed the night they strolled along the river, the night Myra Skaggs decided it was time to introduce some excitement into their heretofore pure relationship by suddenly throwing herself into his arms and sliding seductively down his body to the ground, where she lay in the warm grass along the river.

The look on his face was one of shock, she later recalled, then horror, followed by a strange animal-shriek as he threw himself down beside her and began muttering fragments of Bible passages, his body convulsing with sobs, until she raised his tear-streaked face and kissed it, first his eyes, then his nose, then his trembling mouth until she felt his arms tighten around her and his hips push against her.

"O ye..."he sputtered, but she stopped him with a passionate kiss that left him weak. And there in the dark of the night in Bakersfield, California, Nebulizer Smith found what he had never known before, and what until then had assumed meant bodily evil and spiritual death. And before the last stars winked out in the slow-moving water, Nebulizer Smith shouted with new-found joy: "Henceforth, and forever more we are married, joined this very night in all-consuming love, a love blessed by Jesus, Mary and Joseph and all the Saints past and present who now..." but her mouth found his again, and the last words were a groan deep in his belly as he rolled against her in the dark while a bird watched with one bright eye from a cottonwood tree, and the long grasses hissed and hissed.

III

When Brother Hoss Marucci and The Rev. Connie Wrench put up their Old Time Revival Tent, featuring the "rare and the exotic" just off Highway 99 on the outskirts of Bakersfield, they knew they would prosper when the locals flocked to the two-headed goat (seen through a thin sheet), and the Pygmy Fetus from Borneo, "pickled by its own mother," and other wonders from their researches into the "dim corners of a hostile world." The singing and praying on the street corner quickly ceased to be an attraction to the citizens who, tired of their Basque dinners of under-cooked local lamb, with large red beans, were ready for the rare and the exotic.

When he saw the flyers announcing "Prayer Meeting and Healing Service" to be conducted by one Hoss Marucci and the Rev. Connie Wrench, his throat tightened and he shook with righteous anger he had not felt since his youth. He knew instinctively the pair were bogus, con men who exhorted the crowd with descriptions of the lost but now recovered film of the love-making rituals of the Opolos, "a tribe time forgot"... "film so graphic, so strange as to inflame the loins of the viewers,"--viewers who were required to sign a form absolving Brother Marucci and Rev. Wrench from any liability should the viewing of said film cause "marital dissatisfaction or bodily mal-functions."

Nebulizer Smisth brooded over this obvious call to bestiality and blasphemy while Myra Skaggs sat braiding her hair and humming an old Methodist hymn, now and then glancing at her husband, recognizing the furrowed brow and the tight jaw. The novelty of standing beside him on a street corner, singing and yelling proof texts to passing motorists had long passed, and after the first blush of romance with this strange man, Myra Skaggs yearned for something better, and she had all but decided to go back to the truck stop where she had perfected the art of carrying two long-necks with glasses on their heads to the laughing truckers who watched in amazement as she leaned over their table and turned the bottles over into the glasses without spilling a drop, while they stuffed bills into the top of her dress. Singing on a corner was not it. She, too, saw the flyers announcing the "rare and the "exotic."

"You had best let it go, Neb, " she said. "Them two are not worth your frustrations. Maybe there's more we should talk about, you and me, about how things have been going lately. I don't see much of anything looking like money coming in. I was going to tell you anyway: I enrolled in one of them arty classes at the local community college. I'll be gone most nights for awhile." He watched her and wondered.

"I met a man there who said I looked like I could dance, and he asked me if I wanted to be in a film he was making." He stopped underlining particularly vehement passages in the Old Testament. She is changing, he thought. Satan may be working on her.

The night was warm when he stood in line with his ticket to see the strange and exotic love-rituals of the Opolo Tribe advertised on the giant poster held at each end by Flora and Fauna, the Artichoke Queens from Coalinga, who smiled and jiggled the poster while doing a waltz clog in their patent leather pumps with bright toe and heel plates. As they told their parents, this was their first gig after their success at the Greater Coalinga Artichoke Festival, and they planned to use this work at the Prayer Meeting as a springboard to Hollywood. It is only a mere two hundred miles away, the twins told their worried parents. They had confidence, they said, and could dance. A little.

After his eyes grew accustomed to the darkness, he made out a cheap painting of a forest scene with strange animals peering through large ferns at something on the ground; as he watched, a large sheet unrolled from the ceiling, and the whirr of a projector brought a hush over the audience. Men who had been there before joked about what was coming, and nudged each other. A man turned around and saw Nebulizer Smith and giggled, and whispered to the others, but he looked straight ahead, his Bible clasped to his chest. He had come to witness the evil he expected to find. He would denounce Brother and Reverend, and their immoral show, and call to account all who sat transfixed and groveling at the film just beginning.

At first it showed cottonwood trees and scraggly bushes which might be seen anywhere around Bakersfield. Then two men and a woman dressed in animal skins danced into the foreground, long dirty hair covering their bodies. They danced faster and faster to the rhythm of drums played in the corner by The Rev. Connie Wrench, and the strident blasts of a flute from Brother Hoss Marucci who ran the projector.

Nebulizer Smith hugged his Bible and watched as the gyrations grew wilder, more sexual, as they bounced against each other in time with the drums and shrieks from the flute filling the hot tent. He looked over the rows of hunched shoulders at the film that stopped and started as the dancers came together in frenzied embraces, their arms and legs entwining around each other, their long hair flailing around their heads and down their backs, and he recognized Brother Hoss Merucci, and The Rev. Connie Wrench, bumping awkwardly against the woman, until she fell to the ground with both men on top of her, raising her hips, squirming, turning to one then the other, her long hair over her face as she flung her bare legs over the back of one man as the other lay beneath her, thrusting his hips up and down in time with the drums and the shrieking flute.

Nebulizer Smith could stand it no longer. This was abomination, blasphemy of the body and the soul, and as he stood up, his dark bulky shadow was thrown onto the screen, the convulsing dancers overlapping onto his back.

"Sit down back there!" came the yells, "Down or get out!" from others. The man in front of him turned around and Nebulizer Smith recognized him as the man in the Bakersfield Gazette truck who threw the morning papers at their feet as they began their service of song and prayer on the corner. He gaped at Nebulizer Smith and snarled, "Wait a minute, old buddy and you'll really get an eye-full," and punched his friend again.

He sat down, unsure, ready to denounce the sin and vulgarity, when the men in the film sprang up and pulled the woman to her feet, her hair cascading down her back. He stared in horror and disbelief as Myra Skaggs grinned foolishly at the camera, then quickly covered her face with her hair as the men threw her to the ground and sprawled on top of her as the film ran through the sprockets and the screen went black.

Hoots and hollers followed, loud clapping, whistling as the men moved to the open flap of the tent, slapping each other. The man sitting in front of Nebulizer Smith winked at him. "See anyone you know? old buddy?" and burst out laughing as he followed the crowd into the hot night air.

Nebulizer Smith did not remember the ride home through the musty smells of cabbages and artichokes, nor did he remember lying in bed, waiting for his wife to come home from night school, but he remembered his father's strap cutting into his back as he tried to hide under the covers on their southern Illinois farm, his mother sobbing in the parlor where the ghost sheets of winter covered the chintz couches and chairs. And he fell asleep, dreaming of a wild animal carrying his wife in its mouth as she smiled grotesquely at him. When he woke, Myra Skaggs was frying up some eggs and potatoes, the smell of strong coffee lifting him out of bed. He splashed cold water on his face and looked at the wizened man in the mirror. He was wrong. The wild woman could not have been his wife. That kind of perversion could not happen to a man of God.

When she left for her class in Communication Arts, he put on his black suit and hat and drove to the outskirts where the dirty tent leaned against the wind. He would see what he would see. He would certainly denounce Brother Hoss Marucci and The Rev. Connie Wrench for blasphemers. He would call out a she-bear from the sweating fields to devour the watchers and partakers of blasphemy, and as he swerved to avoid a pothole in the county road, he visualized the squirming dancers, and the way they threw themselves upon the woman like wild beasts. He would call them whores and warlocks, sinners unto the ninth degree, he..."Watch that tractor you son of the devil! Where did you get your license to kill, to maim, to..." but the driver stuck out his hand in the usual salute and rolled slowly across the road, leaving Nebulizer Smith sputtering oaths and shaking.

As the strong beat of the drums began, followed by the shrill pipe, the crowd quieted. He waited for the woman to appear. His Bible was in his right hand, half-raised in the air. And then there she was, long hair flying about her body, her arms and legs moving suggestively around the two male dancers. The music grew louder as the dancers gyrated and threw themselves in and out of embraces. Then the climax as the men grappled with the woman and threw her to the ground. Nebulizer Smith stood up.

"O Ye sons of Satan!" he yelled. "Ye fornicators of life, ye blasphemers of the body. May ye…" but he was cut short with curses. Two men rushed him and threw him down on the bench as the film rushed toward its exotic climax. And when the woman stood up and threw her hair down her back he saw her: Myra Skaggs. His own true wife!

"O Ye strumpet, ye whore and slut of the sewers! I call on Belzebub and all the powers of darkness to confine you forever to the chains of hell!"

"Shut up, you nut!" said one. "Somebody kick his ass out…" The cries came fast as the film wound through the sprockets and the screen went black. In the hurry to get out of the stifling tent, several men pushed against him, and someone punched him in the ribs and snarled, "You hypocritical old fart!"

Nebulizer Smith watched the Artichoke Queens role up the screen, giggling and tapping as they went, the white ribbons on their shiny black shoes like butterflies skittering across the dark stage. He watched from the darkness as they went arm-in-arm with Brother Hoss Marucci and The Rev. Connie Wrench out the flap, and into the warm night, laughing, stopping to tilt their heads back for the bottle. And when they roared around the dirt road to the highway, he sat back down on the bench and put his head in his hands, listening to the tent snapping and popping in the wind.

It was early morning when the patrol car pulled off the highway to the tent. "I'll check the car, "an officer said. "Take a look in the tent." When the man returned he lit a cigarette and exhaled loudly. "Bugger hung himself from a spike nail up on some kind of stage."

"Is that it?" the other asked. "No. There's a piece of paper stuffed in his mouth, and a Bible on the floor with a page torn out from something like Levi…Levetic…"

"Leviticus."

"Huh?"

"Leviticus. It's a chapter in the Old Testament. Full of 'O ye this and that. And vipers…stuff about sin…"

"Looks like he used an old fashioned razor strap, like barbers used to have. I wonder where he got it."

"Better leave it. Sure as hell we take him down the Sergeant will have our ass!"

Out on 99, trucks formed a long, sensuous line as they roared past, bending the sickly trees in their wind, the policemen appearing and disappearing in headlights as they made the long S curve before the straightaway to the Grapevine, and south to L.A . "Who is he, anyway," the first one said. The other shrugged, his face half in shadow. "I hear the ambulance," he said. The high whine rose and fell, dying away somewhere on the highway, as they stood beside the tent flapping in the hot wind, listening to the bugs eating their way through the artichokes, heading for Bakersfield.

Charles Fesque opened the Tulip wood library doors of Willoughby College and peered uncertainly at the grey Tennessee drizzle that wasn't expected. "I ope mine dewy lashes and what do I see in this pastoral part of what others name Tennessee? This vernal wood, these gentle rolling hills awash with green to the slippery banks of the beautiful, if sluggish, Loosahatchie River."

"What did that man say?" a student asked. "He said something about his lashes. My Gawd!"

"That's Creeping Fesque," another said. "He always says weird things like that. Don't take his History of English Poetry class. He jumps around, hides behind the lectern, and says things about his dewy lashes all the time."

The rain that wasn't expected fell steadily through the tall maples that ringed the student park, and ran in a small stream 'like a silver ribbon in the dark tresses of some Pre-Raphaelite beauty,' as C. Fesque muttered, among old buildings housing the choir and physical education at Willoughby College on the out-skirts of Dog Fouling, Tennessee, serving as a faculty lounge (which no one used) and the monthly faculty meetings-- toward which Fesque moved, coat pulled up about his chin, grey fedora scrunched down over his ears, his umbrella held at the ready to parry any untoward or unwelcome student who might be wanting an essay graded and returned. "All in good time," he would tell them. "All in good time."

"Going down to the Pub later, Fesque?" Charles Fesque looked around to see Dr. Browne of the Geology department bearing down on him in that hell-bent-for-leather stride Browne was famous for. Fesque hoped Browne would not clap him on the back, but it was too late. The large ham-hock hand already shook him to his 'nether foundations,' and took his wheezing breath away.

"Why, yes, maybe just for the odd moment. Are you going? Art thou, in a word, wending thy way wearily westward for the odd potable, Brownie?"

"Nah, I think I'll just drop in for a quick beer, Fesque." Browne smiled that wide, clean All-American smile so familiar to the geology majors, the Regents and the Administration, and veered off toward Myron Heffer, Professor of Theology, walking with Gwinneth Jones, who directed the choir--Gwinneth Jones, as Charles Fesque observed, who always wore rather longish dresses and stiff white blouses, and occasionally ate with Myron at the Pub, where she ordered strawberry daiquiris and helped Myron with the ketchup on his home fries as she talked about Brahms, whom she liked, or Wagner, whom she did not, believing him to be a "nasty man."

The room was full of over-heated and tired teachers, copies of the agenda propped in front of them as they graded the latest batch of essays -- essays, as C. Fesque offered, that could have been written by any pre-teen whose life had not been already ruined by television and bad music "Had we world enough and time," he muttered under his breath. The new German teacher leaned close: "Say again? I'm sorry…" But Fesque's eyes had achieved that glazed quality that meant he was not of this world. The meeting droned on. Roll call votes, standing votes, and secret ballots were taken and retaken, but Charles Fesque bothered about them not a whit.

"Is he asleep again?" This from the secretary. She prided herself on knowing all the faculty names and where they sat, and now she pursed her lips and glared at Professor Fesque as she read her minutes, waiting impatiently for someone to move approval, almost anyone else, knowing Professor Fesque held them up to a fine scorn and refused to read or approve of them.

But she heard him say,"Time is too short, Madame Roll Caller. Too short, alas. Would that time unrolled before us like yonder freshet which, even now, has found its gallant but not unexpected way into the gentle Loosahatchie."

"I suppose that means you're here!" said the secretary, who peered over her half-glasses at the semi-recumbent scholar. "Why he gets away with this, I certainly don't know," she whispered to the Dean. "If we all slept through these meetings where would this college be now, that's what I want to know. That's what I want to know. He's never available for committees." The Dean looked at her as if for the first time, marveling at the wonder of speech, thought, whichever came first…his mind on the new mortgage he undertook only one month before his wife discovered their life together was not altogether what she imagined when she accepted his proposal and gave up New York City for Dog Fouling, Tennessee. It was a grievous shock, she told her society friends back home, one that she was not at all sure she could survive. And when the man from Memphis appeared in his stylish little M.G., she threw away her Mrs. Dean-type scarves and the button-down house dress the Dean fancied "should do her;" and off she went, leaving house, home, fields and cattle behind her. The Dean stared at the secretary, trying to place her, her job, her intention with this calling of names of people in front of him, people he thought he ought to know, might have known in some happier time.

Someone reached across to give Fesque a nudge. "Let him be," said Elaine from the psychology department. He's had a rough day. Someone in the P.E. department told him Catullus was a committee, and he can't work it out. It's killing him. Let him alone." The stunning Elaine, as Fesque liked to chortle from his chair in the corner of the pub, "of the size two dresses and designer jeans; she of the cutesy hair-do and mini-butt: oh, she of the progressive, liberated Sisterhood. Oh, yea, oh yea, oh yea…" watched over him, giving a motherly nod to the young German teacher.

The rain fell steadily, and teachers listened to it sluicing through the rain gutters as the Dean intoned something or other about tenure and how they didn't need it (he had it), and should eschew it (a word Fesque delighted at hearing from the Dean's mouth, since he was sure he did not know the word from a roast beef sandwich) because, after all, the Dean said, using what he considered a Dean-like voice, they were all professionals and did not need to store up treasures in earthly vessels, etc,-- all to great rhetorical effect, while the Administration in the front row beamed their collective approval.

The young German teacher glanced sideways at Fesque and noticed the line of saliva running from his hanging mouth, the rumpled state of his clothes, and the apparent disregard for his glasses falling out of his tweed jacket. He passed the reports and dot charts which showed who made what, casting a pall over the assembled academics as they wondered who was the lone dot high in the right corner, indicating a higher salary than anyone, and glanced accusingly at each other behind their reports. But when Fesque did not take the reports, he winked at the stunning Elaine and nodded at Fesque, mouth agape, one arm hanging at his side, the other across his desk as if waiting for the odd '*bon mot*' he loved so much and so rarely heard.

And still the meeting droned on, until the motion from a tenured Professor to adjourn, then papers were shuffled, people unstuck themselves from chairs, and Gwinneth Jones smoothed the pleats of her dress for the hundredth time, and Myron Heffer dreamed of ketchup on his home fries. But Fesque did not hear the motion to adjourn. He would not hear any more motions. Charles Fesque, scholar, lover of language, campus enigma, was dead.

The faculty sat or half-stood in a kind of irritated wonderment and watched as the young German teacher cried softly. The rain slacked off and a fresh evening breeze swept in from the river beyond the green hills where hawks rode the warm, moist currents off the tallest bluffs over-hanging the slag heaps. "Bluffs," Charles Fesque often said "where the fragrant magnolia and the dreaded kudzu brush the dewy flanks of deer as they tip their tulip ears into the wind and follow their secret paths deep into the hollows to lap at the cold moon floating in the water where fish hover wonderfully and eternally awake beneath the falls."

Such were the thoughts and words of Charles Fesque, "Professor, lover of language and nature," said the Dog Fouling Gazette on the Obit page, quoting an anonymous German Professor, "one who thought much, eschewed even more, but loved it all, oh, loved it all even as he loved his little corner of the library and the vista unfolding from his small round window overlooking the sloping lawn to the green hills of Dog Fouling, and beyond, always beyond, to the silent, rolling Mississippi."

Someone said they should raise a statue. Others thought a scholarship might be in order. A small one would do, they said, nothing extravagant, as if someone of note had died. Professor Fesque, they thought, was not of note. He was a loner. He was funny, in his way, they said. He was demanding in class, the good students said. He was one of ours, the Dean said at Commencement. "Quite a guy" said the President, trying to talk like a guy, and suggested a plaque for his cubby- hole in the library where, he guessed correctly, he did nothing but stare out at the river.

But when Helmut Rathburger, former Fesque student, who made his money building a glass mall under the Red River between Fargo, North Dakota and Moorhead, Minnesota gave five million dollars for a new Humanities building, to be called Fesque Hall, they applauded and dressed up in their hot gowns with the multi-colored hoods for the ground breaking ceremonies, having already begun the in-fighting over office space, proximity to the new xerox room and the lavish bathroom.

Four years later no one asked who Professor Fesque was or why the building was so named. The President, Provost and Dean are all Interim positions, the late President, Provost and Dean having retired or taken other positions at colleges with other names on the buildings, and other cafeterias where, on Wednesday afternoons, they betake themselves of the steam-table lunch and the complimentary beverage. The students at these schools, they were surprised to learn, were just as dull, unprepared by high schools, and wore the same odd garments: boys with sweatshirts with the hoods over their heads as if they expected a sudden snow storm inside the classroom: girls with tight tops which came nowhere near their jeans, worn on their hips, affording the casual eye a glimpse of the tops of their tattoos, the rest, as Fesque would have said, having disappeared down the *via media* to their nether regions.

The young German teacher is now Chair of his department, and has devoted himself to collecting the writing of Charles Fesque, and hopes to bring out a book. His tenure is assured. His office has a small window that looks over the sloping green lawn to the lazy Loosahatchie River where students stroll hand-in-hand on Sunday afternoons as music floats from the bandstand in the City Park adjacent to the Happy Rest Cemetery where, beneath a bower of flaming bougainvillea, Professor Charles Fesque rests, unknown, unbothered, unavailable.

Doyle McNutt watched the dogs copulating on the Courthouse lawn when the call came in about a woman beating her husband with a telephone. Three months on the job and this was the first time he had heard anything on his radio.

He watched the dogs break free, yet still connected. How do they do that, he wondered. The dogs stood side by side. It was a wonderful thing to see, he thought aloud. Then he remembered the call and he picked up his microphone thing and said, "OK, got it," realizing there were other words he should have used, something about "Roger" or maybe "4…" he forgot the numbers after the 4.

The corner of State and Maple was quiet. A man mowed his yard, a woman pushed a baby carriage into the small park where the Marmot, Michigan Band played every Sunday. He thought of going next Sunday, maybe taking a girl. He remembered the dogs on the Courthouse lawn. He wondered if he should have honked at them, or thrown a rock or something. What would a policeman do?

When he knocked at the door he could hear thudding noises, then gasping. This might be serious, he reasoned, thinking back to the policeman's manual. But he could not recall anything on thudding or gasping. He knocked. "Come in if you want to, but step over my husband," someone said. He took a deep breath. Two deep breaths, and turned the knob.

"Hello, Mam, I'm officer Doyle McNutt of the Marmot, Mich…"

"…I know who the hell you are. My name is Modine Dubbers and this is my husband, Carl."

Carl Dubbers raised one hand, weakly. His face was very red. The gasping was coming from his mouth, Officer McNutt reasoned. The red was no doubt from the telephone cord wrapped around his throat. All this he saw in a flash. He had been trained to recognize and remember. There was an acronym that went with it, but he got the letters out of order each time he tried to remember it. The training had been brief. So far he had not had to recognize or remember anything. The town was quiet. Peaceful. This was the first sign that things were falling apart, he thought. He would recognize and remember this.

"Mam, stop hitting Carl with that telephone. There's blood coming down the right side of his head. No, don't hit him on the other side either." Doyle McNutt wished the Chief had heard how fast he got that out. Carl Dubbers gasped again and slithered across the throw-rug to the couch.

"Ma'am, Mrs. Dubbers, whichever person you prefer, what seems to be the trouble here? What makes you feel you have to take a telephone to your husband's head?" He paused, tasting those words in his mouth. They tasted good. He wondered if this would go in his jacket at the station. He had never seen his jacket and wondered what was in it. Now this would be in it.

"Carl here has been speaking in tongues and I've had it up to here," indicating with her hand just how high 'here' was. McNutt wrote in his little pad that her hand was at her throat. "I would have cured him of speaking in them tongues if you hadn't barged in. He would not have had strength, blood or tongue to carry on after I was through with him. What do you want?" Her question flummoxed him severely. Surely she could see he was responding to a call over his radio. He thought back to the dogs and how they stayed connected like that. He thought it a wonderful thing and meant to tell some girl how wonderful a thing it was.

"Ma'am, I have been sent over here to put a stop to you hitting your husband with a telephone. And I have to make a report. Though he was no doctor, Doyle McNutt knew a cracked head when he saw one. He looked over at Carl curled up in a ball on the chintz couch beneath a picture of Elvis fighting a bull on black velvet. Doyle McNutt was momentarily stunned. He did not know Elvis ever fought a bull. This call would prove the making of him, he thought. And the dogs, standing there, yoked together that way. His mind often ran to such heights. His aunt Eff told him that many times. Even now he could see the black beady eyes of the fox thing she wore around her shoulders. He wondered who shot it and if it had babies, but when he asked her who shot it she said she didn't give a red rat's ass who shot it. He hardly ever understood women after that.

How long you been policin', anyway?"

"Three months, come next month, since I got my badge and gun and uniform with hat, a black tie for winter months, and the car you see run up against that fire hydrant. It has been my life's dream up to and including today to be an officer of the law right here in Marmot, Michigan."

"You can call me Modine, if you want to."

"Ma'am?"

"I said 'you can call me Modine,' if you want to. You look a mite done in, Officer. Have you been chasin' evildoers today? I'll just bet you have. Your shirt is all stickin' to your chest, thataway. I'm from Georgia, and we like our men like that. Would you like a nice, tall drink of ice water?"

Doyle McNutt's hair began to rise on the back of his neck. What was afoot? He had heard Sherlock Holmes say "afoot" to his friend, Dr. Watt, or something. He liked words and language. 'Whilst' was another favorite, but he seldom used it. The Desk Sergeant asked him if he was a communist as a young man and maybe picked it up from a cell meeting. So he stopped. But the hair on the back of his neck kept rising. He knew something was afoot whilst she took so long to get him a nice tall drink of ice water. He was flummoxed as to what she could be doing.

Carl Dubbers groaned and slid off the couch onto the linoleum floor the throw rug missed. Doyle McNutt wondered if he should call 912 or whatever. Maybe a policeman. "Mr. Dubbers, you had best be still. That blood is still oozing out of that last crack." He knelt beside the prostrate Carl Dubbers and wondered if he should take his pulse. Maybe put a rag on his head to stop the blood oozing onto his Moorhead Cobbers shirt.

"I see by your shirt you are a Cobber. Maybe you would like to hear what I saw on the Courthouse lawn." But Carl Dubbers was speaking something in a low voice. Doyle McNutt leaned closer. "What are you saying, Mr. Dubbers? I cannot fathom it. Is this one of the tongues your wife was talking about? I cannot translate it, though I respect your right and ability to utter it. The words. Maybe you could make pictures with your hands?" Something silky brushed against his arm and he smelled something strong and strange at the same time. His nose never lied. He smelled it once in Texas where he worked on a sheep ranch and had to dock tails. He remembered those times with relish. Or he relished those times. He made a mental note to look it up. He docked over a hundred sheep that day, then held their heads against an iron rail so somebody could brand them. It was the smell of their little heads burning he remembered. Sometimes he recognized a sheep he had just docked, remembering the way it looked up to him as he rammed its head down onto that iron rail, stifling a bleat.

Those were good days. He ate good, rode horses, and docked and rammed sheep. It was a character-building year, and he was loathe (loved that word) to leave it, but it was time. One sheep in particular loitered by the water tank as he rode the strawberry roan through the bleating sheep, scattering them like cotton balls, he thought, as they bounced around amongst the cactus or fell over a cliff.

Now here he was, uncoiling the telephone wire from around a stranger's neck, watching the little trickle of blood run down his double chin onto his Go Cobbers shirt. And now this smell!

"Hi, officer!"

Doyle McNutt was born at night, but not last night. He knew a seductive voice when he heard it. Now he had to face one of those situations the Desk Sergeant talked about. He had to think on his feet, so he stood up.

"Mam, it's the uniform. You will be sorry tomorrow. Carl here will probably file for divorce. I will be fired. You will drown your lust in drink. I have no other words with which to speak to you. Back off. Change into that wrapper you had on with the picture of birds driving their little beaks into some hard ground or other whilst a red fox peered out at them from the bushes."

"You are very observant, Officer McNutt. It came from St. Louis when Carl here…just press your fingers against his neck…and I went to eat in one of those little floating cafes on the river and got sick and was up all night and so Carl got no just reward for being sweet and telling me the fish from the Mississippi contained who knows what kind of bacteria and pee from cows and little boys on rafts and students clear up in Moorhead, Minnesota throwing dead cats into it. It was not a good time."

Doyle McNutt sighed. "Ma'am, I aim to take a girl to the Sunday Concert in the Park this Sunday. They will play music recorded from KMOX, St. Louis, where Pappy Cheshire introduced Ferlin Husky to the great radio audience. So you can see, I am not at liberty, as they say in those magazines, to take up with another. Especially and particularly one already married to this man who is now bleeding onto the throw rug and gasping again. He is trying to say something but it is in a strange tongue. I think I heard it the night Jimmy Swaggert gave the Commencement address at Dog Fouling High School in Tennessee where, for a time, I deballed—I believe there's a polite name for it but it escapes my notice—hogs destined for your dining pleasure."

"What"

" I say I am not free to take up with a married woman wearing a silky garment and smelling better than the sheep I noticed loitering at the water tank."

"Officer, you mistake the garment and the aroma. It's for Carl, my husband and light of most of my adult life, give or take a year or two. Seeing him bleed all over the floor and his "Cobbers Kick" shirt has softened my heart to the tongue-speaking he started when I began the Jane Fonda Exercising for Life and Love videos. He felt left out. Abandoned. He whined and pulled at his garments and still I bounced and stretched and stood on my head and wiggled my feet. I heard him not. So he changed mental stations and began the odd speech. But now, looking at him there on the rug, the blood and all, why it's much sexier than your sweaty shirt, Officer Nutt. McNutt. But thank you for being attracted to my silky garment and aroma. I will call your superiors and tell them you came and talked and fixed up Carl's neck. For that we are grateful, aren't we Carl?" Carl grimaced in pain and said something that sounded like "a-rump-a-rolf-a-do-rumpa-rimp, bollocs-a-barumpa-rump." Doyle McNutt looked at him in amazement and said, "You bet, Carl."

Driving back to the station, Doyle McNutt tried to put the day into some kind of perspective, but he didn't know how many perspectives there were to put days into so he stopped trying and parked his cruiser beside the Courthouse. There, to his amazement, stood the two dogs: side- by- side. It was a sight he would carry with him all his days. Something to share with a girl at the concert after he told about Modine and Carl. It was great to be alive, he said, and rolling down his window, he sang "America, America…" Upstairs the Desk Sergeant raised his eye-shade and looked out the window. The dogs turned their heads, wagging their tails. Still connected.

The Mysterious and Probably Inevitable Rise of Verias Toggs III

Verias Toggs III swizzled his beer and watched the yellow foam hang against the cold glass. From his seat at the end of the bar he could drink his beer and watch the passing parade at the corner of something and O Street. Life, he concluded, was good.

Verias Toggs III had not always thought life was good. In Dog Fouling Junior High School he was humiliated by a coach who, the Principal reasoned, could teach English because he spoke it. The coach, glad for the rest between periods of watching students do jumping-jacks and push-ups, showed films of high school football games and other educational films, such as "The Saturday Club" and "Girls Gone Wild." When he took roll the first day, he called out, "VERIAS TOGGS III! Who is that? Stand up, and let's have a look at a real Roman Emperor. What a moniker!" The students laughed and threw erasers at Verias who stood, head down, tears at the corner of his eyes.

The two years went by, leaving the usual scars from bad teachers, unruly students and a principal whose golf game had improved during his stint as Principal. At graduation ceremonies, Verias Toggs, III was introduced as the boy with perfect attendance and lowest GPA. The audience cheered as he was led to the center of the stage by a sweet little girl on each arm. The Principal and the District Superintendent laughed and slapped him on the back and presented him with a football helmet, many sizes too large, and asked him if he had anything to say. He did. " My fellow students, my favorite teacher, Coach Manussi, and our golfing Principal, Mr. Suggs, I want to thank you for this silly helmet, my two miserable years at this shit-hole, and to all you parents who don't care who runs this school and to everyone connected with it, including the janitor, 'Old Sleazy,' I just want to say, PISS OFF!"

His mother wept and watched Masterpiece Theatre, but his father beat him and sent him away to Mount Hope Boys school in Rising Water, North Dakota, housed in an abandoned Souix Indian meeting house. There, with fourteen other boys he learned how to read cheap novels, smoke pot and drink bad whiskey obtained from Nebraska University students who visited the school as part of their sociology class. Looking back, it was a good four years, Verias thought, and swizzled his beer. How the yellow, bubbly foam stuck to the insides of the glass fascinated him. Why didn't it run down like the rest of the beer? It was his third, and final beer. It was time to go to work. He had a life. But he had not always had it.

After his years at Mount Hope he got a job sweeping out the new gym and spa built by money from the new casino connected to the library connected to the cafeteria kitchen, and promoted by outside interests, to "Keep Native Americans Native." That was OK with Verias. No one talked to him, no one bothered to ask his name. He got to peek into the women's locker room as he swept the halls. And he was delighted to find someone had already been there and seen this and that through two small eye holes in the wall behind a bulletin board where the coaches, who also worked as Personal Fitness Trainers, put signs to stimulate and inspire. Verias had his favorite messages: WORK IT ON OUT! TAKE NO PRISONEERS! WUSSES WILL BE CASTRATED! and BE AN ATHLETIC SUPPORTER:WEAR YOUR JOCK! The coaches thought these were very funny. Quiet, skinny boys passed the bulletin board with heads down, but if jocks were around, they straightened up and felt their pects as they shuffled, ape-like past them--just some of the boys.

The winds off the Bad Lands bothered his eyes. He hated wind. Someone told him he should get away, see some of the world. He had seen enough of southern Tennessee to last him. Try Nebraska, they said. When he left Rising Water members of the "LaCrosse and Indian Heritage Youth Society" left a card in his locker: 'To Verias, the ass-hole with the stupid Greek-Geek name.' Other fond remembrances included, 'Get stuffed you little turd, and Who gave you that dumb name? Crotch-Face'

Nebraska's snow, sand, and chaff from burning silos constantly assailed his nasal passages and burned his eyes. He missed North Dakota the way you miss a bad tooth. His mental tongue played around and over it in his mind. But here in Lincoln, beefy girls plodded through the snow to their dorms where he earned a little money cleaning the walks. They rushed past him, hair flying, skirts (if they wore one) lifted by the sudden rush of air as he opened the door for them. They smiled their wide, clean Nebraska smiles. One girl said "Good morning" so sweetly that he forgot to scrape the steps, and she fell and broke her ankle. Her father, a local legislator and holder of season tickets to Big Red football games, threatened to sue the school, but withdrew the threat when given an Oklahoma game ball with a passable signature of Bud Wilkinson made by the water boy.

As luck would have it, Verias was transferred to the English Department, given a new broom, and told to keep offices clean. They brightened him up with blue pants and shirt and "Cornhusker" cap, and turned him loose in the three-story building where he rubbed elbows, as he said in a letter to his mother, with real people,--people who knew how to talk to a man with a broom. At least the graduate students. A couple of Professors skipped nimbly over his active broom and asked him to please sweep and dust when they were not there. A check of their schedules told him he need not worry. And when he wasn't making things "tidy" as the Renaissance man said, he spent his lunch hour at the Natural History Museum next door, where he walked the quiet marble halls, looking at the stuffed moose and prairie dogs, and the beavers gnawing their everlasting logs on the third floor.

Verias Toggs III was ready for a change, and when his life began to change, he was still ready. He lingered at the back door at a conference of writers held in venerable Andrews Hall, where he worked, broom in hand, as poets read their poems, fiction writers their stories, and other people read other things. There were many of those. And since he had access to the xerox room with stacks of nice white paper, he took to jotting down the odd phrase or image that came unbidden and mostly unrecognized to him as he made his rounds from the basement classrooms to the upper floors where professors bent over books or smoked odd pipes or just stared out their windows at whatever was blowing by.

It was during one such daily journey with the broom that he came upon books set out for students to take. He picked up one or two each week until he had amassed a respectable shelf of poetry and fiction in his new digs, as the Chair of the Department liked to call them, in the basement, next to the furnace. It was in this small, darkish room that Verias Toggs, III first heard the Muse. He listened. They became fast friends. He wrote poems and stories. And they became better friends. He sent poems out to the magazines he found listed on the bulletin boards. And he was rejected. And he felt rejected. But he persisted. Thus he entered the abject, and mostly futile ranks of writers.

Had it not been for Harley Oldfield, a good old Texas boy who liked to teach ALL the novels of James Fennimore Cooper inviting him to the Departmental party that New Years Eve, nothing might have come of his reading and writing past the personal wonder of it all, and the sweet agony of tearing open his sases to find the usual rejection notes. But things changed. Fast. The party was a turning point he would look back on as the turning point. That's how he put it in his memoirs he thought he would someday write. When he had more time.

The party was nothing special. The Victorian spilled beer on the head of a graduate student's wife and recited lewd verses from Swinburne. The Deconstructionists drank only white wine and shared meaningful glances with each other while they listened to a visiting Romanticist discuss Keats' Great Ode, proclaiming then and there that even his oafish freshmen knew what Keats jolly well meant. The gulf between them, while limited to the space of the crowded living room, was palpable, as one generalist put it.

Verias stood in the corner with his beer and watched and listened. Someone asked someone else if that someone standing in the corner looking stupid was the new professor from California,--the one who came from a small Lutheran University and still thought Longfellow could write. They snickered and drank. Someone produced a ukulele but nobody listened as he crooned an old English ballad, so he put it away. The party was really exciting. Everyone watched the new girls in the corner, and wondered who they were and why they were there. The girls in the corner watched the professors and graduate students and wondered if they had the wrong address. So it went until a friendly young writing instructor found Verias half-behind the drapes and asked him how it was going, if he was publishing any of his poems, and would he like to read one tonight. Verias was stunned. He was more than stunned, but he didn't know the word for it.

The friendly young instructor (who is still an instructor, but no longer friendly) pulled him out and got the group's attention by banging on a glass. The crowd quieted, and Verias was introduced. Very few recognized him in the shaggy cardigan sweater over his blue work pants and shirt. But they were bored and ready for something to take their minds off the Deconstructionists who had taken up positions in groups unfamiliar with their *raison d'etre.*

Verias pulled a wad of poems from his sweater pocket, mumbled apologies appropriate to the occasion, cleared his throat and began. The first few lines quieted the whispers in the corner. A senior professor and critic's critic, long and happily immune to faculty parties, clamped his pipe into its holder at his belt and listened. By the end of the poem everyone stood, mouth agape. Those who were not sure how to do that just stood quietly. Verias waited. Nothing. No clapping. Silence. So he began another poem, weaving his own volatile brand of profanity into one obscene and violent poem after another, until all were cowed, bowed, dulled and blasted into …what? One hardly knew. One and all felt somehow liberated, lifted into some other place…a place unvisited, uninhabited…some kind of…place.

The next day Verias received an offer to teach freshmen English while he worked on some kind of degree. The Department knew they had a winner and helped him to publish his first book of poetry, and promoted him to Professor. A phone call here, a post card there, calling to mind "that summer at the lake," and judges of literary contests had their underlings sifting through the stacks of entries to find something by an author with the unlikely name of Verias Toggs, III, and, finding the manuscript, read the first poem, gagged or laughed and pronounced him the winner. They gave him $1,000.00 and published his collection. His rise was so meteoric it stunned even the veterans of literary contests who, by now, knew each other well, having seen each other's names in the lists of finalists over the years as they funneled thousands of dollars into contests where, they were assured, the winner would be chosen blindly…and they were. Blindly.

Verias Toggs, III was given an office on the second floor between the Eliot scholar and a slender graduate student writing on Hopkins. He was an excellent buffer between them, he was told, as the Hopkins' girl hated the Eliot scholar who insisted on giving himself daily communion, often leaving the wine on his desk for his students while he intoned telling passages of the "Waste Land."

The catalog featured their new Poet-in-Residence. Societies asked him to kick off their latest endeavor. He received, and accepted, invitations to read and relax at Breadloaf, and at a neat literary spot in the Catskills just making a reputation as the place to come to find yourself, or someone else. He was a hit in his blue pants and shirt and Cornhusker cap. They thought it quaint. He thought they were weird and said so. They loved it, and they drank and read each other's poems and ran naked through the poison ivy.

Word got around. He was Nebraska's hit! He is still there. Students crowd into his classes to hear him tell them to "Get Fucked!" They clap. They gasp. They write home to parents who write letters to the Dean, who sends memos to the Chair to check out this new poet. But he is a star on the circuit. Their star. The Chair assures the Provost his next book will be a best-seller. Also judged blindly. The Dog Fouling Gazette ran a photo of him giving his old Junior High School's commencement address and called him The Tennessee Nightingale.

He likes his new office, but is often cruel to the janitor from North Dakota who dusts around the stacks of obscenity on Verias Toggs, III's desk. He tells him to straighten up and act like he knows where he is. When he learned the young janitor's name was Tennyson Brown, Verias entertained the Department with "Ode to Tennyson Brown: the Flower of North Dakota." Everyone laughed. The Deconstructionists met to discuss the Ode and planned a paper called "The Unknowing of Everything: the Ode of Tennyson Brown." The janitor hung himself in the furnace room in the basement after eating his lunch on the third floor of the Historical Museum, where they found his notebook in front of the beavers gnawing at their everlasting log. It was full of poems, which they gave to Verias. His next book came out the following spring. It was awarded the Pulitzer Prize.

Leaving the one-bedroom apartment was exciting. My father said we needed to "spread out, give the kid his own room," so when one came up across the way, we took it. I had my own bedroom. No more sleeping on the couch. No more being awakened at 5am when my dad thumped around the kitchen, making his lunch for work. It was a good move, my mother said.

With them both working, I had my days pretty much free. I rode my bike with the other kids, picked on a nerd next door, and scavenged around in the alleys looking for neat stuff. I always found neat stuff. One day, Darwin Vickers and I were walking the alleys when I spied a small wooden box full of coins, all kinds of foreign coins. Darwin Vickers said he saw it first, and since he was older and bigger, he got the box of coins. So it went. I found plenty of neat stuff anyway.

When the alleys were empty of neat stuff, I would walk along the tops of the backyard fences all the way to the next street, cross the street, and begin again. I could go blocks that way, looking into the back yards, stepping carefully around telephone poles, watching out for bad dogs. It was something to do.

One hot summer day, I heard a kid say there was a painter man working in the apartments, so I wandered over to our old place, just across the chain-link fence, and watched a man painting the inside. The door was open, so I walked in and went through the familiar rooms, smelling the strong paint smells where before our furniture and our food smells were. When I came out to the kitchen, he looked at me as he painted the inside of the cupboards. I noticed his mouth moving back and forth and up and down as he painted. It was creepy. Then he stopped painting and looked at me and said, "Hey, kid, do you know how to jerk off?" The hair on the back of my neck rose fast.

I mumbled something about having to go home for lunch and went out the door , around the fence, and upstairs to our apartment where I hid in the closet, holding a yardstick. I wasn't sure what he meant by his question, but I knew it was not good. Besides, the way his mouth worked and rowed made me feel dirty all over. And his eyes were odd too. They were kind of dead looking, as if there were no life behind them. I was scared so I hunkered down in the closet with my yardstick, listening, waiting.

My mother found me when she came home from work and opened the closet door to hang up her coat. At first she jumped back, then : "What on earth are you doing in this dark closet? And why are you holding that yardstick?" I looked around her to make sure the painter man hadn't followed her upstairs. "Well?" she asked. "What are you doing in there?" Something made her stop and bend over to see me better, and when she did she stood up straight and said, "Jerry, tell me what's wrong. Right now! What have you been up to?"

I told her fast, and then went over to the window where I could see the apartment across the fence. The door was still open, but I couldn't see the painter. I didn't want to look at my mother after telling her what he asked me, but I didn't have to because she was already on the phone, calling my father, and, then, the police. I still remember how fast my father came home from the gas station where he worked a few blocks away; the police came just behind him and stopped him from barging into that apartment. I watched two of them hold him while a third went in and brought out the painter, still holding his brush and a can of paint.

That night, my mother talked low to my father in the kitchen, but I could hear him swearing and threatening to kill the son-of-a-bitch. "The police have him now," she said, rubbing his neck and shoulders. "They'll put him away. Jerry doesn't have to worry anymore about him." I was not worried right then. It happened so fast, like in the Saturday movies we saw where Hoot Gibson or Hopalong Cassidy ride up and throw a rope around four or five outlaws and drag them down the street to the Sheriff's office. I wasn't worried then. That came later. And kept coming.

It was about a week later that I came home from school to find a man in a suit and tie talking to my parents in the living room. I found a sandwich already made up with a note to take a Hershey bar with it and go read a book in my room. I was glad for the Hershey bar. My dad brought home a whole box of them from the store when the men at the gas station told him that he could get them with his ration stamps. I heard later that the other men bought cigarettes and nylons. I started into my room, when I heard the man in the suit say, "When we searched him we found a 16inch garrote, a thin wire with leather at each end for a handle, sewn in his pants." I stopped, not knowing what a garrote was, but scared anyway. My stomach did that flip-flop stomachs do when you think you have to go to the bathroom.

The man talked low to my father who sat with his fists in his lap. I could see the sweat on his forehead. I couldn't see my mother, but I heard her crying softly. I put my sandwich down on my bed and walked across the carpet. The man in the suit was still talking, but all I heard was "...and he had been locked up in the State Asylum for crimes against children, but somebody with lots of money got him out. He had that thing sewed up in his pants before, and used it. He would have used it again."

That night, I watched the moon come closer to my bedroom until it filled the window. I had never seen a moon in my window before, so I got up and looked out, but all I saw was my face staring back. I wondered if my reflection could see me. And then I wondered if my reflection was me, or another person, watching from outside my bedroom window, or the car window when we went for Sunday evening rides to the San Fernando Valley, my face coming out of the long green rows of trees, the eyes framed by smears of orange.

When I was fifteen, fishing in Stoney Creek in Sequoia National Park, I bent down to pull a trout out of the creek, and saw my eyes staring back as the cold water ran over my hands and arms, and I waded into the creek, thrashing at the eyes with my pole, hearing, "somebody stop him," as I fell face down in the rushing water until my head went under the water and into the eyes, dead looking eyes. It will pass, said the psychologist; he needs to play football, said the coach. Wait until he meets Suzie Creamcheese, laughed a cheerleader at Inglewood High School. Join the Army, said the Scout Master. My mother covered all the mirrors. "Get the hell out of that closet," said my father.

Months later my father moved all the furniture out of the rooms so the apartment could be painted. It wasn't hard to find his 16 guage shotgun and the box of shells he had hidden. It took a minute to realize the painter had found my note, saying "come in" and was moving through the apartment, opening drawers and closets. Pulling back the hammers was easy, and when his shadow slid under the closet door, I held my breath and took up the slack on the triggers, and when the doorknob turned I fired both barrels, the recoil slamming me against the wall. My father's body was wedged between the door and the couch, so I reached through the hole and opened his eyes, but they were dead eyes and I could not see myself in them, so I shut them again and leaned back against the wall and reloaded the gun, and waited for the painter man. It was cool and dark in the closet, and I did not have to see anything at all.

The Thirteenth Chair
(for Dan Geeting)

I

In the gently rolling hills fifty miles east of Memphis and far enough from the hustle and bustle of the big city, but close enough for the Chamber of Commerce to talk about the benefits of "soft sweet airs wafting eastward from the Father of all Rivers," lie small towns and hamlets connected by blue highways and in some cases by dirt roads not on any map. Such a town is Badger, Tennessee, home of tiny Willougby College, a small Liberal Arts institution with a faint church connection, more-or-less ignored until a wealthy member gives money for a new building.

Badger boasts of their apples, peaches, and long, hot rows of corn and soybeans, and winks at the strong smell of mash in the summertime, evidence of the small brewery that bottles a limited number of Old Backwater, sometimes sampled in a barn on Old Risley Road. There are the usual churches at the corners of the Square, and one synagogue next to the Post Office where cars wrecked out on the four-lane are stored. It is worth a walk uptown, the locals say, to see the new ones.

Straggling out from the Square on tree-lined streets are small clapboard houses built in the 30's and 40's on huge lots with maples full of mockingbirds, towhees, grackles, cowbirds, and "lovely meadowlarks who wind their silver thread of song among the moon-rinsed trees" as the local poet puts it,-- and some catalpa and cypress, liking the warm moist air of summer. Farther out is poor town where people struggle with truck farming or work as hired hands on the big farms in hay time.

Old timers still take part in the Great Palm Sunday Rat Kill held at the Nostrum Tierney farm on the Loosahatchee River, at which times they like to remember the day when a handful of farmers gathered together to make a town that bright Sunday afternoon when they placed the cornerstone where they hoped a Courthouse would someday stand. It still stands, and they are proud to remind folks that Lincoln, or somebody who looked a lot like him, once stood before it as he speechified his way through the state.

There is a fine sense of civic pride in Heston's feed store, Bridey's Cafe, the new ADVOCATE offices on the third floor of the Courthouse--and in Willoughby College, where the fine arts flourish in the shape of the Badger Symphony made up of local players, outlying musicians who own their own instruments, and pick-up players from as far as Cairo and Golconda, and, when called for, a tuba player from Nokomis. The Fundle twins from Muscle Shoals, Alabama will come if allowed to sing their duets from The Methodist Song Book, and selections from their uncle's one-act opera: "Quivering Dewlaps: A Tale of Lust and Revenge in the Kennel."

Not all the news of the world gets in the newspaper, so it was considered by some a musical miracle when THE ADVOCATE announced the renowned violinist, Shlomo Mintz would perform with the local symphony, with the equally renowned, Michael Tilson Thomas conducting.

II

Shlomo Feinman belched. "Damned pizza. Why do I eat it?" He threaded his way between a tractor and a catering truck with the sign BIG PIZZA, and lifted his hip to pass a little gas, smiling at a lady in a taxi, who smiled back. Shlomo gunned his big boat, as his friend Russell Pashky called it, down Badger's main street past the Odd Fellow's Hall and up the long lane leading to Willoughby College, stolid and serious, wreathed in a fine mist from the rain that wasn't expected.

Russell Pashky unpacked his violin and glanced at his watch. "So, traffic? Who would have thunk it in this burg?" Shlomo raised his eyes in answer as he lifted his violin to his chin and worked his fingers back and forth in mock runs on the taut strings, feeling the music wanting out. He held the violin under his chin while he rubbed his stomach, and belched.

"Indigestion, Shlomie?" asked Russell Pashky, who missed nothing. "Pizza again? I eat anything. You want to eat anything, you eat it all the time. All the time, Shlomie. You hear what I'm talking? Eat it all, but eat it regularly, REGULARLY!" Shlomo Feinman half-listened. Pashky had an answer for everything: violins, raising children, eating. "You are Mr. Thirteenth Chair. Let your fiddle sing. Just think, two Shlomos on the same stage. Mintz is one of the greats. He could be Stearns, or Zukermann. Hell, he could be Midori?" Shlomo Feinman tried to laugh but his breath was short and his chest hurt.

Shlomo Feinman buttoned his tuxedo coat and walked onto the huge stage of the Willoughby College Music Center. The Hall was full. It was Shlomo Mintz playing the Brahms D minor Concerto. It was…he stopped near his chair and grasped his chest, swallowing several times to get his breath.

When the lights dimmed, Shlomo Feinman was ready. He unbuttoned his coat and stroked his beautiful violin. Not like a woman. Bernie Hartz, who played tenth chair said he fondled his violin like a beautiful woman. He did so now, and Shlomo watched him run his hands up and down the violin, bending his ear to the tuning as if accepting, as Bernie Hartz often said, "whispered words of amour" from his lover. Shlomo tried to do that but he always felt someone was watching.

The stage door opened and Maestro Michael Tilson Thomas walked to the podium, preceded by Shlomo Mintz. "He's got red hair," whispered Russell Pashky. "How can you play the fiddle if you've got red hair?" Shlomo Feinman stiffened his back just a little and kept his eyes on Mintz as he walked to center stage. There was a moment of silence, and it began. The serene, austere main theme in low strings always transported him. He noticed Bernie Hartz's head bobbing and weaving like he thought he was first chair. The gentle oboe melody gave way to the passage Bernie Hartz like to call "assertive." Such talk offended Shlomo Feinman. He knew his scores as well as anyone, but he disliked the way Bernie Hartz bobbed and weaved. He didn't think a number ten chair should be assertive. "Leave that to the first chairs," Russell Pashky said. " Up front you can be seen bobbing and weaving. What's the point back here?"

Schlomo Feinman felt the tightness in his chest and wondered if he could fish around in his pocket for his mints. The pizza was killing him. The movements swept by, with Shlomo Mintz standing in (to use his father's baseball expression) like the star he was. He watched the guest artist attack the cadenza in the first movement and hoped Bernie Hartz was watching, because Mintz did *not* bob and weave.

The final movement was the big one. All stops would be out and Shlomo Mintz gathered himself for the assault. Schlomo Feinman clutched his throat and swallowed hard. "God, it hurts. OH! Not now. Not now…"

"Mutterings? During the finale?" breathed Russell Pashky at his elbow. "Some respect. Show some respect for your hero," throwing a glance at his friend, but Shlomo Feinman crumpled in his seat just as the "Hungerian temperament of Brahms and the flashing virtuosity of Shlomo Mintz combined, giving the coda a truly bravura thrust, as the strings," THE ADVOCATE said, "rose in all the power and majesty of the symphonic world."

The house sat transfixed as the final notes sprang from the instruments, soared upward, and it was done. Michael Tilson Thomas jumped from the podium and grasped Shlomo Mintz's hand as shouts of bravo echoed to the third tier of seats. The faces of the orchestra were suffused with joy. Shlomo Mintz glowed beatifically. Bernie Hartz jumped to his feet as they were asked to rise, but his eyes caught the back rows where Russell Pashky held Shlomo Feinman, who was not going to rise again. Russell bent low and whispered, "You wouldn't eat regularly, would you? Not you. Now look at you.Shlomo Mintz hurried from the stage, smiled at the back row, and nodded. "So, now you're happy, Shlomie? He smiled. He smiled at you! Hear that applause? It's music." The applause reverberated from the rich wood of the Hall, broke against the high ceiling and fell to the stage below where the violin section tapped their violins with their bows,—and Shlomo Mintz, poised and smiling at the door, nervously thanked the stage manager, and patting the shoulder of the seated violinist in the thirteenth chair, strode onto the stage to accept the standing ovation.

III

It was the talk around the Square for a while, then people returned to their poor crops and bad weather. Babies were born and people died in the River View Home. Young people searched for quiet places, and small boys gigged fish beneath Shoal Creek Bridge. Michael Tilson Thomas and Shlomo Mintz left kind regards for the town, and told the orchestra they had rarely heard better strings. As the Editor said: "If it's happening in Badger, it has already happened everywhere! Until now!" Those who did not see the New York humor, wondered what that meant.

On a beautiful Indian Summer day, painfully rare even for that part of Tennessee, Russell Pashky sat drinking ice tea, remembering the concert in St. Louis when he and Sholomo Feinman played their violins under the Arch, but came home sick from something they ate on the river. He held the cold glass against his face, and watched a boy come down the street, carrying a violin case in his arms. "No bobbing and weaving," he said more to himself than to the boy, and picked up his newspaper, skimming the piece about the freighter going aground at Memphis, "its cargo of Carousel horses swept under the Chain of Rocks Bridge, heading for the Gulf, their painted mouths open, gasping for air," so he did not see the boy stop at the corner and look carefully around him, his hand running along the case, feeling the music wanting out.

Arundo Donax at the P.O.

Arundo Donax was Postmaster for Five Oaks, California for twenty-nine years and, according to all accounts, a fine man, hard worker, and friend to all. One of the carriers named her truck the Donaxmobile, and he was a sure bet to win Postmaster of the Year before he turned up one Monday morning with an odd looking belt around his waist and waving a shotgun.

At first the people behind the counter laughed and told those in back throwing packages at various bins to come look at old Arundo. People standing in line were not amused and said so. One lady scolded him loudly and said she was not in the habit of buying stamps from a terrorist. That dampened the enthusiasm quickly. Two workers put "Next Window" signs on their counters. Most of the customers walked slowly outside and stood talking. One man used his cell phone.

"I just want you to know that I'm retiring as of today, and right now," Arundo Donax said in his normal, firm, but convincing manner, made even more convincing when he raised his shotgun and fired off a round into the newly painted mural of a long line of letter carriers winding up and down green valleys to the Pacific Ocean. The blast wiped out half the carriers and dotted the ocean like raisins.

"Arundo!" called the Supervisor from under the counter. "What on earth are you doing, man? Have you gone mad? Put down that shotgun." Arundo leveled the shotgun at the head barely showing and the other barrel went off, blowing the paint off the counter and opening a hole in the wall behind him, showing a number of workers huddled together, some of them still chucking packages in the direction of carts. Then it got quiet. Not a sound. No voices, no pleas, no people wanting to look through the stamps in search of the 1919 Blythe Romance stamp minted in Caledonia, with the picture of Queen Nettie and her

Consort the Royal Prince Rupert. It was one of their hardest sells.

"I am here today to bid you all a more-or-less fond goodbye. I have toiled with some of the most incompetent people on the face of the earth." He stopped and listened. Silence. Then a package missed a bin and fell with the sound of broken glass. "That would be Stanley, unless I miss my guess. Good job there, Stan. You have the eye and the arm to become Superintendent some day. Some of them make it and some of them don't, Stanley. It's the breaks of the postal game."

Arundo Donax, child of the Postal Service, Social Servant and winner of the P .O. Foot Patrol in 1985, fingered a cord attached to the bulky looking belt around his waist. The counter people dropped. "Never mind the theatrics, friends. I haven't pulled it. Yet." When the heads came up he broke the shotgun, inserted two more Super X shells, and snapped it shut. The heads dropped before the snap and well before the double blast that took out most of the counter, missing the workers who had spread themselves sliver-thin along the ugly linoleum.

"Got your attention?" Arundo Donax put down his shotgun and yanked hard at the belt around his waist. It fell off with a thud, one of the red bricks inside breaking on the floor."Just wanted to make sure we're all on the same page," he said, chuckling softly. It was a nice chuckle they said later, one they often wished they had instead of the horse-like nicker or nose-blowing chuckle they thought they possessed. Arundo Donax's chuckle was soothing. It made the hearer glad to be American. And alive. Mostly alive.

All these memories flooded or seeped in well after the police had come and gone, Arundo Donax having left before that. The whole event took less than fifteen minutes, one told the police. "He was not in his right mind," offered the newest worker, still prone on the linoleum. The crowd outside began murmuring. They had schedules, a man shouted from within the crowd. "I want a 1919 Commemorative Stamp of Caledonia, the one with Queen Nettie and her Consort, Prince Rupert," said an elderly lady recently out of a tanning machine.

It has been some time since Arundo Donax, Postman Delux, and runner-up to the "Can We Help You" Award went through rain and sleet and dark of night. The counter has been replaced with metal sheeting behind the wood. The linoleum is still there, and sometimes the Super can be seen marking just where this or that worker lay quivering or praying, or both. A committee was formed to write a "treatment" for television, but they cannot get together on the details about who should play the one who leaped over the counter at risk of life and brains to wrestle the shotgun out of the villain's hands. It is in hiatus.

Stanley has improved his aim to the point where there is no longer any need to put three or four bins together for him. A few packages, *sans* tracking slips, are still missing, though one showed up in Finland at the home of a man who drove reindeer across the frozen lakes while his wife and two children scooped up the dung, dried it and burned it in their Finnish Yert on those rare chilly nights.

This may not be the end of this story. But unless you know who and where Arundo Donax is, it is.

Afternoon in Cornwall
1664

Suppose the fishing was bad. It happens. Then suppose a fisherman has time on his hands instead of fish, and hears the news that HM Charles, I will take the airs high above the Fowey River. Consider the pleasant path through the trees made by deer winding their way to Pont Creek, hooves clicking on rocks, cool and smooth from mist off the water.

Now you are to consider our fisherman, fresh and refreshed from the pub, who, with a wave to his mates on the quay, ascends to the heights above the boats weaving lazy patterns on the bay, when suddenly the silky flanks of deer coil and explode at a sharp sound echoing through the trees and down the green hills of Polruan—our fisherman,hands smelling of Stout rather than fish, dead at the feet of the Monarch, the assassin's lead not caring whose heart it found, the deer fled to the hidden copse of beech beside Pont Creek—HM Charles I astounded at the sudden beauty of death, not his.

But consider once more the poor fisherman, (nameless on the Plaque commemorating the King's Walk), happy with his stout stick and his dog, waving to all who drank his health and knew his wife, eating his meager lunch beside the path, so close he could, and did, touch the sweating rump of the Royal Horse moving slowly through that sun-dappled Cornwall afternoon, considering nothing.

Then consider the wife waiting on the quay with her children, shading her eyes against the trees catching fire in last light across the bay where, the water running in a white V behind her, the family dog swims to shore where she gives birth to seven puppies. Six females and one male. Consider that! His mates drink him into the night, crying and playing darts. It is late. It is time to stop considering.

Tomorrow the sun will come up over Portsmouth where a lookout watches the white sails in the channel, and the sun will go down over Gribbin Head, splashing gold over the Scilly Isles before dropping off the cold grey sea into, what? They hardly know. Nor do they care overmuch as they shove their boats down the shingle to the water's edge, cursing the cold.

The shops on the quay show early lights. A cat watches seagulls circle and land in the wet street where a woman moves from doorway to doorway, searching, adjusting the sack and shading her eyes as morning spills over the hill across the river, touching the tops of copper beeches, uncovering masts, seawall and town, upwelling like a golden sea behind her as she climbs to her house where children stir in the shadows.

A Mild Variant of Normal

I watch the doctor through the glass window in the door. He is very calm. I can tell because my wife is too. I can't hear anything, but I read his lips. "It's a mild variant of normal," he says. A mild variant of what? I wonder. My wife lifts her head as if she doesn't understand what the doctor is saying and brushes her hair back from her face the way she always does when she's distracted or busy or wants to be busy just when I ask her which cupboard the whatchamcallit is in. That kind of head-lift. The doctor bends his head in response. He's a very tall man, probably six feet six. I wonder if he played basketball in school or if he was a techno-geek. But here he is, much younger than I, telling my wife something about a mild variant of normal. Mine? My normal? I have or am a mild variant? But of what?

There's music playing in the little room where the tall doctor and my wife are talking. I heard it before the doctor closed the door. It was some kind of jazz. The waiting room has three paintings of Peruvian women at various tasks. The fat one sits at a loom with bright threads running over a frame. The colors run close to each other. Too close. I want to separate the lines so I can see between the threads. Before I went into the room with the little glass window my wife watched me touch the painting, and whispered. I could not hear what she whispered, but I knew she wanted me to sit down. She gave me an old copy of Newsweek to look at, but after turning a few pages I was drawn back to the Peruvian weaver. They wear those little hats, almost like something men wore in the 30's and 40's. They were very real and I felt I could reach out and tip a hat off if I wanted to.

The doctor is holding my wife's hands in his. His head is turned a little so I can't tell what he's saying. My wife still has her head tilted back, stretching her neck upward like a flamingo. We saw flamingoes at the zoo in San Diego once. They stood on one leg and craned their necks into circles and darted their beaks into the greenish water. My wife always had her hand on my elbow, guiding me past the cages as if she was afraid I would miss something. The zoo was crowded and I got very thirsty walking up and down. I thought a man pushing a baby buggy sold lemonade and I asked him for two glasses, but he backed up and looked at my wife, and she made some kind of movement with her head, telling him to keep walking.

The doctor does not have a white coat on. Must be a modern doctor. Sleeves rolled up. A kind of beard. He is still talking to my wife, but now he's drawing some kind of diagram in the air that she can't follow, so he draws it again, this time slower so she can put her hand on his as he draws. She drops her hand and takes a handkerchief out of her purse and dabs at her nose. The doctor lifts his head as if he's studying something on the ceiling. My wife has the handkerchief to her eyes, wiping, and wipes her glasses.

I like the doctor. He tapped my knees and elbows with his little rubber hammer and called in another person and asked him to tap my knees and elbows. He must have been a doctor too because he strung a lot of big words together and tapped some more. When he left, the doctor asked me to walk down the hall and turn around and come back, but when I got to the end of the hall there was another Peruvian picture of a row of houses curving around a corner and down the street to other houses. I wondered how those houses could curve like that and I touched them, trying to feel them turning, but the doctor turned me around and we went back into the room and I sat on the table again while he wrote something down.

Watching the doctor and my wife through the little glass window in the door is like watching people in a painting. It's framed so there is no distraction from other people or things. They sit, then they stand; he bends his head, she cranes her neck upwards, all inside the frame of this little glass window. I think I could reach my hand into their picture and move them around if I wanted to. I could put them beside the weaver with her bright threads or in one of the houses curving around the corner. It was very pleasant to think of it. If I put my right index finger on the glass I will not be surprised when it goes through the glass into the room where the doctor and my wife stand talking.

My hand will follow my finger the same way it did at the zoo when I climbed over the railing and reached my hand through some ferns to touch the big tortoise. It was very heavy and moved slowly, and my hand came and felt its hard shell and my other arm touched it and then my legs moved inside the pen until I could wrap myself around the tortoise. My wife cried so we went home to our house next to the train track and she gave me a pill and I slept a little. I tried to touch the train once. I reached my finger toward it, and my hand followed my finger, then my other hand moved toward it and my legs and feet moved until I was on the tracks and waiting to touch the train as it came around the curve, just like the Peruvian houses curve around the corner, but my wife found me and took my elbow and guided me down the gravel from the tracks and cried until we were inside the house.

I can see a clock on the wall just over their heads. It reads 5:00. The doctor looks at it too and lifts his head again as if sighing. He scratches his head and then pulls a white pad of paper out of his shirt pocket and writes something and hands it to my wife. She does not look at it, just folds it up and puts in her purse. She acts like she has read it before. His face has turned to me looking at them through the little glass window in my door. I can read his lips again. He is talking about a mild variant of normal, but my wife lifts both her hands up as if she's angry, and pulls out the little paper and looks at it and shakes her head. He shrugs his shoulders and they both put their heads down, then they turn so I can't see them.

Two men just came in. One has a large white jacket behind his back. They say they have come for me. The doctor nods and points over his shoulder at the room with the little window. He's looking at his patients standing in front of the paintings, talking about the life-like people in the windows, all wearing wonderful colors. One laughs and turns my wife to the painting, pointing to the man with no clothes on, running down the curving street. The stones are cool beneath my feet. Music plays from the houses fading around the corner, and the trees lining the street bend as I go by, my arms and legs longer, reaching for the end of the street that curves around the houses weaving into colors as I go past, the bodies and faces bending, curving around the cool street where I run, the street narrowing, darker, the shade coming closer as my legs lift me into the air, floating me through walls and bright colors, past people staring at paintings, their arms long and reaching for me as I pass through them, seeing and not seeing the woman standing alone, her hand to her mouth, crying, watching me running, running, curving around the colorful bending houses, lifting and floating into the cool, dark shade.

Frank and Paul and Min. Frank and Paul drinking beer. Min doing dishes. The time is late afternoon, and Paul is not bowling today because his back went out. "Where did it go?" Frank asks. "The theatre? New restaurant in the Mall? Where do backs go when they go out?" Paul sips his long neck and watches Min dry a white porcelain bowl.

"Nice bowl, " Paul says.

"It's a bowl," Frank says, "and Min washes it and dries it. End of story. Which reminds me, what did you really come over to talk about? Your back? Min drying a white porcelain bowl? What?"

"Can't I come over for a beer and some conversation? Is there a law I missed somewhere? What's the matter with just drinking and talking?"

"When you have so little on your mind it usually means you're having a dry spell with your novel, or you're thinking about it right now, wondering if you should talk about it. Which is it? What do you think, Min?"

She turned to them, sleeves rolled up, suds on her hands. "If he wants to talk about his book, I'm listening. I'll wash quietly. I hate to go to bed leaving dirty dishes in the sink."

"Ok, ok," Paul said, "How about I just tell you about it, and then we'll see if you want to hear any of it."

"What kind of story is it? You happen to have it with you?" Frank smiled and finished his beer and went to the fridge for two more. He held one up to Min, but she shook her head and stepped up on the stool to put the bowl on a top shelf. Paul watched her stretch, the bowl over her head, the calf muscles tightening as she raised on her toes.

"When you're through ogling my wife's legs we can talk about your story, Paul. If you're sure you're quite through. Drink your beer, and let's hear it. What's the theme this time? Pirates on the African Horn? Froggy's Sleepover? Who's the intended audience? How about Chester the Molester Comes to Your Neighborhood? That should find an audience of some kind."

Paul took a long pull on his beer and fumbled in his case. "Here's what I've got so far. I had hoped for more by this time, but I'm stuck. Maybe you can help me out."

"Shoot. I'm listening. You listening, Min?"

"Listening," she said. She turned around and dried her hands in her apron and leaned back against the sink. "I hope you don't mind if I stand. I sit too much."

"This story sounds pretty average, Frank. Guy falls for his friend's wife but can't tell his friend. Naturally, it puts a strain on their friendship because this guy acts different, doesn't look at his friend's wife because he's afraid that'll give it away. That's the idea. Ten pages. Nothing good yet."

"It's a simple love story, but a tired one, my friend," Frank said. "Not that you can't do something different with it. I'd say that's the trick. Do your own thing with that old theme. What's the wife like? Home buster? Sexy? How do you describe her in your not so good ten pages?"

"She's pretty, for one thing. But pretty in an unusual way. She's easy to talk to and fun to be around. The guy in my story has seen her with her husband for a long time. Old friends. You see the problem."

Frank tilted his chair back against the wall. Min made a face and he put the chair down. "She hates it when I tilt my chair back," Frank said. "She's afraid I'll bust it and maybe break my neck while I'm at it. Old habit. Hard to break. Tell me some more about this couple this guy is about to break up."

Paul got up and walked to the window and stood looking out at the two kids playing on the jungle gym. He had watched the kids from babies. Earaches, bruised bones. He wondered if anyone noticed that the girl looked like neither of her parents.

"The couple are average, two incomes, two kids, dog. They eat out about twice a week, go on vacations together, and go to church occasionally. Nothing going on there, they go in, they come out, nobody shouts hallelujah. The other guy is getting nervous because he can't see anyway out except to 1. tell his friend he loves his wife, or 2. run away with her."

"Is there a third option? Or does the husband just shoot him?"

"Option 3, he keeps his mouth shut, and things continue as they are. But that's where I'm having trouble, because first of all, the guy can't keep his feelings hidden from the other woman—her husband's too smart not to see it, and second, his feelings for his wife are bound to fail because his mind is split, his attention is divided and fast going the other way. That's the dilemma."

"Well, old sport, I'd say you have a problem. Three options and all of them bad in one way or another. Can this woman leave her husband and children? What kind of woman are you portraying here? She sounds pretty shallow or callous to me. What do you think, Min?"

Min turned to the sink and worked on a skillet with a scouring pad. Her hair had gotten inside her glasses, and she shook it, finally taking them off and pulling her hair back and winding it tight with a rubber band.

"What about it, Min? What's the woman's point of view here. Help our buddy out of this mess. He pulled two more beers out of the fridge and closed it with his behind. "I know which option I'd choose if it were my story. Easy choice."

"Tell me, Frank. I'd like to know what's so easy about it. Looks like a no-win thing for this guy. He loses no matter which way he goes. Where's the easy come in?"

Min finished the skillet and banged it into place beneath the sink, then took off her apron and went into the bedroom. "I don't think she likes this story of yours, Paul. Too much like what's on TV, divorces, people throwing things at each other, yelling…she's tired of it, and I guess I am too. So, the easy choice here is for the guy to go away and get help, a new city, state, country…"

"He's married."

"All the more reason to get the hell out of Dodge! Take his wife or leave her, just leave. Let it go. End of story. That's —30— as we used to put at the end of our articles in J classes in high school. Remember? I never did find out where —30— came from. By the way, what does your wife think of the story? I'll bet Susan has an opinion. She's sexy and sensitive."

Paul watched the sun ease through the blinds in the living room and start down the chintz couch toward the sleeping dog. He had watched sunrises and sunsets in this house for years, but now he looked at it as if he hoped for an answer somewhere in the sunstream, or the dog. Something.

Min returned in a fresh dress, her hair down about her shoulders and smelling of White Shoulders. Frank pulled out a chair for her and pushed a bottle to her, which she pushed back. "I'm just an interested bystander, " she said to the dog. "You boys hash it out. I'll take mental notes." She lifted her eyes to Paul then back to the dog.

Frank noticed the look and said, "Well, Paul, just watching Min here, I think, if this were my story, mind you, and if I were the woman's husband, I would be quick enough and sensitive enough to take that one look Min just gave you as a dead giveaway."

Paul gripped his bottle, put it down, then held it up to the light. "Then what, Frank? What would your next move be? If you were that person and if Min were the wife. I'm going to take a few notes." He opened his yellow pad to a blank page and selected a pen from several in his briefcase. "Dead giveaway…is there a hyphen somewhere in there?"

Frank stared at the table and moved the salt and pepper- shakers around, flicking dots of pepper off the table. "The dog will find those," Min said, "and she'll sneeze her old head off for five minutes. A wet paper towel will take care of that before I have to get down on my hands and knees to scrub the entire floor." They both looked at her, half in shadow at the end of the table.

The next day Paul put his house up for sale and spent the next month making small repairs. Frank watched him from the window. Min scrubbed the kitchen floor. The children played on the swing set until it broke, and the dog had loose bowels again.

It rained the day it sold. Frank and Min waved from the porch as the car turned in the cul-de-sac and followed the moving van around the corner. That night their TV went out as they sat at the table, listening to the old dog trying to retch something up on his pad behind the stove. "Dog's still sick, Frank. Better take him to the

Vet." He nodded, watching the window behind her where Susan's face appeared and disappeared in the rain. "Do you think they'll made it to Albuquerque? Frank?" He tipped his chair back against the wall, then brought it down again.

THE DREAMS OF CLAIRE HARDING

When she was a little girl she told her mother she could fly. Her mother smiled and said, "That's nice, dear, now go to sleep," and shut the door. Claire Harding buried her face in her pillow, closed her eyes tight to keep the tears back, and after awhile she felt herself rising from the bed. When she felt the air billow beneath her nightgown she knew she was flying, so she opened her eyes and saw their Southern Tennessee farm beneath her, the house and barns and tall silos moving together as she rose higher and higher over Turley's Woods.

When she was sixteen, she met Arnold Havilke in school and he told her he would take her to a dance down by the Loosahatche River if she could sneak away some night, so she told her mother she was going to a church supper, met Arnold Havilke at the end of their lane, danced for hours and hours until she drank something he gave her when she was thirsty, and fell asleep in his pickup.

The next morning she woke in her bed and knew she had not been flying, that she had been hurt. She pulled the sheet down and saw blood on her legs, and shut her eyes tight to keep back the tears and wished she had been flying.

Nine months later her mother lied to her father and told him she was taking Claire to St. Louis to see the Arch, and that if they could afford it they would stay a day or two in one of those little floating motels that go up and down the river. That would be nice, her father said, and Claire shut her eyes tight again.

The neighbors around Dog Fouling knew Claire Harding was different, but she soon learned not to tell them about her flying. She told her mother once more just before she married Harlan Geeting who owned the farm down the road. But her mother told her to just make his biscuits and gravy and sew his underwear, and try to behave herself and packed some nice clothes for her and kissed her good-by because her father had lost his job at the Western Cartridge Company in Memphis, and they had to sell the farm and move away, Florida, maybe, she told her, and to call her Aunt Mary Marantha of Jackson if she needed something.

The wedding was quick with The Rev. Fimbarrus Nobs presiding. He looked like a witch, she thought, in his long black coat and black hat. He read some scripture she did not recognize and whispered to her to obey her husband no matter what, and she felt Harlan squeeze her hand, and when she looked over at him he was grinning at Rev. Nobs. Claire can fly, her mother said to her husband as they pulled out from their little farm in Dog Fouling and headed east. "That so?" he said.

She cut the horse weeds like Harlan Geeting told her and fed the hogs and tried to milk the cows, but she didn't have the knack and spilled milk, so he pushed her aside and mumbled that if she wasn't going to be the kind of wife he wanted and thought he had she had better stay busy in the damn kitchen where she might know how to do something useful. She lay awake at night wondering what had gone wrong, and why he stayed in the barn drinking so much, waiting for him to stomp up the stairs to their room beneath the eaves and make violent love to her. She always gripped the sheets tight and kept her eyes closed to keep back the tears, and wished she was dancing with Arnold Havilke, baby or not, and it wasn't long before she began to feel the cool air billowing beneath her nightgown,--and when she opened her eyes she was sailing above the farm, her arms outspread, her hair streaming behind her as she swooped through Turley's Woods, laughing at the quail scattering through the leaves, making their soft whirring sound as they took flight, rising through her outstretched arms and legs. It was not something she could tell Harlan Geeting. Nor could she tell him how her life was not like she had dreamed it would be when he brought her to his forty acres. So she rose higher over the trees, her eyes wide open with laughing.

"Did you let the dog out?" Claire Harding shook herself. She watched the snow gather on the window edge. His voice came through the scenes and memories she was dreaming.

"Or did you let the dog in? If you'd quit that damned day-dreaming all the time, you might just hear what someone says to you."

She went downstairs and crossed the cold room into the kitchen to look behind the stove where the dog slept on a gunny-sack during the winter. There she was, thumping her tail on the floor, her nose tucked inside her flank. "Good dog, now go to sleep. That's what I'm going to do."

When she turned back the covers, he was already snoring, his breath holding deep inside for long seconds before exploding through his thick lips. She noticed he had taken his work shoes off, and thanked God for small miracles. She held herself stiffly between the cold sheets and watched the snow through the heavy dotted-swiss curtains, wondering how long it would snow this time, and if her Aunt Mary Marantha knew she was in this cold attic room, shivering between cold sheets, her eyes closed tight to keep from crying.

Sometime in the night she got up, went to the window, and pressed her body against the cold glass. The farm was dark beneath her, but the snow had let up and only random flakes touched the glass, briefly, then disappeared, leaving thin trails of water on the window. She reached her hand to touch one of them, but it was gone, and her hand seemed to push through the window into the darkness, and through the lightly-falling snow, pulling her out of the room and over the two silos leaning against the ruined barn and through the tall thorn trees that marked their property from Turley's Woods.

She no longer felt the cold. She was flying somewhere into the night sky, the land with its little hills and deep gullies was white and still. As she flew over the small lake deep inside the timber, she saw foxes lifting their slender legs in and out of the drifts. One large fox stood at the edge of the water, his thick brush stiff, his ears tipped into the wind. She felt the wind caress her body as she dipped closer over the trees and soared down the dark tunnels of elms, brushing feathery tips of ferns waving in the breeze that lifted the hair on her neck and cooled her body, warm even in the snow, and she thought her life was now warm and safe and beautiful, flowing, sailing beneath stars winking on as the clouds lifted and the snow ceased.

The next morning his biscuits and gravy were hot and on the table served in his favorite blue bowl he brought back from Springfield, a color, he said, the woman he should have married wore the last time he saw her. She moved quietly from table to sink, scraping the leavings into the dog's pan. He rarely talked about her anymore, but the blue bowl was talk enough. She knew she was second choice, not even choice, — more an accident of being in front of him when he woke to the fact that his first love had turned him down — so he took her hand and told her his farm was the place she could be happy, and that he would provide for her in all weathers, and that they would spend evenings on the old wide-board porch and watch the birdbath catch fire in last light. His words were wonderful, she thought, romantic like in her dreams, and she told her mother she had found the man she had been praying to meet at long last.

"When you get through with them dishes, clean them rabbits and don't get blood all over the sink this time. You'd think you never learned anything at home. Use the new knife I got you, and try not to cut your fingers off with your clumsy carving." He slammed through the screen door, the old dog behind him, following his white plume of breath to the barn where she saw him in her mind's eye, moving among the cows, cursing the cats that came out of the dark barn for the milk that he would spill as he fumbled at the teats, pulling too hard, causing the cows to swish their tails or kick over the bucket full of warm milk. Once she stood at the barn door and watched him pick up the three-legged stool and bring it down hard on the head of a cow who kicked over the milk. She went down in a heap, and he just looked up at her standing in the doorway, her body outlined in the fading light.

She washed the dishes, and put them away in the cupboard, trying to remember her dream. She remembered some of it, the flying over the woods, her nightgown filling out around her like a sail, soaring and diving into the woods and up over the tall dark trees. But she could not remember how it felt at the end, or if there was an end. There was just the sailing and the dark trees and the cold air on her fevered body, and then his heavy hand on her breast, his body against her back, pulling her into him, his breath on her bare shoulder before he threw back the blankets and turned her over beneath him. The rest she blotted out with chores in the house, straightening the drop-cloths on the furniture in the parlor he refused to let her use, then the root cellar where she arranged the fresh eggs on a clean towel, and dusted and counted the jars of things she had put up from the garden she kept, pushing through the harness hanging from the rafters like black snakes over the old chest with her good clothes she came to him in and had never worn since.

That night, she raised on an elbow and listened to the wind try the white porcelain doorknobs downstairs. There would be no moon tonight. She would not dream of flying over the dark farm, or watching the kit foxes growl at the new ice, so she got up and stood outside their room on the landing, and looked down into the empty house. There was only the wind, no sound of someone's soft breathing next to her after love, no talk late into the night about the future, children that would surely come. She remembered her Aunt Mary Marantha's one visit after the first year, and how he scowled at her for being there and refused to talk, even during dinner, but only hunched his shoulders over his biscuits and gravy and fried rabbit. She felt the questions her Aunt wanted to ask, questions about the bright red welts on her shoulders, but she feared the leather strap he kept on a nail beside the sink would come out when she was gone.

"If you've made a mistake," her Aunt had said, "for God's sake, leave him now and come stay with me. He's going to kill you one of these days," and she waved as she drove around the white-rock road to the highway. That night, after he had eaten his supper, he pushed back his chair and said, "I don't want that woman here again, you hear me? She can just stay the hell in Jackson where she belongs. If you need somebody to talk to, talk while you slop the hogs. They'll listen…" he laughed, and banged through the screen door to the barn.

When the leaves began to turn and the air felt cool and crisp, she wondered if maybe this time it would be different, that he might come in from the fields and wash the chaff from his back from the silo where he had gone to shoot rats, that maybe they would have supper off the plates she had from her mother, that…but the door exploded and he stood there, mud and cow dung on his shoes. She stared at him and knew he had been drinking. She turned to take a dish- towel from the rack when he hit her in the back of her head.

He stood over her, his mouth turned back from his teeth. He held the leather strap and grinned. "This here's what you been waitin for? Huh? Well, here it is and this is what you're goin to get. I told you I didn't want that woman here again, didn't I? Didn't I tell you that? Well, you had to go and invite her again, didn't you? You didn't think

I knew that, did you? I opened the damned letter you sent her. 'I need you, Aunt Mary Marantha, bad. Please come and stay with us for a few days…' that's what you wrote, missy…and other lies about how mistreated you are, and how you thought things would be different here on the farm…well, this here's goin' to be different." He swung the strap over his head and brought it down on her legs.

Claire rolled over onto her stomach as the strap fell again and again across her back. She clenched her teeth and tried not to cry or scream. The strap fell while he cursed the two-bit farm he had to work, the rain that kept him from getting into the fields, the lazy woman he gave all this to and the ungrateful way she treated him after all he had given her. He ranted on about the silo about to crash through the barn, the old dog dying of consumption or somethin, until his voice broke and he stumbled against the sideboard, knocking her mother's dishes out onto the floor, and with one more swing with the strap he collapsed onto the broken dishes and began to snore.

That night she soared high above the farm, her nightgown wet with the gentle rain, her hair flowing out behind her. The silo leaned against the barn, but flowers grew up the sides and bloomed in pinks and blues and bright reds and gave off a delicious fragrance as she swept low over the barn. The cows moved easily against their stanchions, their heavy bags swaying against their legs as someone milked, and she could hear the steady swish-swish of the milk going into the bright pail. Someone knew how to milk, she thought, and she swept through the open door into the barn and over the bales of sweet hay and saw her father sitting on the three-legged stool, his strong hands pulling gently, easing the milk from the swollen teats. Beside him the stray farm cats waited for him to squirt a warm stream of milk into their open mouths, and she heard his wonderful laughter as the warm milk ran down their whiskers and wished he had laughed for her.

The room was cold when she got up and looked over. He was not there, and she knew he was still be in the kitchen where he passed out after the beating. Her shoulders and back were red and sore from the strap, and as she stood naked in the bathroom, she looked at herself in the mirror. She did not cry this time. Something inside her refused to let the tears start. Something told her to leave the bedroom, go downstairs, and take down the long knife from the holder over the sink and carefully make the neat incision at the back of his head, the way he showed her on the rabbits he shot in the cornfield, and she could feel his hard hand guiding the knife as she carefully peeled the warm fur down off their bodies, being careful not to spoil the meat, until they lay pink and clean on the sink.

Later, she remembered the bright blood sluicing around and around the moon floating at the bottom of the sink. She remembered, too, flying over the farm towards the moon caught in the empty cages of the wild plum orchard on the hill, and she thought she heard her mother calling to her, and something about the Gazette wanting pictures before they took her away, and neighbors she had not known before standing under the big elm, watching her being led out, still in her blood-splattered nightgown, and how they stepped around the old dog asleep on the porch to see into the kitchen where something lay under a blue tarp.

There was warm air beneath her now, soaring and sweeping in and out of Turley's Woods, where peonies and blue bonnets spread out in a great circle next to the clear blue lake, where foxes lapped at the moon in the cold water, and her mother's voice from a long way off, calling her to come back, to talk to her as they got in cars and left the farm. But she could not answer, for she was soaring high over the tall thorn trees into the clean air and the sweet smells of alfalfa and clover, higher and higher until she became part of the streaming clouds moving over the farm and woods and beyond.

"I was in the neighborhood, looking for friends," was his line if someone asked him what he was doing in their house. Austin Fount was not a reflective man. He acted or reacted much as a jellyfish acts or reacts. So when he found himself walking up the driveway of a house in another part of town, he barely hesitated, didn't breathe slowly or any of the things one is supposed to do before giving birth or making difficult decisions. He just walked up the driveway, past the unlocked gate, and through the sliding patio door that was, what else, ajar! Like in the movies, he thought.

Once inside the strange house, he felt a curious but not un-pleasant surge in his bowels, a bit sexual he opined, but without the usual finish. Or hoped-for finish. Lately, there had been no finish at all, more of a flush, with a huge exhale and perfunctory peck on the forehead, and off to sleep. He never watched sex scenes in movies anymore because they reminded him just how far he had slipped, or lost, or gone over the bridge in such matters. Magazines in offices always had 10 Zones one needed to know about.

He stood in the middle of the room and looked about him. His eye fell on a framed faux Picasso, and a signed cartoon from The New Yorker. The furniture was heavy and old. He picked up a photo of an attractive young woman wearing a bikini bathing suit. Behind her was the Hermosa Beach pier, a pier he knew very well from his Inglewood High School days. Southern California was crowded with such beaches, he mused, and crowded with people and traffic. But here she was, in a skimpy bikini looking pleased. Who was she pleasing, he wondered.

When he walked into the bedroom, he opened the bureau drawers until he found women's underwear. He slid his hand beneath a stack of panties, slowly, enjoying the surge low in his stomach, and picked out a pink pair with little objects that might have been flowers embroidered around the top and put it in his pocket.

That night, Florence Fount served diced-beets and tuna. When he stuck a fork in the tuna, he looked across the table at her. Who is this woman, he wondered? How long have I looked at her without knowing, until this moment, that I didn't have the least notion of who she is. Or why I'm looking at her.

"Doncha like the tuna? How 'bout them beets? Got 'em at a little roadside stand in Malibu Canyon where we used to get the corn. Remember the corn? You said you liked that corn." He watched her eat the beets, sopping up the tuna with a piece of bread. He stared at the diced-beets. He hated beets, and wondered why she served them. Was there a breakdown somewhere? His mother never served him beets.

"I thought you liked beets," she whimpered. "I try. God knows I try to fix you things you like. Is it the tuna? There's some pop-up waffles in the fridge. I could put an egg on top. You like them." He watched a hummingbird hit the kitchen window, hardly making a sound.

The following week he drove five miles to the other side of Fern Oaks and parked his car in a cul-de-sac. No one was stirring, except two Hispanic gardeners digging a ditch, two houses down. What are they digging for, he wondered as he passed unseen and unheard through the back gate. The kitchen held smells of breakfast. He opened the fridge and took out a bottle of chocolate milk. He loved chocolate milk and wondered where they found it in a bottle. Everything is in these tedious little flimsy cartons nowadays, cartons he could never open without ruining the top. Florence had to open them for him. Like the boxes of cereal. Otherwise he opened them at the wrong end and cereal flew all over the floor. Florence Fount looked grim as she knelt on the floor, scooping the cereal or coffee or sugar into a mini dustpan she kept for walks with the dog who pooped little turds on their neighbor's dichondra.

He washed the glass and put it in a cupboard where there were no other glasses. He would have liked to see the woman's expression when she found a glass with the plates. He knew what Florence would look like if she found a glass in with the plates. He turned on the TV in the family room and put his feet up on a hassock. The news was bad as usual, republicans and democrats arguing, the moderator trying to moderate, but not knowing how. He watched them on the split-screen, grinning as the other spoke, as if he or she couldn't wait until he or she was on again and could tell the world what an asshole the other he or she was. He turned it off.

In the bathroom, he opened the medicine cabinet but shut it again. He thought of leaving a message on the glass, something enigmatic, he thought. Maybe his nickname. But he couldn't remember what it was. The bedroom smelled like perfume. He ran his fingers over the little bottles on the glass-top dressing table, then took the stoppers off several bottles and put the tops back on the wrong bottles. He left one off, feeling that little tickle down deep again.

"Austin, I think maybe you should see Dr. Aufgrabe. You haven't been yourself in some time. Our conversation is between games or news, and then it's not much. We used to talk .What happened to our talk?" Austin looked at her. Who was this woman? He remembered seeing her at breakfast. He fished around in his mind for words to say but couldn't remember any.

"Austin, where are you? I don't know you anymore. Have we slipped into that black hole? What do they call it?" He saw her in a black hole, her eyes shining in the dark like a ferret, her words floating up and up to the tiny circle of light.

The next day he parked his car and walked up the street, saying hello to people. He even stopped to enquire about a chocolate lab pooping on someone's manicured lawn. "Nice dog," he said. "What is it?" He knew it was a chocolate lab but he wanted conversation. Good news. The dog's owner yanked on the leash and pulled the dog off the lawn in mid-stool. It was a sad sight, he thought.

He picked out a house and rang the bell. First time for that, he thought. He half-hoped someone would come to the door. "Hello, I'm home," he yelled. A noise from the back of the house startled him. "Just a minute. Be right out. The ceiling fan's in the bedroom. I'm just finishing this load of laundry. I don't know what's wrong with it. Makes a burring noise, but my husband couldn't fix it."

Austin Fount liked the sound of her voice and felt a tremendous rush of excitement through his stomach and down his legs to his toes.

He sweated as he took out the pink panties with the little embroidered things on the border and flipped them up onto one of the blades, then walked slowly through the living room and closed the door.

That night, he smiled at Florence and his meatloaf. It was one of her specialties. He liked meatloaf with mashed potatoes and peas. He thought her meatloaf was the glue that held them together. He said that once in an adult Bible class at church and they laughed. One woman didn't laugh and afterward told the pastor she thought such a comment was indicative of a sick mind. Maybe a communist. She never went back to the church, but sent Austin a note saying she would fix him something better than meatloaf if he was interested.

All things must end, he mused the day he walked unannounced into a nice home in an upscale part of town. A maid was vacuuming the floor and barely glanced at him. She jerked her head to the back as he stepped over the vacuum cleaner and walked down the vaulted hall with plants growing at the top. He wondered how they got up there and who cleaned them. Someone had to get up on a ladder to water them, he thought. Who would do that? He paused in a service porch and saw people playing in a large swimming pool with a slide. Two children sat crying at a little table with ice cream cake in front of them. He never had ice cream and cake on his own little table, he recalled. Back on the farm it was pork chops and gravy. His mother served him after she served his father, who never spoke, never asked him how he was or if he learned anything in school. He never told them he skipped much of school and sat in an old tub in a shallow creek and watched fish hovering just below the surface. If he didn't eat, his father beat him and locked him in his room beneath the eaves until he cried in hunger.

Late that night, she came up the stairs with a tray. He knew his father was in the barn, milking, and would go into the silo with his little three-legged dog to kill rats, so he ate fast while she sat on the edge of the bed and read him a story about a little boy who had no friends at school and so walked through town into strange houses, looking for friends, but could never find any because they were all out doing other things with other people. He knew it was a sad story, but he liked to hear it and would not let her skip pages.

When he heard his father's steps on the stairs, he pretended to be asleep, knowing he stood just outside the door, his great balloon face floating in the dark. Sometimes he stood on the landing, curling his toes back from the cold wood and listened to his mother crying from their room down the hall. When he saw him he chased him back to his room, beating on his back, then went to the tool shed and came back with hammer and nails and two long boards and nailed him into his room.

The people watched him open the door. They were playing volleyball in the water. The ball landed in the corner and sprayed the two little children and made them cry again. They all stared at him, naked, in the doorway. One of the men laughed. A woman climbed out of the pool and walked toward him, but stopped. "Excuse me," she said, "and you are…"

"I was in the neighborhood…" he said.

He walked to the pool and let himself down easily into the water and opened his eyes. All the torsos and legs were pumping up and down, like pictures of hippos in some African pool. The old feeling settled in his body as warm water filled his eyes and the pumping bodies appeared and disappeared as he sank lower into the water. He exhaled a little bubble of air and watched it rise and sit on the surface like the moon in his window at night that watched when he dropped his nightshirt and pressed his body against the cold glass, the farm covered with moonlight, the animals asleep in their shadows.

Here were friends, he thought, playing a game in the water, and children with ice cream and cake. Faces were coming closer, saying something under water, their mouths opening and closing like the fish he got in a small bowl for a birthday, that his father bumped into, laughing as they opened and closed their little mouths in the thin layer of water on the linoleum floor. He blew his breath out and inhaled, settling on the bottom, and thinking this is a nice house, he watched the bubble grow smaller as it floated to the surface, exploding soundlessly in the sun.

Across town, in a mid-upscale hotel, a lady with jewels around her neck sits in a cashmere-type chair looking out at the East River. The man, her husband it turns out, watches her. He is smoking, but puts it out in a conch shell, a gift to the hotel from a shopkeeper in New Zeeland. After three martinis the man is talkative. She is not. She had a rather poor dinner and hasn't got the energy to drink.

Their conversation ended minutes before the maid knocked at the door to ask if there was anything wanted before she left for the ball game, where her intended said he would show her what a shortstop was. She almost curtsied, but instead bowed her head and walked out backward.

The woman in the long yellowish dress starts to rise, then settles back into the arms of the chair with some book or other. Her husband notices her at once. "Get you a drink now?" He lights another cigarette and pours himself two fingers of scotch. A storm is brewing outside. "Why don't we just go to bed, dearest?"

His voice, while honest, carries little of the passion she found in her book. Something to do on a stormy evening away from home. After considering how long it will take to divest herself of the dress, and glancing quickly at the TV guide, she decides she will.

It is the last night at the hotel. It is raining. It will be good fun, he muses, already loosening his tie. The cigarette is snuffed out. Looking at his reflection in the full-length mirror he fancies he looks like Cary Grant. One quick glance at the TV guide before nimbly hopping over his brown suitcase, he dances through the large white doors, with a wink at the fellow undressing in the window. Let's just see, shall we?

Two blocks away, but still in the shadow of the hotel, a young man in a sweatshirt, with the name Jeter on the back, fields ground balls in the light from his car. The maid watches and thinks of the couple in their fine clothes. She does not want to marry a shortstop. The young man with the sweatshirt does not want to play for the Mets. It is too early to predict how not-wants will work out.

In Dubuque, the Editor of Doublewide Digest waits for his man to return from holiday in the hotel to lay out the new catalogue. He has not heard of the elevator accident.

On a fridge in Nebraska a magnet holds an evening picture of her daughter standing beside a policeman on a horse in front of an old hotel. A letter has gone out on the sign. The woman stares at it in the moonlight and wonders which letter it is. Tomorrow she will serve desert and ask her neighbors to guess.

The policeman has retired to Kentucky where he raises goats on a farm just down the road from the Abbey of Gethsemani. The monks pray for him and for his goats. The man prays for them too, although he is not sure it works, since he is not catholic. Father Louis, who receives the goat milk in a shady spot under the loblolly pines, asks if he knows a quiet hotel for a Zen Master. The man tells him he knows just the right place, but doubts there will be one in every room.

The horse has been promoted to Major and does not work the night shift anymore.

ROOTS

When my wife screams that something grabbed her in the bathroom I come running … it was stranger than anything she says… felt like string or something … look in there … could those nasty grabby things be roots? (later) rooter-rooter man proceeds at length unknown in my language to tell me of roots and bad pipes and drains and stub-outs and other things I know nothing about … big fellow, hitches a thumb into his jeans and hoists them up over his butt and spreads legs and proceeds among much snuffling and spitting of bad juice on my patio to ask if I want to peek into his tv camera he had run under my house avec the rooter…so I look, he is pleased beyond all imagining … he tells me names of thin fingerling roots invading pipes and how all will collapse sooner than later …

he tells me he is pleased I looked into the nether world of pipes... my water heater is not the problem he says … drain it … watch out for the hot water bib…dangerous thing that…turn the blue handle off first then a 9/16 wrench for the other thing…I am east of Cleveland at this point ... mr. rooter watches for signs of incomprehension…I tell him that is ½ miles east ... (there is no laughter here)

watch the bibs he says … spits near the dog who licks it and vomits … you ought to do something about that dog, he says… shouldn't ought to vomit in the middle of the day … all the while the tubs and terlits are running so we can look down into the Dante-esq third level of roots invading my cheap pipes,—like blood flowing like water through the roots—not unlike the beads of wine spilled at the altar when the priest received the knife easily and cleanly between the third rib…it's a novel I say … he looks at me and wants to know what Christ has to do with my pipes ... we all sin, I say weakly, and come short of something … he is not short he says...maybe a little and do I have 50 I could loan him … I tell him no, that such things are harder to find than love … mr. rooter hitches up his pants and spreads his legs and tells me the horrors of hot water bibs … the dog watches now for the spitting, being a lab and smart ... mr. rooter asks me what I do and I tell him I sit and look out upon a park ... he backs off and asks if I'm a komnist or something …

I watch my pipes overflow into the street carrying this and that plague from rats and three golf balls…aha, he says, then adds to the bill … something runs red out of a rusty pipe … like blood I say,-- water and blood bleeding across the stiff corn stalks … rabbits hiding in the shadow of my father's rage … the 12 guage coming up, the cow with head down and flies gathering around the distended teats dribbing milk onto the hard Illinois ground… water screeching down the drainpipes … the hot water bib overalls filling with my brother's crying and my mother downstairs crying and me crying and the leather strap falling in the darkness across our legs and my father hitches up his jeans and the cow looks up at the 12 guage, two small moons in her eyes … the sound echoes over the spitting man and the vomiting dog and the cow is dead and my mother is crying and my father is waiting for me in the barn ... the darkness swallows me up and you too and all is almost lost due to the dark times coming and going but the water bibs faileth not, yea, they turn the blue handle this way and that …

Hosanna to the bibs! … Eureka to the water flowing and the blood of the labs swishing through the roots thin and thick as you plod your way…(tremendous silence) mr. rooter edges away from me with his tool belt around his knees making back peddling difficult… it's a novel I'm working on I say … just free-associating sort of… imagining … he throws his gear into the back of his truck and backs into my driveway and burns rubber out and down the street…bill is for $275.00. 75 for bibs and snake the rest for the tv show …

my wife watches from the house … she is quaking, visibly upset … says she will go down to the Mall to use the ladies' room … it's nice there, she says … AC works there … can get a latté she says … nothing to grab on to her just when she settles in, she says … I'm to let her know when our bathrooms are safe for women and children… you men, she says, can just use the nearest bush or tree if you want to but civilized women shouldn't have to worry that something will grab

them at any delicate moment …
the chocolate lab continues to retch on the patio … broken bibs and the odd wrench are left behind by the retreating mr. rooter … the house is quiet … my wife is ripping paper in my office … something about metaphor stronger than thought…chapters one and two go down the hall into the loo … mr. dog sleeps … roots gurgle and romp, rooting along in the dark.

THE BIG BANG
(TENNESSEE)

I

When Womack Dobbs woke up, he thought he had it: THE BIG BANG! He knew! He understood it all. God had come to him in a dream. "Wantcher oatmeal?" his wife asked. "Yer not touchin' it." She stared at him over her bowl of oatmeal. She was concerned. He had taken to "strange fits" as she said to her friend, Dolly. "He's taken to readin'," she said, hiking up her bra with her thumbs. "I ast him for some smokes and he says to me, he says, 'I'm thinkin on a problem and prefer not to be disturbed.' He's up ta sompin." Dolly looked at her over a Coors longneck and said, "I know it."

Lyle Burjoice, plumber, lay preacher and Dolly's fifth husband said, "I will ferret out his problem or know the reason why not, in which case you owe me a bottle of Maker's Mark and an ice bucket so I can stretch out in the sun in front of the double-wide I keep down on the Loosahatchee River."

The girls, preferring the third person plural, watched for signs that Lyle might miss, but he was on the job, peeking in their window and driving his pickup around the Womack house, and other sly things. But Womack Dobbs continued to keep his own counsel. "What does he keep?" Asked Dolly, "and where does he keep it at?" Merle drank off her third beer and belched into her armpit. "I seen doctors do that," she said.

"What does he think about, Merle? I used to think, but I gave it up when I married Arno. Now Lyle does it for me. Have you ever seen him do it? Next time he fixes to do it I'll ring you up and you can watch while you wash your dog. Lots of times he does it right on the porch where anybody might see it and disclaim."

But when Lyle finally cut it too close on one of his passes around the house, and bumped the curb and careened into Merle Dobbs' peonies, Womack came out just as Lyle was scraping a chicken off his hood. "Now there's what I think about, right there. That's it!" Lyle blinked at him, and threw the chicken in the drain that said "Do not throw things into this drain because it drains into the ocean." Lyle Burjoice knew there was no ocean near Dog Fouling, Tennessee, and regularly threw his old oil from his pickup into the drain, along with melon rinds and bones. "Going Green," he said.

"What is it, Womack? What are you telling me?" Lyle squatted down and watched a mother hen and her four chicks peeping among the rotting cabbages. "My Grandmother kept a garden, Wo," he said, spitting tobacco juice at the hen. Womack Dobbs squatted near Lyle and jabbed at his teeth with a toothpick. Lyle knew better than to rush a man thinking, having interrupted his Uncle Bogus causing him to come down with what the doctor said was a brain fart, but that Medicare would cover it. In time.

"Lyle, I have decided what the Big Bang is and why. It came to me when I heard you ram into those two defenseless laying hens. Doubtless you have heard of the Big Bang or seen it on that crazy channel that shows planets and other objects spurtin' around the universe. They all say it started from the Big Bang, but they never say who or what started that!" Lyle pulled his hat low over his eyes the way he did when the preacher started on predestination. It seemed to help.

"God started the Big Bang with one little-bitty particle of some kind or other, and then he watered it and dug all around it and staked it up, just like them peonies you just plowed under and it grew." Lyle showed interest by whistling in the manner he'd learned from his grandmother who whistled through her dentures while wringing chickens' heads off for dinner. "It's life and death and back to life again, Lyle. You done demolished them chickens and plowed under a line of Merle's favorite peonies, and you done chucked the chickens into the great mother earth, and tore them peonies from their stakes, and now everything will return to that little bitty piece of particle of something or other and start over. See? You liberated them! Now we have to be liberated too, Lyle, and find someway to be both part of this earth and part of the stars. We must be ready, and help the Big Bang to take us!"

Womack Dobbs looked away, his face relaxed and, well, relaxed. He had reached a state from which he could not be yanked back. Lyle stared at him and wondered if his friend would soon be seen on one of the science programs where people juggle apples and oranges to describe how things go around and around. He always hoped they would juggle eggs and drop some. That would be funny, he thought.

Lyle and Womack spent more and more time together, studying the ways of God and the rest of things and the girls went on with their smokes and beer while they watched "When the World Turns" on the Hoffman TV they shared. "They are beyond us now, " Merle said. "I know it," said Dolly, flipping her cigarette into the sink. "He's on a planet somewhere, Dolly, and I can't reach him, and now your man is too. I even went into downtown Dog Fouling last week and bought Willy Nelson pillow shams in the hopes he would start into strokin 'em, and finally find me in my silky step-ins. But he don't seem to care for it anymore. He just stares out at the little patch of peonies he worked up, watchin 'em twine themselves around the little stakes he put in."

When Rev. Nobs from the Rose of Sharon True Light Gospel Church came over from Mussel Shoals, Alabama to see for himself, Womack started in with the little seed and how God planted it and watered it and staked it up --and now just look! Brother Nobs watched for signs of the devil in him. "He has found the answer," he says, and is just waitin' for God to stake him up and fling him into the great universe of life to be seed for young plants and planets and people and hounds and lactating bitches and hogs what eat chicken heads and old grandmothers who still serve fried chicken and women who wear silky undergarments and those who go bare to bed and men who raise chilluns and wonder where it all comes from. That's what he says."

II

The day after the Memorial service by the river, and after Womack Dobbs, in Rev. Nobs' words, "became whatever it was he became," the girls sat watching a fly kicking in a spot of pancake syrup on the linoleum tablecloth. "I tell you, Dolly, he saw the promised land and is now mucking about in it! The last thing he said was that he, Womack Dobbs, *is* the Big Bang. I was and remain, dumbfounded, or whatever you are when you don't know what to say."

At night you can hear the night birds singing from the garden, and the answering boom of owls from the bottoms just before the cicadas begin their arching whine in the tulip trees and along the marshy backwaters of the Loosahatchee. And if you don't mind walking in the graveyard at night, you will come to a bower of clematis growing around the statue of the Confederate Soldier, and a little further on you'll find a plaque nailed to a cottonwood tree that reads:

In Beloved Memory of Womack Dobbs
Thinker, Sometime Husband and Lover
R.I.P. Big Banger

What possessed Womack Dobbs to stand ankle deep in Merle's wet peony patch in the middle of a thunderstorm, holding up a pitchfork, no one knows. "It is likely to remain a mystery," said the weekly paper, adding that "the remains cannot be viewed at Dewey & Sons because there aren't any." Lyle Burgoise signed on as Rev. Nobs' acolyte and taken to reading the books of Daniel and Revelation as penance, "to try to understand the marvelous thing I was briefly but dimly part of, in a bodily sense."

Or you could just drive slowly and look through the window at Merle and Dolly smoking and drinking beer, watching "As The World Turns." They do not talk about the Big Bang or taxes or death or the weather. They carry on, more or less aware of their place in the universe, --or at least in the small patch of peonies they tend together, planting, watering, staking up.

Pisaller Moult prodded his bear claw with a thick finger. "This here's yesterday's bear claw." A cat stared at him through the window. "Rosacia did you hear what I said? This here bear claw is yesterday's bear claw. What do you think of that?"

"That's interesting, Pisaller." He tilted his head to read the back of the magazine she was reading. "What's ezombia zones, anyway?"

"That's *erogenous* zones, Pisaller. But never mind that. You haven't managed to find any of them in years."

"I'm thinking of enlarging my business enterprises," he said to the cat. "I'm going to have business cards printed up that say:

Pisaller Moult
Venture Capital
On a truly International Scale

What do you think?" He looked at the cat curled up on the hood of his car." Rosacia, are you listening? I just told you about my new business cards. I could say something about my drain-cleaning business on the back."

Rosacia Moult toyed with her BLT and watched the cat uncurl itself in one long languid and very fluid movement. "See that cat, Pisaller? That's the way I want to look when I move around. Do you think I look like that? Be honest now."

He looked across the table at her and tried to imagine her getting out of bed in one long very fluid movement. It was hard to imagine. But then, he could not imagine cooking his own breakfast either, or washing his own underwear. "The way you look when you climb out of that bed of a morning would put any cat to shame." He hoped that would serve. He waited, not looking so much at her as through her, lest his eyes reveal his soul, as someone suggested they probably did. He hoped they would say what he could not: I loved you then and I love you now. He rolled that around in his mouth with a bit of stale bear claw. Rosacia had been ready for a man who stretched like a cat and made love like Bolt Upright or somebody. He had failed in both categories, not from a lack of interest, but from a short stubby body used to bucking bales of hay in southern Illinois.

Rosacia put down her What's Happening Now magazine and studied his face. It's a quick study, her mother said as she ironed her nightgown before her father drove her to the wedding in his pickup with a Redbone hound in the back. Try to show some interest in what he's going to want tonight, her mother said, and if he's wearing an asaphydia bag, ask him sweetly to remove it before surrendering yourself.

Rosacia thought about the sweet surrender she had read about in the movie magazines. But after Pisaller had milked four cows on their wedding night and cleaned out the silo before he came to bed, she was half asleep and dreaming about a muscled man ripping her bodice off, his castle rising out of the sea behind him. But it was only Pisaller pawing at her nightgown. It was not a night made in heaven.

Their life on the farm was a life on a farm, she wrote her mother. And when they celebrated their 50th, she made him turnip pie and put on the red nightgown she ordered from St. Louis, hoping he would forget the silo and conquer her just one more time. She knew she had lost her youthful looks, and that she was not the dying swan they saw on TV that night. But she could not flap her hands up and down like that, what with the arthritis in her wrists. And Pisaller would not fit into those tights, and would wonder what the little bulging cup was for. Marriage is what it is, her father said about everything from a calf still-born to his W.W. II memories in the prison camp. The farm was not a place to exclaim.

Pisaller Moult watched the cat rise up, hinder end first, then stretch and curl itself down again. Time was he could just about tie his shoes without passing gas, remembering their wedding night in the

Brite Spot Motel in Elsah, where tankers sounded fart-like noises far out in the channel when the fog covered the Mississippi from St. Louis to Cairo. It was a time of inching their way together, he remembered, each move memorized from the pamphlet Rev. Nobs of The Rose of Sharon Baptist Church gave him as a wedding present. In it were hints on how to inspire the loved one to action (Hezikiah 3:12), and what to do immediately following. Prayer was urged.

Pisaller Moult regretted saying I'm no Barys Kov, and you're no dyin' swan that night. He had drunk too much, and she had danced with the Havilke boy just back from Iraq and had fallen, throwing up her skirts, allowing all and sundry a long look at her new step-ins. He regretted it mightily, and glad they turned from the fallen swan to a TV therapy program where couples threw chairs at each other.

Still, they were a couple, he thought. There was much to be said for that. Now with #55 coming up, he thought he might join the gym and tighten up what had slipped and fallen. Maybe a husband and wife discount. She could join the ladies in the shallows he had encountered in his one and only trip to the pool. It was like swimming through dancing hippos he told his wife. She looked away from him and into the mirror, then walked upstairs and brought down her new bathing suit and threw it into the trash. Pisaller was chagrined (a word he had come across in a magazine featuring Prince Charles) and ashamed. He would make it up on their 55th. He would buy one of those new Speedos. Maybe fashion that little cup out of some leather harness.

That night, she waited in bed for his coming, and when she heard the creak of stairs, she slipped the new nightie down and kicked it across the room. Pisaller wore a red thing that looked like a girl's bandana. The abnormal bulge could be some rare kind of hernia, she thought. Their toes touched beneath the covers as friendly night covered them. "You are my swan," he said, very softly. "And you are my Barrys Kov," she cooed. Then they laughed and rolled against each other. He hoped the roast pork would not cause gas, but it did. When he woke in the night, he turned over, feeling his toenails tearing the sheet, then he sat up and stared at the window where his wife stood naked, etched against the moon, flapping her arms. He wanted to tell her to come back to bed, but he could not stop watching her shoulders, arms, hands and fingers moving up and down, up and down as if she were swimming into the moon, slowly, easily, until there was just one bright shimmering swan swimming into the center of the moon. He couldn't stop watching. He just couldn't stop watching.

Grace Fundle watched her husband at the window. He looked at something in their back yard, but she could not see what it was. He's acting strange these last two days, she thought, stranger than he usually acts, what with his insisting that he can't eat the same food two days in a row, and has to save his clothes for something special, wearing instead older worn-out things. She wondered if this was how it would be now, her wrapping and unwrapping her hands in her apron after the morning dishes, him staring out the window.

"Ruhlon, you've been staring out that window forever. What in the world do you see out there? I can't see anything but that old wheelbarrow you moved into the flowerbed. Did you hear me? I asked you a question. You *could* answer!" She had been asking him questions for fifty years, and the last ten or so brought few replies. Ruhlon Fundle, retiree, lover of silence and privacy, retreated into himself by degrees, as one might slide into a warm bath, slowly, until the world was seen through a thin film of water and odd shapes moved above as in a dream.

"Ruhlon, are you going to stand there all day? Your pancakes are cold, and you know how particular you are about cold food, though God only knows what different it makes to you. What in the name of thunder are you looking at!"

"The apes."

"What?"

"It's the apes. The apes are here."

"Apes? What apes? Where do you see an ape? This is Thousand Oaks, California, not Africa or wherever apes live. Did you take your meds this morning?"

Ruhlon Fundle did not hear, or feel his wife breathing on his neck as she stared over his shoulder into the back yard. He had not felt anything like a warm breath for a long time. For years he sat in his tiny cubicle at work and stared at a screen with numbers and lines and descriptions of bolts and flanges that had to spin just this way and not another, and then only with the right amount of pressure of the fingers or else the warranty went up in smoke and they would be sued and he would be fired. He lived in his cubicle. He ate lunch there and stared at his screen and the only conversation was the clickety-clack of other fingers whacking away at their computers. It was a sound that soothed him, made him part of the great machine. We are all wired together like brothers and sisters, he thought. This building is the mother-board and we are little bits of the body, small bird beaks pecking away at the great universal egg, tiny bones whistling in the drafty walls at night. He never talked like that at dinner, or on Saturdays when they pulled weeds out of the dichondra, scooting (as he thought) along like dogs scratching their butts on the ground.

At first he failed to notice his boss standing behind him, nor did he know that he had been reciting lines of verse as he worked – things he had picked up in school, bits of information about prehistoric man, and the sounds the great gorillas made from their secret bower inside the cloud hiding the summit of the great mountain. But the pressure of the boss's hand on his shoulder snapped him back, and when he turned his head, he knew his career was over.

They gave him severance pay and a waterproof watch that stopped when he took his bath that night, and offered to let him come to the gym when no one else was using it. The man next to him sent him a funny card showing a dog wearing sunglasses, floating on an inner tube in a swimming pool. "Happy Retirement" it said. Martha from two aisles over sent him a box of candy.

"Ruhlon. Are you going to tell me about the apes you think you see out there? I know there were animals in a place called Jungle Land when Thousand Oaks was just a place in the road between Los Angeles and Santa Barbara, but I don't remember anything about apes. Talk to me!"

"Do you see that leafy bower – overgrown bushes, as you call it – no, there, in the southeast corner." Ruhlon Fundle liked to give directions because he secretly rejoiced at how many people said, 'Oh,

I don't know north from south, just tell me the name of the street.' Having grown up on the farm, he was used to it. All the farmers talked that way. Grace Fundle did not. He loved the farm. The quiet. The sunsets. The animals. He remembered vividly the time he carried the newborn lamb out of the fields where the mother had given birth, and her large, sad eyes as he picked the baby up and held it close, blood running down his shirt.

"Where? You mean that mess of tangled bamboo you said would not spread? That tangle? I see it. But I don't see an ape." He was glad the bamboo spread. He liked it back there. The ground was soft. A man could dig there.

"Keep watching, Grace, and try to use your imagination." Grace Fundle had not used her imagination in years. She had one, she knew that, but where it went she had no idea. The last time she remembered having it was when, after thirty-five years of marriage, Ruhlon said, "Gracie, try to imagine a little place, maybe five or ten acres, up in the woods somewhere, or down south, maybe Tennessee, with a stream running through it and no traffic. Do you think we could get used a place like that?" She tried to imagine it, even in Tennessee, but nothing came of it and they never left their little house in the middle of the growing city that threatened to choke life out with cars, noise and ugly signs. She never tried to imagine anything after that. "There. There he is. See him…?" She craned her neck at the window, shielding her eyes. "See who? Where…?" "…There…you can make out his eyes staring out of that bush next to the wheelbarrow."

"Ruhhon! Ruhlon! What *is* that thing? Something with a huge head and dark eyes is coming toward us. Is that an ape?"

"That's one of them. The leader. He's a gorilla, the largest of the apes. A Silverback. Isn't he magnificent? Look how he throws the bamboo around and crashes through the vines. Isn't he something?"

"I'm calling the police. I thought you were crazy, now I think I'm going crazy. What is an ape doing in our back yard. Are there more of them?"

"It's a small pack, maybe eight of them. They're well out of sight back in the bushes and vines in the corner where that old tree dips down and makes a kind of bower. Remember? We put a bench out there to sit in during the hot months so we could drink lemonade. We sat on it once, then forgot about it. Why is that?"

"I don't care about the bench. I want to know how that ugly ape got in my back yard. I'm calling the police."

"No, Grace, don't do that. Just stand here quietly beside me and watch."

Grace Fundle fidgeted beside her husband and watched the apes. The biggest gorilla walked on his knuckles onto the patio and pressed his huge face against the glass door and breathed heavily on the glass, fogging it up. Behind the Silverback came two smaller apes, one carrying a little one in its arms. "Is that a mother," she whispered. "An ape mother? Carrying an ape baby?"

"It is," he said. "You don't have to whisper. They're friendly and won't be frightened by us talking. Just watch." The apes gathered on the patio and took turns at the patio door, spreading their great nostrils against the glass.

"Ruhlon, tell me where they came from before I call the police or animal people or whoever you call when you wake up and find a yard full of apes that weren't there before. Is this some kind of joke?"

"No, Grace. It's no joke. They won't be here long, and then… oh, look, the baby's feeding." She watched the mother sprawl on the hybrid-Bermuda lawn she spent hours on and pull the baby close to her enormous teats. "That's disgusting, Ruhlon, right here in our back yard. What if the neighbors looked over the fence right now?"

"When do you remember the neighbors looking over our fence, Grace? Or knocking on our door, or asking us how we were. Do you know our neighbors? Besides, what's wrong with a mother feeding her baby? I think it's beautiful."

"But what are they doing here? Why are they here? What's it all about?"

"They're here to see us. They arrived day before yesterday, but stayed hidden until last night when I saw one of them drinking out of the patio fountain…" "…out of *our* fountain, Ruhlon? My God, they could contaminate it. Why didn't you shoot it or something?"

Ruhlon Fundle sighed deeply and sat down. He knew Grace would not like the apes. And he knew that they knew it too. He also knew they would leave very soon and then everything would be different. He didn't know just how things would be different. But he felt it more strongly than he had ever felt anything in his life.

"I want them out, and I want them out now! Gone! Take them wherever you take apes. Today, Ruhlon. Runlon? Are you listening?"

But Ruhlon Fundle was not listening. He had not listened for some time, marking time with little lists she left under a magnet on the fridge for him to do. The days went by with coming and going and the evenings went even faster: dinner, the evening news, then each to a computer until they finished the evening off doing exercises on the living room floor while a young man in a zebra workout suit stretched and pulled himself into shapes they could not imagine, let alone do, all the while smiling out at them, telling them it was all great fun. Then to bed where they read their novels until she fell asleep with glasses sliding down off her nose, the pillow wet beneath her mouth.

"Grace, I think they've come for you."

"Rhulon?"

"I think the apes have come for you. I think that's why they're here. They want to take you with them to their home and show you how to live and how to love. I think that's why they've come."

She stared at him for a long time. "Ruhlon, that's not funny. I know we've had our differences in the past, and maybe we haven't set on that old bench you built out there, but its not funny for your husband to think…or WANT, great apes or gorillas or saddlebacks or whatever you call them to take me away to…to…where? Where are they from and where are they going? And WHEN?"

The apes gathered outside the door and watched. The great silverback stood up, filling the door, and thumped his chest. The sound frightened her. It was like thunder, or guns, but close. Too close. Rhulon remembered thunder rolling in the bottoms of the farm in southern Illinois when he was ten, and how he would drop his pajamas and press himself against the cold window of his room under the eaves, and watch the farm appear and disappear in the dark rain, afraid yet loving the terrible and wonderful sounds of the thunder overhead, and the crack of lightning as the storm moved over Turley's Woods.

The females came closer to the door and sniffed. The mother put her baby down and scratched at its head. Then they all looked at the door, waiting.

"Runlon, what are they waiting for? What are they looking at? I'm afraid."

"Don't be afraid, Gracie. They know what's best for us. Trust them. They are gentle, loving things, these apes, and they want to show us how to be gentle, loving people. I don't know where they came from. It seems crazy, I know. Like a dream. Like they are not really there. But they are there. They've come to do something. Something important, and when they've done it, they will leave and everything will be different."

"Ruhlon, what are they going to do? Kill us?"

"No, no, of course not. Look at their eyes. They are gentle, and strong, and love their young. And each other. I think that's the way it's supposed to be, Grace. Let them be, here on the patio, and let's go to bed. In the morning we will see."

Grace Fundle did not sleep. Sometime in the night she rose and went to the kitchen for water, then slipped behind the drapes and peeked out into their back yard, awash with moonlight. The grass she pampered and loved above all things was bright, bright green. The new patio furniture covers looked like little bouquets she thought. But there were no apes. She slid back the patio door and carefully stepped barefoot onto the dewy grass, curling back her toes at the cold as she walked towards the bower.

When Ruhlon Fundle woke up it was almost noon and he felt wonderful. He was hungry! He had not felt hungry in a long time. The house was quiet. He thought of asking the neighbors to come over for brunch. He would look into the Civic Arts Plaza Concerts this very day. He had not heard good music for years. He pulled on a workout suit he bought and never wore because he did not work out. Today he would run through Sycamore Canyon to the beach and wiggle his toes in the sand. Maybe wade into the cold Pacific! Something. He would do *something* today. Maybe dig in the garden.

THE HOUSE OF DUNDAS POINS
(FOR JOHN MOORE)

Dundas Poins opened the door of his house expecting, what? He hardly knew. Something. Something wonderful. It was, after all, his house. Others might assume he would know what lay behind his own door. Others might. Let them be the others, Poins mused. When he opened his door he was ready for anything. Any surprise.

The drive through the stand of oaks was marvelous. It reminded him of his parents' home in England. Though he lived on the outskirts of Dog Fouling, Tennessee, he often referred to his own home as "Oak Haven," or simply "The Oaks." He remembered vividly his first trip to England with his parents as a child. The names of houses, glens, rivers and even government buildings filled him with delight. It was adventure—chivalric, he thought. He liked to tell his American friends that his parents came from Trout- Rich upon Whippet, Over- Hill from Retching. But they made fun of that too, so he told them they were from London. Some cocky bikers in front of him brought him back "to the moment" as he liked to say. He glanced at their bright yellow jerseys and clever little snap-on pedals as he passed and thought of saying something about riding in the bike lane, but he rolled up the window and honked as he went by. That upset him, but he knew his house waited for him, snug and cozy among the dullards surrounding his. No imagination, no color.

When he wheeled into his parking structure (not really a structure, he said to himself each time he pulled under the overhang), more of a nuisance, really, blocking out, as James might have said, the salubrious effect of the oaks growing in the ravine. But there it is, you see. Nature is never spent, as Hopkins rightly opined. More than opined. Fairly screamed it for the beauty bursting from him, from his pores, his eyes and heart…how rare a thing, Poins pointed out to the children drawing a hop-scotch thing on the driveway. How rare a thing. But did they look up from their hopping? No. Perhaps it is not so rare a thing after all. What did they know or care about Hopkins or the Oaks, or thoughts on what comprised structure and what did not. Not they. Nor their parents, with their bar-b-cues on weekends, and uncouth music rattling the windows of his serenity.

He walked slowly to the door, pausing to nudge the neighbor's cat off his porch. The poor thing, Poins thought, never sleeps on its master's doorstep. Why is that? Poins thought of cats and their proclivity for strange behavior; how unusual and almost unnatural, in a natural sort of way, they were. How… but he sighed, stepped over the cat and inserted his key in the lock, his heart racing. The cat rubbed against his leg and mewed. An odd sound, mewing, Poins thought. Must want milk in its little blue bowl it knows I keep on the window shelf. I shouldn't do it, I suppose, but then, succor all the little creatures someone said. Poins wondered who said it. Then he bethought himself of the pork chop he had put in the special place in the fridge for tonight's supper, and took it from the rest of the animal parts in the freezer and moved it to ready access! That's the ticket, Poins thought. Let it know its time! But there was much to think about before thinking about his supper. There was the matter of the cat still rubbing against his leg, fur sticking to his good pair of grey slacks. The slacks that went so well, he was told, with his blue blazer. The secretary in the English Department had crooned something about him and GQ. It sounded terribly like a compliment, and he made a mental note to find out what GQ was. Probably a rock band. He never listened to rock and roll. What is the roll part, Poins wondered. The key clicked in the lock.

Poins opened the door a crack and paused. This was the best part. He savored it. He made himself wait. Beyond that door lay miracles, well, maybe one miracle. His day was spent in unseen tension, imagining, sometimes remembering his time on a sub, running underwater at night in red light. Dundas Poins' eyes never adjusted to the red light. It gave him nightmares; him in his wooden rack anchored and chained from the bulkhead, hanging three inches above a torpedo in the forward torpedo room. More nightmares. The people around him wondered why he would suddenly grin, or scowl or grind his teeth. Sometimes it was the sudden pain in his chest that made him grimace and catch his breath, but he laid it to the constant state of excitement he lived in.

Inside, the room was cool. He kept his eyes shut and stepped halfway in. He held himself there, barely breathing. He put his hand inside his shirt and held it against his heart. The pain was intense. It was getting worse. Perhaps he would see a doctor. Probably not. He would not go all the way in just yet. Dream awhile, he told himself. Let it come slowly. Imagine what's waiting for you in this dark room. It is not a hayloft; there will be no sharp corn cobs whistling past his head, no naked boys pushing him in the deep end. He waited for the surprise.

The cool draft covered him like it had that night in Tijuana when he had liberty from boot camp in the navy and some of them had gone to the forbidden city over the border. Poins thought it was dangerous. After all the Company Commander told them to stay away from Tijuana. Some got tattoos there and told him he should get a skull on his arm with the words "Dork" or "Pudgy Poins." They reminded him of the boys in the pool. Or the boys on the farms. They were not nice boys, his mother would have said. And she would have fainted had she watched him go inside the dirty tattoo parlor and present his right arm for the needle. The man asked him what he wanted, and the others said to make it up... go for it, Poins…be creative… and he had laughed and said, "yeah, be creative…go for it…" so after two hours of pain, the first real pain he had known since the paddle with holes in it, he came out with the boys into the bright Mexican sun with his sleeve rolled up over a multi-colored American flag with the words "Don't mess with my fuking flag." He was disappointed and the others laughed.

Their tattoos were still painful when they returned to the base and Poins had to show the S.P. on duty why his sleeves were not where they were supposed to be, and he told him they had been to Tijuana to drink and get tattooed and everyone stared in disbelief at him when they were carted off to the C.O. One punched him on his arm and made him almost cry, but the C.O. said it was a cold day in hell when a recruit had the cojones to tell the truth about shore leave, and by god, Poins, you got 'em! So everybody got off, and they laughed and called him dirty names, but patted him on the back and said he was both stupid and lucky, and they would take him to town with them next time for sure.

Both feet inside now and the dark room was fragrant with the smell of bougainvillea and green growing things he had not smelled since his sub patrolled off Viet Nam, hoping their work on the sail would make their boat look like a nuclear sub from the air. Though he never quite understood who might be up there looking for a nuke sub, and he leaned against the door, remembering the big storm when a rogue wave hit, and they heeled over until the sail almost touched the water, knocking a man into the water. The Officer of the Deck fell down and he knew it was up to him, so he jumped in and swam hard just as the sub righted itself and pushed water into his mouth and he thought he might drown. His chest pounded then, too, but he held himself still in the water until he could breathe evenly, then dived, and through the bubbles he saw legs and grabbed one and kicked hard for the surface, sputtering and clawing at the water, dragging him along until he could get an arm under him and turn him on his back and float toward the small craft putting out from the sub.

He got a medal for it, and his mother called her friends and told them he was a hero, and died the next day. He disliked the idea of death. He also disliked the submerged idea, in or out of the sub, and thought he would get out as soon as he could. But before he could transfer to another vessel they told him to take a lieutenant and two sailors in to reconnoiter. He listened carefully as the lieutenant went over their mission, and how he turned to Dundas Poins and told him he was to return to the sub if things got crazy, and tell the Skipper there was enemy in the area, like he thought.

It was, he remembered, a beautiful day, with high clouds and a turquoise sea spreading over the shoals north of Nha Trang. He ran the rubber craft quietly onto the beach and waited, admiring the ferns and tall trees, and the flaming bougainvillea that swept like a red wave to the beach, — but when guns opened up he pushed the rubber boat into the water and kicked it over — but instead of returning to the sub, he stood off shore and waited for the officer and the two men to return, his chest hurting worse. When they didn't come back, he beached it and ran into the jungle and found them shot, but not dead. The officer was badly wounded, but tried to raise on an elbow as he told him to follow orders and get his butt back to the sub, but he clamped his hand over the officer's mouth, and felt his own heart pound under his wet shirt as if it would burst. The enemy was still in the area, so he laid his body across the lieutenant, and when the sailor groaned he threw his life jacket over his head. When there were no more sounds in the trees along the beach, he dragged them one at a time back to the boat and made it to the sub.

More medals came then. His mother would have been proud again. They took pictures of him with the men he rescued, but all he could remember or think to say to the reporter was how the bougainvillea flamed out in a perfect aurora of color and about the stunning cinnamon smells of the dense jungle foliage, deep, deep green, and how the low moist clouds hung in diaphanous folds over the mountains--and how all he could think of was how he loved the fresh homemade donuts coming out of the galley when he got back to the sub and the sweetness of the hot glazed icing. But the brass didn't like his response to the reporter and took it all out and put in something about duty and his love of the service.

It was time to open his eyes. He expected to be surprised. And he was. The room was full of people. His mother sat on the couch, weeping softly. Next to her were two uncles from Nashville he met when he was young. He remembered how one shook his hand and told him he didn't have milking hands. He never forgot that. The other uncle didn't do anything. Never had, his mother told him. Don't turn out like that, she said. A parrot was perched on the back of the chair and reminded him of the pet parrot he had when he was ten. It always perched on his shoulder and ate off his plate at supper, until his father whacked the bird off the table and it landed upside down and never flew again, but sulked in its cage and refused to eat or drink until it died. His father said he would buy him a dog, but he said he didn't want a dog and never had another pet.

The two little girls were marking his hardwood floor with chalk and throwing their lags into squares, hop-scotching barefoot down the hall. His old swim coach stood naked in the kitchen, surrounded by some of the boys he swam with in high school. They wore suits and hats, and one had an overcoat on and carried a brown suitcase with

Cincinnati stickers on it. They looked at him and smiled. Their teeth were all green. The coach had his paddle with holes in it between his knees because he didn't have any arms.

People from the English office at Willoughby College crowded around a giant water cooler, talking in whispers, and he ducked when they began clicking their staplers in rapid fire. Women cried and looked toward the corner. He saw a casket on two sawhorses, with candles burning at either end. This was strange, all right, he thought. Nothing like this ever happened in his house before. He looked out the patio window and saw two sailors sitting in his hot tub, their white hats squared just so. An officer stood at attention behind them.

He seemed to float over the thick carpet to the casket, as if he were barefoot, or walking on air. Then the cinnamon smell came again, and bougainvillea he had not noticed before flamed out against the open window and the candles sputtered and danced in the evening breeze soughing through the oaks. The sun was going down, leaving a beautiful smear of color on the eastern sky. Music floated through the window --the sailors were standing in the hot tub, singing The Navy Hymn-- he had sung it many times while standing watch, always softly, knowing the others would throw things at him and call him Admiral Caruso. He felt the tears hot in his eyes and the old excitement beating painfully in his chest.

Everyone was outlined in black, the last sun behind them, their hair flared out like exposed negatives... the women waved their arms, their hands like leaves in the wind that billowed the white curtains into the room ...a shrill keening sound began...he felt like crying, but didn't know why...wanted to talk to the people staring at him in the fading light, their bodies rising and falling in beautiful diaphanous folds above the furniture...and for once that day, and in a very long time, Dundas Poins was happy, glad to be in his very own house where...what?... what was it he always expected, but could not name each time he felt the heavy knob, turned his key in the lock and slowly opened the door? Now through a heavy mist the men stood in suits with heads bowed...women pressed around him, their mouths open wide as he closed his eyes and leaned over the casket... arms across his chest... the candles failing...now, he whispered...now for the surprise!

I

The afternoon breeze rolled up from The Helford River through the tall beeches and oaks, cooling the upper gardens and the house where Jean Aldington sat reading in the window niche. James Clevelly watched her from the sofa where he smoked, his book on the floor at his feet. He liked the way the afternoon sun splintered in the heavy leaded windows and cascaded around her in shimmering bits of sunshine that caught in her auburn hair.

"I can feel you thinking, James," she said. "What's going on in that mind of yours? Why aren't you reading that poor discarded novel I bought for you in the village? I'm reading mine, as you can see." She looked at him, wondering how long it would be before he told her what was on his mind. She knew he was going back to America for graduate school, but she didn't like to talk about it. The summer was flying by too fast and they had things to do together.

"Would you like to take tea outside? It's still nice." Jean Aldington smoothed her long dress and walked through the tall doors to the patio. James watched her arrange some pillows on the chairs and couldn't remember when he first knew he loved her. She looked at him standing there, his pipe in his mouth, hands thrust into his flannel trousers. "I think from childhood, I've loved you, James Clevelly—"she said to herself "-- since childhood to this moment."

"Good morrow, sweet Prince, may flights of angels sing you to your rest..." James grinned, and followed the butler through the doors. After arranging things on the old wooden table that served for quiet outdoor teas, the Butler stood at attention. "Thank you, Beasly," Jean said. At that the butler turned on his heel and walked away, sighing " Mens sana in corpore sano..."

"I see Beastly hasn't changed much while I was in America," James said. "He always was a silver-tongued fellow." Jean squenched up her nose at him. "Beasely is such a figure here, I'm sure we couldn't do without him. Besides, he loves us all so much, you too, James, though he shows it in odd little ways."

"Jean, you know how I feel about you," he began, but she put her finger on his lips. "Will you take me walking, James? The cornflowers are covering the fields, and I want us to see them together before you go off to the Colonies again."

They walked hand in hand in silence, save for the swhish-swhish of her dress among the tall grasses. Poole worked on the hillside, his sleeves rolled up, sweating over a bed of daisies. "Good morning, Poole," James said. "I see you're giving us some new color for the hill."

"Oh, yessir, Mr. James, color it is, Sir, yessir, Sing Hossaner… morning Miss Jean … Sing Hossaner, I'm sure …"

They walked a ways and stopped, looking back to the new flowerbed and the house beyond. Both knew what the next day would bring. Finally, "Jean, I want you to marry me, now, today, right here on this bluff overlooking the bay. Let's tell your grandmother to call Father Ford, and get some flowers from Poole, and have Beastly carry the rings, and the organist can play whatever you like … let's …" But Jean was looking away toward the sea, her head bowed.

"James, do you see that corner of Helford estuary down there? See where I'm pointing? Remember the monuments that commemorate the men and women who died in the two wars? And close by is that big rock with the poem we always read out loud when we came up from swimming. Do you remember it?"

> They shall grow not old,
> as we that are left grow old;
> Age shall not weary them,
> nor the years condemn.
> At the going down of the sun
> and in the morning
> we will remember them.

Can you imagine what went through their minds the day before they embarked for France? I'm sure I can't imagine what they must have felt. I daresay you can't either. But something of that is what I feel right now knowing you are boarding a different kind of ship tomorrow and sailing out of my life. And what homecoming will there be? And when? And what am I to do whilst you are studying your poetry, and whatever it is…oh, I know, horticulture, and soil conservation too… and here will I be, walking with Grandmother through these beautiful cornflowers, sharing your latest letter over tea on the sunny verandah while Poole grunts away in a garden patch with his 'Sing Hosanner,' Beasley hovering behind our chairs, muttering Latin phrases. I know you have to do this. Only please don't ask me anything so important as, as…good-by is all I can stand."

Letters did come with news of housing and tough classes, and pictures of the beautiful sun-drenched world of Santa Barbara. They sighed over a photo of him in shorts and floppy t- shirt, with some kind of odd looking slippers on his feet. "It looks like he's changed his wardrobe for the States," Jean observed. "I think I preferred him in tweeds and hunting boots."

"Everything changes, my dear," her grandmother said. "James will no doubt change in ways more than dress before he's through with this adventure. I don't think he sees, now, what kind of changes. But I feel in my old bones that change, perhaps unpleasant change, is coming for him. I just hope he can make it through whatever it might be."

Jean looked at her, trying to read something in her face, but she turned away, her long grey hair falling down her back. "Yes, I washed it too late, this morning. I should go into the house and put it up before we walk." Jean marveled at her ability to read her thoughts. Their bond had always been close, and after the death of her father that bond had become even more special. These lazy summer days spent in long walks in their garden in the late afternoons with the sun catching fire in the birdbath were wonderful; and now with James gone to America they became moments of glad grace that she could wish might last forever.

In his room, overlooking the university lagoon, James tore the edge off the letter, and looked inside before he eased it out. The draft board has news for you … he threw it down on his bed and stood by the open window, breathing in the sea air off the Santa Barbara coast where the water changed color by the minute as tides came in or went out, swaying the tops of seaweed anchored below. And he saw Jean, skirts billowing in the wind off the channel, her parasol shielding her ivory complexion as she walked to the crest of the hill, and looked east toward the broad expanse of flowers, ponds and trees of Trebah Gardens, and the Helford River below.

"Grandmother, here's a letter from James. Thank you, Beasley. We'll take tea outside, I think, by the fountain."

"Very good, m'lady. Old Sol will soon find you deep in the arms of Morpheus. I will watch for the signs and place the umbrella to shade you as you read the letter from Master James: Omnia vincit amor, m' lady."

"Jean, where does he get that? You would think he reads the classics up in his room. But I never heard him quote anything I've heard before. He just seems to make it up. I wonder if…what is it, Jean? Don't tell me he did poorly on his exams this time. Or is he out of funds? Perhaps we should send him something. Poor dear, so far away from friends and home."

Jean put the letter in her lap and poured the tea into her grandmother's porcelain cup, noticing the way the sunlight penetrated its sides leaving a tiny sun floating in her tea. She poured the milk, added the customary lump of sugar and placed the biscuits nearby.

"Grandmother, where did these cups come from? They are so fragile and…" Her grandmother stared at her. "Jean, what is it? What does James say in the letter. Tell me quickly. Is it bad news? Has he been hurt or…?"

"James has been drafted. Into the American Army! He's going to report soon. He doesn't know what will happen yet, or where he will be. He says he will write just as soon as he knows something for sure. He also says we are not to worry, that there are a million things he can do in the Army, and he is sure his drama and literature skills will show themselves —maybe even his botany and soil conservation studies— maybe they'll ask him to do shows or something. Possibly write a newsletter, or whatever they have in the Army. And of course, he sends his love for us both, and says I'm to kiss you on the forehead, and that you should fire Beastly the next time he comes to serve dinner in that outlandish Scottish costume he keeps hidden in his closet. That's all. There isn't any other news."

The air had cooled beneath the yew tree and Beasley removed the umbrellas. "I think we had better write him right away, Jean. He will need news from home now more than ever. Evan told me my letters were the only bit of sanity left in the world. He read them over and over, by moonlight, or light from a cigarette. Even in the trenches he read them. Terrible thing, war. But having said that, what is one to do? Oh, Jean, let's make a list of things to send him. Warm and comfortable sweaters, and maybe those trousers he wore at the party last summer. He said he thought they fit him better than anything in his wardrobe."

She looked away, remembering those days of World War I when life was so fragmented. When Evan went off to war her world stopped, then started again in a single heartbeat. But differently. Everything changed. The fields she walked through from Burton Water were green as ever. The sheep grazed as before on the hills surrounding the tea house in Lower Slaughter where she read his letters from the front, though he tried to disguise the brutality of the war, the shooting and killing, the gas attacks, and the infrequent rests in some dreary French hamlet. Or, as she found later, a small field hospital where he was treated for wounds. Just that. Wounds. Nothing more. The days and weeks went by in agony as she wondered what kinds of wounds he had suffered, and what their consequences might be. Then the letter came telling her he was coming home, that he had suffered permanent damage to his legs and would be on crutches when he met her.

Their life together after that was different in ways she could not understand nor explain. They took easy walks, had tea at five, watching the sun catch in the oaks and beeches, but the days were strained; there was less conversation and laughter. Little by little, he grew easier at being home, slept better,—and when he could trade the crutches for a cane their walks became longer and their life returned to something like the life they had before he went away, when they sat on the hill among the sheep, watching the shepherd's dog moving quietly among them, and said, almost together, "It will always be summer," laughing at what Evan called infernal romanticism as they ran hand-in-hand down the hill, weaving in and out of the sheep to their cottage near the river.

Jean Aldington watched her grandmother arrange the azaleas in the blue vase, a gift from Grandfather on their 50th wedding anniversary. She noticed her right hand tremble as she cut the stems, and how she put the scissors down and stood looking at the flowers as if she wondered why she was there, and what she should be doing with the flowers. "Grandmother, let me help you with those stems. They can be awfully hard to cut." Her Grandmother looked at her, but said nothing as she felt behind her for the chaise and eased herself down.

"Thank you, my dear, " she said. "I felt a little faint just for a moment. It's probably that new medicine Dr. Bryn-Jones gave me. Very light-headed for a moment. I'm quite all right now. It's nothing to …" Jean gasped as her Grandmother rolled sideways on the chaise. "Grandmother!" she cried. "Are you ill? I'll ring for the doctor this minute. Beasley. Oh, Beasley! Come quick!"

That evening, she sat by her bed, watching her sleep. The doctor paused at the door, putting his heavy coat over his arm. "You must expect more episodes like this," he told her. "Your grandmother is almost ninety, and, unfortunately, things begin to break down. You have been a tonic for her, Jean. She might have slipped before now were it not for your love and care."

As the first sun came up the hill, out of the beech woods, Lady Aldington opened her eyes and looked around the room at the familiar heavy furniture—the stiff brocaded draperies, the teak chest inlaid with mother-of-pearl, a gift to her husband from the family of a man whose life he'd saved in France. It was the only piece in their house he loved, and here she kept his uniform, cleaned and carefully folded on top of the ceremonial sword with his ribbons and medals.

"Good morning, sleepy-head. Hungry?" She turned her head to see Jean standing at the door with a tray of tea and scones, and a long-stemmed red rose. "Beasley is put out because I insisted on bringing this myself. He's downstairs muttering something to the cat. In Latin. He's really getting to be too much. But he loves you so, and …"

"Jean," her grandmother interrupted her. "Put the tray down, dear, and come sit on the bed. And thank you for the lovely rose, and the tea—and cook's fresh scones!"

"You are not to talk today. The doctor said …"

"...piffle on what the doctor said. I was feeding Doctor Bryn-Jones his porridge before he could walk. Now, sit down. I want to tell you something, and I want you to just listen. Jean, when James comes home… no, don't say anything…when he comes home I want you to promise me you'll be married right away. You love each other and there's no reason to put it off. He can make this place his own—your own. Perhaps build a new house—though you might want to keep this old place for company--and Beasley--and Poole of course. Jean, dear, open the chest and bring me that packet of letters under Evan's uniforms, will you? Yes, that's it. I want to share something with you. As you know, your grandfather wrote me as often as he could during the war--I've kept all his letters of course, but there's one I think I'll read to you now. Just sit beside me. Now, if I can find it. I've folded it so many times it's close on tearing. Would you close the curtains just a little, the bougainvillea is casting a shadow on my bed. I don't think I like shadows today. I may not be able to finish this letter.

Dearest Hilaria,

July 10, 1916
near Arras, France

Last night, we slept in the trench again for the fifth time this week. We manage to hollow out a depression in the trench wall but rain washes it out as soon as we're done, so we mostly just stand with our heads bowed. The rats don't like the rain any more than we do, and they run over our feet in droves. We don't mind them anymore anyway, there are so many of them in these trenches.

Flares go off every now and then in case any of us are coming over the wall. And we may well go over. The bosch send up the flares just in case. Two days ago, five men went over in a downpour just after the flares died out, but their machine gunner must have guessed because he opened up and cut the men down before they had gone ten yards. They are still out there. The Captain was ordered to send out a burial party, but he refused to send us. It may not go well with him for refusing a direct order; still, the Colonel who gave it is not a bad sort. We will soon know. It's hard to work up any interest in anything when you are inches deep in mud and filth, hoping they don't send over gas while you're stuck here. I miss my pipe. I miss my tot of sherry too, and ham with fresh baby potatoes ... so many things.

My darling, last night I dreamed we were walking on the hill overlooking the bay through acres of cornflowers. Their blue was bluer than the sky, and your eyes were bluer still. You never looked more beautiful--unless it was the day I left on the troop train, my head stuck out the window as it pulled out of Victoria Station, and saw you wreathed in smoke from the engine, your eyes still shining. I took that memory with me and have it still. Do you remember what we talked about that last day on the hill? You worried about us finding each other again after the war, and where we would be, what town, what fields of flowers ...all the things we took for granted growing up would be changed terribly, you said. Nothing would be or could be ever the same again. Would we be the same people? you asked. You remembered a lovely quiet place outside Brest where we took a cottage for the summer, and wondered what I would see when I got over there. We will be there again, I promise. Tonight I'll try to imagine the muddy wall I'm leaning against is a hilltop overlooking a bay with little white sails on it, and hearing the faraway sound of seagulls crying. As you must cry too, I know. As sometimes I do. As sometimes I do.

My love, always,

Evan

"Jean, I wish now we had talked more about your father's death—and Evan's. You were fifteen, I think. The news drove you inside yourself, and I knew talk would not answer this time, that healing would happen in its own time and in its own way if we stayed together and made this place a home. But Evan's letter has put me to thinking about that awful day. Your father was crazy about flying. I can remember standing on the bluff, holding my breath as he did loops and spirals over the headland. And when he took you up for your fourteenth birthday I thought I couldn't stand it! I couldn't, and went into the house and poured myself a brandy. I remember poor Beasley watching me drink it off, aghast."

"I loved it though, Grandmother. I loved the loops and spirals even though it was just that one time. My father was a grand pilot. He always wanted to be in the Royal Air Force, but his heart kept him out of the action that he yearned for. Yes, I remember that awful day. James and I were playing badminton on the new grass court Poole made for us. We were whacking the shuttlecock this way and that and having a fine time of it when two men pulled up in an official looking car. James threw his racket down and came under the net to me and we just stood there like ninnies, wondering what it could mean. What it meant was I was now an orphan. And you, too, in a way. I don't remember my mother at all. Father rarely mentioned her. A picture of the two of them standing beside my father's first airplane is all I have. I think he went a little mad when she died. He sent me to Aunt Julia's in Devon for the summer, and when I came back James told me he watched my father put everything they had into a van and drive away without a word to anyone. I learned he drove the van to a cliff somewhere near Land's End and pushed it over the edge into the sea. I think he was charged with something, littering, if nothing else."

"Yes, your grandfather took care of it. Everything sank into the ocean of course. It's somewhere in the middle of the channel by now, covered with silt. Your father never fully recovered from losing your mother so early. But that outbreak of influenza was terrible in Great Britain that year. It took so many lives. So many."

"Daddy usually flew alone. I don't know how he talked someone at Cauldrose Field into letting him take that experimental ship up. And dear grandfather wanted to support him, didn't he? Otherwise, I wonder if he would have ever gotten into that thing. And that's the last we saw of either of them. "But we have each other, grandmother--and James. I can't remember not having James. When we were growing up he spent more time here than at his house at Trebah. Though with his father as head gardener there, we had the run of the place when we wanted excitement-- running around those absurdly huge plants that looked as if they came from another time, as indeed they did. Remember when he suggested we put in a dovecote and a stew pond! You shivered at the thought of a pond full of eels and little fish that could be harvested for breakfast! I don't know if he was serious or not."

"The dovecote, though, was a grand idea, Jean, and when he

comes back I'll ask him to build one halfway down the hill, where it levels off, you know? We could hear the doves from there. It would be wonderful to have him working on a project again."

"Yes, it would. But we will have to be patient and see what he wants to do. He may not want to do anything. He may need time to just be."

"I wish he had talked about his mother. Why she went back to America."

"But we know that, Jean. Since she was an American, she wanted James to be born there, in Santa Barbara, as I remember. She wanted to be sure he was American. When his father insisted he not become an American only, they quarreled fiercely about it, until his mother decided it by leaving England when she was six months pregnant. Then, to everyone's surprise, she brought him back to Cornwall, and for awhile we thought all was well, things forgiven and all that. But it was not to be. When she went back alone the following Christmas we never heard from her again. To this day I don't believe his father ever knew what became of her. But he raised James wonderfully well."

"And now he's in some awful war halfway across the world where we can't see him or touch him or take care of him. I'm counting the days. I wonder what he will be when he comes home."

II

August, 1969
Long Khan Province

Dear Jean and Grandmother,

Sorry to be so late with this, but we've been busy training and training and now we're finally here, and I have a little time to write. My first impression of the jungle coming in by chopper was the incredible green, with small patches of fog against the mountains.

When I arrived at the firebase the First Sergeant said "Put a round in the chamber and welcome to the war." And that was that. I've been on a few patrols already, assigned to the 17th Cav. I walk behind a track for the most part, but I'm hoping to get a crack at a gunner's job on an

ACAV. Nights are very warm, like the days, and my shirt is more off than on. My M-16 is becoming second nature to me now—which is lucky for me and for the men I'm with. Nothing much to report. I hope all is well at home. Tell Beastly to go easy with Poole. I'll try to bring Poole some seeds. And something pretty for you and Grandmother. My love to you both,

James

October brought rain and weepy flowers on the hills, and the return of the flycatchers who set up house keeping under the eaves. Most days the sun rose behind thin clouds, lingering briefly in the wet trees before vanishing into darker clouds on the west. The annual flower show at Trebah Gardens excited Poole to fits of "Sing Hosanner" until he learned his entry of a miniature bog-garden had suffered an attack from seagulls and herons who took most of his fish and a large toad he loved for its deep bell-like voice. Beasley did his best to console his loss by talking cook into making her best scones, which he served to Poole on the patio, while Jean and her grandmother stood at the library window, watching the postman ride his bicycle around the circle drive, waving a letter. It was two letters! Jean thanked him profusely and followed her grandmother up the old stone steps to the library, gave the fire on the hearth a vigorous poke and pulled an ottoman close to her and opened a letter.

September, 1969
near Dinh Quan

Dear Grandmother,

This morning we completed a long patrol over steep hills covered with hedgerows and jungle. Very hard going. But, just before sundown, we stumbled on a small field of red flowers. We all stared at them. Beautiful red flowers in the middle of all this brokenness, filth and horror. I wanted to pick one, but we just looked at them, happy to see beauty at all—these bright red eager flowers coming up out of the muddy fields. We were, to a man, grateful for that.

The night noises are beginning and I will not be able to see what

I'm writing, so I'll close and send you all my love and, if I could, one of these red flowers. But I couldn't pick one now anyway since we've set our claymores on the perimeter. I can still see them through the trees-- this small field of red surrounded by green--and now I see only one, fading into the dark.

> All my love,
> James

She glanced at her grandmother and handed her the letter, and opened the second and read to herself, savoring each word. "Oh, I'm sorry grandmother. Let me start again."

> October, 1969
> near Highway 20

Dear Jean,

The monsoons are here at last with heavy wind that blows the rain sideways. In the morning as we move, heavy fog keeps us jumpy because the next bend in the trail might be just where Charlie is waiting. We can't see more than 15-20 feet in the daytime.

We set up cyclone fence each night against RPGs (rocket propelled grenades). Sometimes we're low on food and water but we have plenty of ammo. Last week we set up beside a trail and looked for a POW to take, but a fire fight broke out and I was firing as fast as I could, but we were hit with grenades and automatic weapons. Some men were hit by shrapnel and I was nicked in a couple of places, but nothing serious. It went back and forth for two minutes until the VC broke contact.

After the firing stopped I was shocked to see how badly my hands shook as I reloaded my weapon, but I guess you react in spite of the fear, which is REAL, because if you don't react the other guy is going to kill you—so you don't have time to think about right and wrong, good or bad. And when it's over you know you're OK for now. Just for now.

I hope you and Grandmother are keeping each other steady over there. Just mark your calendar—three months in country. Nine to go. The rain clouds are coming up again, and the wind is blowing. Stay warm.

Love from here to you!
James

Fall crept by, and they talked of Christmas, and who to invite in for Christmas teas, and whether Beasley should have new serving clothes. They were still talking when their neighbor from the bottom of the hill rapped on the sunroom window. "Good Afternoon, Lady Aldington. I didn't mean to give you a fright. But this letter came to us by mistake, and when I saw the postmark, why I knew right then who it must be from, and I came right round this minute, seeing as how you and your granddaughter loved to get mail from Mr. Clavelly. Goodness, me, how I do run on and you wanting to read it. I'll just see myself out by the garden gate, if you don't mind, and see what your Poole is planting that could possibly survive this damp and cold. Well, ta."

"Why, it's from a Charles somebody. It's dated last month. He says, 'Dear Miss Aldington, I'm writing to tell you that Flip (we found out his middle name was Philip so we call him Flip) was injured by a booby trap last week'. She stopped and looked at her grandmother. "Please go on, Jean. Don't worry about me. Please read it all."

'It's not serious, but he took some shrapnel in his chest and arms. He's at the field hospital now but should rejoin his unit before long.'

'He would probably be mad at me if he knew I was telling you this, but we've become pretty good friends, and I knew you would like to know he's going to be OK, in case someone sent you a telegram or something—' "—you see, Grandmother, James is all right—" '—and I wanted to let you know how it happened. We were on patrol at the edge of the jungle and everyone was jumpy anyway because the VC were pouring it on us all night, so the next day we followed their trail, and just before noon Flip tripped a wire and a grenade exploded. He wasn't close to the bush it was hidden in so his wounds are not bad. He hurts like hell (pardon the French), but he's a tough nut for a former English major. I'm from a farm in Illinois, and poetry was not high on my list of things to do in high school. But Flip likes it, and takes out the book of poems you sent him, and reads them if there's any light to see by when we're in our night position. Sometimes he'll read one out loud. The day before he got hit, he recited something like How do I Love You, or Thee ... by heart ... it was pitch black and when he stopped all you could hear was jungle noises and a light rain on the leaves and on us. We all liked to hear him read. I better stop now and oil everything that moves on my track. I hope you don't worry about old Flip. He's OK. Just pretty sore.

    Yrs. Truly,

        Charles Fredrick, (Flip's friend)

    Jean looked out the tall windows at the trees and bushes, wet and glistening. She wished James was here, now, sitting by the fire, reading his favorite poems. How she wished it. She thought it strange how she assumed wanting something badly enough would produce it when she was young, or at least cause it to be produced by those hearing her tantrums—not that there were many. No one in the house would have allowed them. "Prayers, yes," her grandfather said, "but no mucking about with whining! One must get on with it, Jean" he said, and gave her curls a shake. How she missed that as well. And isn't it odd, she mused, how many things one missed, in spite of the many things one has.

                                  December, 1969
                                      Cornwall

Dear James,

    Or should I call you Flip? Yes, I know about your nickname. I like it. But I'll still call you James if you don't mind. By the time you get this letter I expect you will have written to me about your accident. I already know you were injured—but not seriously? I'm TRUSTING a friend of yours told me the truth about your wounds not being serious! No, I won't tell you who wrote to me, but I will tell you I'm very glad he did, because if I had received a telegram saying you were injured I would have been very scared—scared mostly for you, but also for myself. At least you have a friend who didn't want me to hear about it without some details, and that you would likely be out of hospital soon. I hope your letter, when it comes, says the same thing.

Grandmother knows too; she's seeing about supper as I write. I think she needed to get up and do something, anything but sit and stare at the rain, wondering about you. I'm afraid she's not doing very well. The doctor says it's just age catching up with her. He gave her some pills which she pretends to swallow, then puts them in her napkin which Beasley immediately picks up and throws away. It's a conspiracy!

Well, it's raining again. I think this will be a very wet winter. Poole says so. He's standing under the grape arbor right now wondering what to do. I know what I'm going to do: it's a pot of tea for Grandmother and me, then I'll put on my slicker and walk to the village to post this letter before supper and see if there's one from you. I love you, James. Please, PLEASE be careful and come back to us soon.

All love,
Jean

P.S. Promise me you won't be angry with your FRIEND who told me. He's my friend now too!

The rest of the year passed with brief notes from Vietnam talking about the terrible weather, bad food and the extra added attraction when the Rome plows come in to clear jungle, plows which can clear up to 150 acres per day, depending on the thickness of the forest, the weather and enemy contact. Sometimes a plow will have to ram trees several times to bring them down, and then all kinds of things fall into the cab such as scorpions, bamboo vipers, kraits, centipedes and other critters.

Christmas was as merry as they could make it, but the house knew it was not really merry at all. They hosted the usual dinners for neighbors, and "Happy Christmas Bake Sales" for the poor and needy, but it went on mechanically and without much spirit until the Helston Chorale Society sent carolers to sing at their front door, bringing the entire household outside to listen to "Good King Wenceslas" while Beasley bustled in and out with cups of mulled wine and trays of plum pudding and minced-meat pastries before they were invited into the library where they balanced tea before the fire blazing on the ancient hearthstone, while Jean moved among them with trifle and cook's special raspberry sponge. When it was over, they watched the tiny band of carolers disappear beneath the tunnel of trees on the drive, their bright hats and scarves wind-blown, leaving bits of "God Rest Ye Merry, Gentlemen" hanging in the frosty air. And when the last things were put away, and the household staff received their gifts from Grandmother—with a festive tot of rum or brandy—and Beasley and Poole retired to Beasley's room beneath the stairs for their Christmas Cheer—she kissed Jean goodnight and climbed the curved staircase to her room. But she stopped at the top, remembering, then looked down at Jean sitting by the fire. "Do you wonder what James is doing tonight? I do too. I try not to imagine, but ... tonight of all nights I wish him God's peace. And safety. Good night, my dear."

Later, while the dying fire snapped and popped behind her, Jean went to the tall windows and watched a light snow outline the dark evergreens along the drive, wondering what darkness James walked in this night, and thought of lines from "Soldiers" by Edison Gage:

> Bathed in moonlight bright and cold as stars,
> they follow others into wars
> with just the moon to see them go,
> their footsteps slow and deep and full of snow.

She pressed her body against the cold window, and watched the moon catch in the empty branches of the wild plum orchard on the little hill beside the house, and whispered, "Happy Christmas, my darling."

As the year wore down, Jean sat with her Grandmother in her room and told her she needed to get away, maybe a trip by rail. "Maybe I'll take my car, I don't know. I will be in touch with you, of course, and I've called Dr. Bryn-Jones ... now don't pout ... he will send a very qualified nurse to stay here while I'm gone. I don't think I could bear to be away more than a week, two at the most."

January proved as wet and cold as December, but a fire on the grate in St. Ives cheered her spirits her first night. She had a letter to read from James that she fingered as she drove, trying to sense the contents. There wasn't much news in it, but she read it over again as she sat with tea in the small hotel sitting room to see if she had missed anything before looking at her map, tracing with her finger the tiny spider web of lines from village to village. Two little girls watched her from their nurse's lap, but when she smiled at them they buried their heads in the nurse's coat.

At Portreath, she watched a man smoking a pipe in the dining room of the hotel. A thin curl of strong, but pleasant smoke curled up from the newspaper he pretended to read; when he lowered it, she saw a pair of grey eyes, like her father's. In St. Agnes, she bought a book about tin mines, read two pages and tossed it in the boot, telling herself she would do better when she got to Newquay. But the quiet she hoped to find was not found; instead a steady stream of busses clogged the streets with people from Scotland in search of better weather. They would not find it in Cornwall in January, she mused.

"Hello, Grandmother, how are you, dear? Yes, I'm fine, but my car's not. It blew something or other that's essential to something else says a nice man here in St. Clement. Yes, I've left the coast and plan to cross Bodwin Moor tomorrow, car and nice man willing. Do you remember that little place we came to after seeing the slate mine with the beautiful subterranean lake? St. Neot? Yes! Well, that's where I'll be if I can make it. Yesterday, I had tea with two delightful people I met at Lanhydrock Estate: Jill and Mac. We chatted about flowers and war. Somehow it seemed a natural combination, though now I can't think why. A wonderful visit. What's that? A letter from James. Oh, Grandmother, read it to me, will you? I'm in this perfectly awful room surrounded by drooping trees and bushes and some kind of flowers outside my window that look as if they've given up the ghost entirely. Please...just a minute...there, I'm ready. Are you all right? I mean, are you up to.... Yes, I know you are, dear. I just didn't...no, I'm not playing nurse. How is Nurse Agnes, by the way? Have you and Beasley conspired against her? All right. I'll be quiet if you'll read his letter."

"Can you hear me, Jean? I'm going to speak slowly. It's from a

place I can't pronounce.
Are you there?"

January
Vung Tau

Dear Jean,

I know it's been weeks since you received a letter. I can write now as I'm taking some in-country R&R in a place called Vung Tau, an old French resort S.E. of Saigon with four men from our company. It's pretty lively at night! The details would make you wonder too much, so I'll just leave it as lively. We almost didn't have any R&R at all because the slick, a re-supply chopper, went crazy as it lifted off-- something wrong with the rotor-- and we spun around two or three times a few feet off the ground before the pilot got us down. No one was hurt--a few bruises-- but we had to wait for another chopper. By then we were really ready for rest and relaxation.

I am now a gunner with Delta Troop. Last week, we met some healthy resistance north of Cu Chi (west of Saigon—in the Iron Triangle), but we poured some serious (deleted) into them. Our Captain of Tanks (I call him to myself) was recommended for a medal for bravery after the big fight. It lasted five hours, with some heavy casualties on the other side. Unfortunately, some men I know are not going home like they planned. A Brig. General got caught in the middle of things and our Captain managed to pull him out of the mess; however, I heard the General died later. The Captain could just as easily have taken a hit that time. No one talks much about it. People who have been here a long time laugh and curse a lot and one can see they are protecting themselves against madness. We don't talk about that either. We just do the mission and hope we'll be somewhere dry come nighttime.

It's kind of comforting, though, to be rolling along with all that clanking of armor close by. After awhile, you can't hear anything but that—until night, then everything is alive with sounds from the trees and bushes. Even the sound of water in the nearby stream comes clear and distinct, just like the stars, diamond-hard, glittering in the darkest sky you can imagine, so far away from this unholy mess. And you know nature doesn't know or care who you are, or why you're here listening to the river and the wind soughing through the tall trees—you can't touch it, whatever IT is behind the mist and the mountains and the incredible green and the beautiful stars. It's just us, looking and listening, especially listening, our weapons and ammo like a second skin. That's it for now. We're moving out.

    Love to all
        James

Spring came, waking the colors one by one in ditches still running water, and on hills where generations of seeds turned themselves into flowers again. It was a time when Jean missed James the most because she knew summer was coming and all that it would mean with him gone. It was always summer for them growing up, and now she doubted the meaning of the word. It held no promise.

It was almost May when a letter came that made her tremble; not the news—she was used to reading about missions and ambushes and choppers in and out of areas of operation—it was something she sensed, some dark thing in the lines at the end, something she dared not look at too closely as she read the letter aloud to her Grandmother:

March, 1970
Dinh Quan

Dearest Jean,

Last week was a classic foul-up, because something went very wrong and we very nearly got shelled by our own artillery. We were in a night defensive position guarding some engineers, but the coordinates worked out before dark by the Engineer Captain were wrong. As a result our artillery was given our location as an enemy base camp. They fired at least ten rounds at us, and all kinds of stuff from shrapnel to leaves, limbs and dirt rained down on us.

We hit the ground fast, some made it into their tracks, but two men setting claymores were hit by shrapnel and later had to be medi-vaced out. The Captain of tanks got on the radio and told the artillery they were too close and that stopped the fire mission before they threw another round. He's going to H.Q. tomorrow to talk to the Colonel about the incident. If any round had exploded inside our perimeter we might have been wounded—or killed. After scaring you to death, I can give you some good news. One of the men got a rain jacket with a hood, so we take turns using it when we're on guard duty. Well, we're saddling up for something you won't read about, so maybe I can tell you about it when I get back.

All my love,
James

May, 1970

My Dearest James,

Summer has finally arrived. Well, May anyway. Grandmother is taking short naps on the patio again while Beasley hovers over her like a mother hen. The cornflowers are popping out all over our hill, and you will want to know that the funny birds you found strutting through the fields that day we picnicked overlooking the harbor were pheasants—or so says Poole. Oh, James, when you get back we'll have to go to Fowey again and tramp for days. Do you remember—of course you do—our hike to Gribben Head that rainy day, and how we had to huddle in that copse of trees with two cows until it let up? The cows never complained about us sharing their tree. We had hot tea, thanks to me, and sandwiches. Weren't they wonderful?

And the day we took the ferry across Fowey River to take the Hall Walk, the walk HM Charles I took that fateful day when an assassin's bullet missed him and killed one of the local fishermen who had been waiting beside the path for a look at the King? The history of the walk, and the number of Monarchs who took it were in our minds as we followed the path beneath those wonderful old trees and skipped across rivulets of water running down to the river. You carried me across a stream and almost fell in! But you were wonderful. And the sunset, James! The sunset over Gribben Head we saw from Polruan!

Everything turning yellow, slowly, like an upwelling of gold across the meadows and into the trees until everything, earth sky and water burned with gold. It was, and is, the most amazing sight I've ever seen. And we will walk there again, James. We will walk there again, my darling. Never doubt it. Never fear. Never, never, never!

I love you and miss you –
Jean

But her intuition was better than she thought, for the postman returned in the afternoon with a letter he found stuck in the bottom of his sack. As she watched him disappear down the drive beneath the great overhanging oaks, she glanced at the return name on the envelope and saw that it was not from James.

"Grandmother! A letter has come for me, for us, but it's not from James. It's from an army person. Grandmother, are you awake? May I come in? I'm opening it. Oh, it's from a Chaplain! Grandmother, don't look for trouble. It's probably one of those form things that have to be done. He's letting us know that James is all right and we should be hearing from him about…" Now she broke down and buried her face in her grandmother's arms.

"Jean, Jean … you haven't even read the letter yet, and we're carrying on like school girls. Dry your tears and let's get on with it, as Evan liked to say. 'Let's just get on with it, Hilaria!' he would say in his Lord Aldington voice. Read the letter, Jean."

"Grandmother, it's dated April, 1970. This is an old letter. I wonder how long it was in Michael's bag. But, I'll read it now."

April, 1970
Long Binh

Dear Lady Aldington, and Miss Jean Aldington,

I am a Lutheran Chaplain with the 199th Light Infantry Brigade. I had the pleasure of meeting your fiance while he was recuperating from shrapnel wounds suffered during an attack at Long Binh. While in hospital, James took communion every day, and we had several talks about his background, his faith, and about his love for you and for your grandmother. Before the war I was campus pastor at the University of California at Santa Barbara. We did not know each other, but I sat in on several English classes, so it was good to find someone who loved poetry and actually carried a book of poems with him.

I know you and your Grandmother worry about him, as I do, about all of them. The "whys" may never be fully answered, so I will not tell you this war, and James' injuries are God's will. But I will tell you that in spite of the battles and the bloodshed, James has not lost hope of peace, nor has he lost his faith. It has been tested—the faith of all of us has been tested—but he has not lost it because it is very deep and very personal.

He won't tell you this, so I'm telling you now. He will need some care when he returns to you. You may or may not be able to give him what he will need for the future—his future. But by the grace of God he will come back to you and you will find the words. The care and love you have shown him already have been vitally important to him. If there is anything you would like to talk about please feel free to write me at any time. Meanwhile, I will keep you both in my prayers.

Sincerely in Christ,
Martin Childs
Major, Chaplain
199th LIB

But June had not ended before the next letter came from the Chaplain, one that would explain the silence and the nagging feeling that something was still terribly wrong. It was the letter she heard in news reports, and in bad plays when the audience knows it's coming.

May, 5 1970
Saigon

My Dear Lady Aldington, and Jean Aldington,

Please forgive me if I've bungled your titles. I haven't had enough practice to remember just how it should go. But I wanted to write to you as soon as I knew anything for sure about James and his condition.

Doubtless he has not written, and the reasons are serious. First, he was badly wounded in a recent action. He was hit by several pieces of shrapnel from a mortar round in Long Khan Province as his unit was stopping enemy movement across areas targeted for land cuts by the big plows. He didn't know what hit him or how badly he was injured because he kept firing until there was an explosion that knocked him unconscious. I'm sorry to tell you he is unable to walk without the aid of crutches; however, the doctors think he may do fine with a cane in a few weeks. They cannot be sure, of course, but they feel his chances are good.

Unfortunately, whatever blew up in his face during that encounter has left him temporarily blind. I say temporarily because the Doctors say so. They are not sure what caused the loss of sight because they found no pathology. They say it could have been from the flash close to his eyes—or it could be a psycho-traumatic problem. In any case, they feel he will recover his sight. When, they do not know. It could be next week or next year. Or longer. I knew you would want the truth, so I've written you what I know. I'm sure you will receive an official and more detailed account of the action and the injuries from someone soon. But now you must be prepared to take care of him and nurse him back to health. And you must do that very soon because he is being sent home to you. I thought you would like to hear that from a friend. And he has many in his company and in his platoon. Captain Tierney, his 'Captain of Tanks' may write you as well, as he is very fond of James.

Now I must say goodbye to James and go back to a busy place where men are in grave danger of body and soul. Please feel free to write to me at any time. I will keep James and all of you in my prayers.

Peace, (pray for it)
    Martin Childs
    Major, Chaplin
    199th LIB

III

Jean reached across the table for James' hand, gripped it tightly and stood up. Neither spoke as she guided him across the large flagstone patio and onto the path through the upper garden. "The sun is out, James, and there are blossoms everywhere. The azaleas are especially lovely today. Poole planted some tulip bulbs years ago and now we have several colors all in neat rows across the top of the hill. Thankfully he is such a fussbudget when it comes to his flowers."

James let her guide him along the path, though he knew where he was, which trees cast shade, which shrubs and vines provided the border to the path where he had cut some sweet peas back. But now he let her lead him, her arm through his. It was strange, this darkness on a sunny day on the hill he loved.

"James, what are you smiling about? I haven't seen you smile since you came home. Was it something I said?" She squeezed his arm and waited. She knew she could not push him to talk. She had tried that and he had retreated farther into himself.

"I was remembering poor Poole's look when I cut some of his favorite hedge. He could not stand to watch, so he walked down to the village and sat in the pub all day. Do you remember? We sent Beastly after him and they both came home tipsy, Beasley singing his old school songs, and Poole weeping bitterly-- more from the drink than grief, I think."

"Oh, James, it's so good to hear you laugh. Yes, I remember that day. Poor Beasley couldn't get out of bed the next day. I don't think he handles Guinness very well. James, would you like to sit awhile on the bench overlooking the bay? I can tell you what kind of boats are in and how the channel looks. Then, if you feel like it, we could walk down the path to the water and listen to the waves on the shingle."

"Jean, stop a minute. No, first, take me to that bench. I know it must be close. I want to tell you something."

Jean watched a crowd of butterflies hover in the sun. "There are butterflies all over. I wish you could …oh, I'm sorry. I know you…"

"… It's all right, Jean. You don't have to be so careful, I won't break. You can see them for me and tell me their colors and how big they are and what they're doing. You're my eyes now. Thankfully, I can see them in my mind because I spent so much time here--more time here than at my own house. It's funny, isn't it, how one thinks of home? This has always been home to me, even after my parents separated and my mother moved to the States because she wanted me to be an American. And I am an American…but England, Cornwall, is where I belong. It is most me." He turned his head toward a sound. "Jean, are the bees hiving? I hear something like a soft motor in the wood just there. I'll bet they're fumbling the goldenrod I put in. I love the sound."

"James, you amaze me. Yes, I see them now, deep inside the wood, swirling in a great cloud around that old burnt-out oak. They return to it every spring. Your ears are very sharp, James."

"My ears are ok. I just can't see." Jean held his arm tightly against her, pushed back her hair and kissed him on the cheek. "You smell like…what? Not gardenias. What is that scent, Jean? I smelled it on your letters and went to sleep smelling it, even in the mud and rain."

"James…you don't have to..." "...yes, I do. I have to say it. But you won't want to hear it. It's something no one should have to hear about, much less do." He waited, then stood up and felt his way to the willow overhanging the bench. "Good old willow. If you knew how much I missed this tree. All the trees. And the hills. And the flowers and the boats in the harbor and the rain that drove us inside to play cards with Grandmother and … Jean … I missed it all … every bit of it. You most of all. No, not most of all—you were everything! I couldn't think of this place, of England … of life itself, without seeing you, feeling you close to me, smelling that scent in your hair. I never thought about honor or duty…not even much about country—though all that was part of it--part of the reason I was there. I could have, maybe should have, skipped the exercise all together. Maybe… I don't know… conscientious objector or something. Why I didn't I don't know. I just didn't. And it doesn't make me any braver or dumber than anyone else. It's just what I did. At the moment. Maybe I would have chosen another path at another moment."

"Tell me what happened to you over there. I'm right here, holding you tight. Tell me now. This minute. I promise you I won't go away, ever. Not ever, James. What you are, we are. That will never change, my darling."

"It was raining. It was always raining then. Mud flew up as our tracks tore down the road to the next position. We made a logger, a big circle, and sloshed through deep mud to set the claymore mines. I've got a shotgun slung over my shoulder, grenades and ammo on my belt. I felt heavy, and a bit silly, like some character out of a B movie. We were in thick jungle. We all listen, hard, harder than you ever listen to anything, trying to make sense out of the night noises, and the hard rain pounding the track and ground.

We lay quietly in the rain, our weapons ready, the detonators, grenades. We had it all. We were ready for anything, and we felt, knew, that something was going to happen that night. I can feel the others on the ground near me, their eyes flashing as they turn their heads. Nobody talks or sighs or coughs. We just wait, tense, ready. I must have dozed, or half-dozed, because I suddenly sensed someone was standing in front of me. I blinked against the rain, then I could make out what I thought was the tree line we saw when we set up, but I knew it wasn't a tree, it was Charlie and he was in front of me, maybe looking at me. I didn't wait to see anymore. I pulled the trigger of my shotgun and squeezed the detonator of my claymores. Then, all the claymores went off along the trail, and I heard grenades go off and felt a concussion behind me that threw dirt on my back. They were pouring Ak 47 fire into us, so I crawled backwards, and then I saw the man right in front of me, black against black and I fired until there was nothing there, just a pile of black clothes, muddy arms and legs spread out, his torso blown apart, his head…"

He stopped and wiped his face. "It's getting cooler, isn't it? Strange how I can feel even the slightest breeze, this breeze especially, with a taste of salt water in it. I used to lie awake at night, trying to remember what salt water tasted like."

"James, should we go in now? The mists are rising up the hill, and it will be cold tonight. Grandmother will have something good and hot waiting. Shall we go back?"

"Not yet. Not until I've said it all. Or as much as my mind will let me remember. That night, all hell broke loose, and I emptied over two magazines into the dark clothes coming at us, my claymores spreading death and destruction, my grenades bouncing in front of me … noise, crying and cursing from my buddies near me in the trees … and then, silence. Just as if a switch had been turned off. It was quiet. No one talked or moved. I don't remember an explosion. The next thing I do remember is the whirr of blades above me, and that I had enough sense left to lie still and let them lift the litter into the chopper. I don't know how long I was unconscious before that dust-off came.

When Lt. Geeting came to see me in the hospital, he told me that the VC had women and children with them that night. We killed all of them. No, I killed them. I pulled the trigger, threw the grenades, and shredded them with my claymores. I killed them because I had to kill them. I didn't think about it. I just pulled the trigger as fast as I could. There was nothing to say or do, and there's nothing to say or do now. In a way it was not real. You don't see it as real. The real world is here, or wherever you aren't. Nothing is real but staying alive. Nothing matters but that. And if you are alive after a firefight then you are still alive for another day. And that's all. All the talk about heroism or fear or duty doesn't enter into it. You have your arms and legs and hands, and your face is not shot away, —but your friend is dead, his blood seeping into the mud, and you help bag him and lay him in the helicopter and maybe ride back to base next to him, the moon finally coming out as the wind at 90 knots hits your clothes, wet and heavy and full of someone's blood."

Jean watched him closely, trying to see into him, to find the hurt and pull it out, but she couldn't. It was beyond her powers, she knew; something had to work itself out in its own time. She shuddered when she realized it might not ever work itself out, that it might be there to stay, deep inside him, festering, hurting. As she cradled his head in her arms she prayed that his, their lives might go forward in spite of the darkness he lived in. Somehow, someway, she would bring him back..

"Grandmother will scold us, won't she, Jean? Let's go back. I can't wait to see—oops, almost forgot—can't wait to *hear* old Beastly rant and rave about the Queen and the price of fish. Believe it or not, I missed him. Poole, too, with his broken wheelbarrow and smelling like mulch. I missed it all. Let's go back. No, I'll go ahead. I know this path and can tell by what's under my feet where I am. You whistle if I stray off the path."

Summer was leaving their hills. Beasley stood tall and gaunt, his arthritic knees keeping him leaning against the sideboard during dinners. Lady Aldington read a little in the afternoons before shadows crept up the stacks of books to the high ceiling of the library where Jean would find her nodding by the fire. Jean pretended not to watch James on the patio as he rested or suddenly stood, his head tilted to the side as if listening for something, something he feared was coming. But it was better, always getting better, she thought. And Dr. Bryn-Jones thought so, too, and suggested he not take one of the pills the Army doctors sent him home with. Such was the end of summer: tired, warm, indifferent summer.

One morning in early September, they thought of fall when they saw Poole digging in the beds, mulching timid leaves that had fallen in the night. The Doctor came more often to talk to Lady Aldington in her library, always leaving by the side door for his car where Jean waited to talk to him. She knew time had already taken its toll, and she spent more time at her side reading to her or and trying, unsuccessfully, to knit, which caused her grandmother to scowl and mutter about the younger generation, so she often just sat quietly, watching her labored breathing until sleep took her there in the dark bedroom, and she could slip out to find James, sometimes strolling with his stick on a path through the trees, or sitting on the bench by the bluff, listening to the gulls crying as they wheeled and dove in the estuary. He always heard her coming, and raised a hand to hers, and they would sit quietly until the last sun touched the tops of the eastern hills, and Beasley's little bell sounded for tea.

It was going to be a fine fall. Everyone said so. The grocer in the village proclaimed all the signs were there: the rare birds seen again, the flights of others heading out over the channel to France, a flower hanging on past its time--all signs, he said of a fine, fine fall. Poole and Beasley had found some kind of peace, or an unspoken truce had been agreed upon; Lady Aldington had improved to the point of little afternoon walks in the garden before tea in the great parlor. Jean read, asking James questions about Frost's "Reluctance, " or an image from a sonnet by Keats or Hopkins. She enjoyed reading to him above all things, smiling as his brow furrowed if she got a line wrong. He was coming back to life, she thought, and back to her as his hand reached across the Rosy Dresden table to hers, holding it quietly.

The first day of October was bright and warm, with long ribbons of sunshine across the steel-blue ocean. Beasley walked out the tall doors with his duster tucked in his arm in the manner of a serving British officer; Poole grunted somewhere in the tangled hedges on the hillside facing Trebah Gardens. Lady Aldington was on the chaise, her eyes closed against the sun when Jean and James came around the house from the gazebo. "It's still summer, is it? No one will believe this can last. Even the grocer will be dumbfounded. What in the world is Poole up to down there? It sounds like a badger rooting about in that tangle. Let's go sit on the bench by the bluff, Jean. I want to smell the ocean today. What do you say?"

"Lead on, James, and I will follow closely." But he had already pulled his arm back from hers and was walking slowly and steadily along the path as it curved through the giant oaks and beeches. "Your feet are miracles, James, how they remember each turn. I'm so glad to see you out walking and not pouting as I stumbled through Owen and Sassoon. And what is that line of Hopkins you love so? 'What is all this juice and all this joy?' That sums up this beautiful October day. Isn't this what you Yanks call Indian Summer?" She laughed, picked up a stone and tossed it aside.

"Jean, do you remember how we used to say this bluff would be the ideal place to get married? Remember?"

"Of course I remember. I think we each dreamed our wedding. This bluff that runs down to the river, and the seagulls crying and the wind whipping the long grasses, lush and green like another sea rolling down to the estuary. Of course I remember."

"Well, then, since our memories are not impaired, perhaps we should dream again. I've always loved you, Jean. You must feel that— as I feel your love." He reached to her and she held his arm against her body as she guided him to the wooden bench on the rim of the bluff.

Poole had finished his rooting and grumbling in the hedges and came up to the patio for the lemonade and cookies cook had promised. Beasley dozed standing up, and hearing Poole, roused himself and looked over at Lady Aldington on the chaise. Seeing her book on the ground beside her, he tiptoed across the patio to retrieve it, but as he bent down, he stopped, shading his eyes, frowning. Poole watched as he carefully removed her sunglasses. And when he stood up at last, he looked at Poole, making no attempt to stop the tears as he carefully drew her shawl over her face.

"Sic transit gloria mundi," my friend Poole. "Thus passes the glory of the world." Then he straightened, cleared his throat and said, "Poole, pray fetch Lady Aldington's maid. Tell her to bring the sable comforter on Madame's bed. Then go wash your dirty hands, because we will be having visitors. I shall call Doctor Bryn-Jones, then fetch the children from the bluff. Go now, Poole, then come back and stand with me through what must come next."

High billowy white clouds piled up over the river and a low-flying plane came through them, and dived low over the channel, hugging the rocky western coast. "Jean, we should go back and tell Grandmother we've decided to be married right here, on this very spot. She will like that. "

"Oh, James, she will be beside herself with planning. It will be a wonderful wedding. So many people from the village will come, and your friends at Trebah, so many things to do. So much to … James, be careful there. What are you doing? You're too near the cliff!"

"I'm just wondering what this small patch of cornflowers is doing on this hillside this time of year. They must think it's still summer!"

She walked down and stood behind him, looking over his shoulder. "These cornflowers should not be ..." She stopped, her hand to her mouth. "James, how do you know there's a patch of cornflowers still growing? How … James! You can see! Can you really see? Why didn't you tell …" but he pulled her to him and kissed her hair, her nose, her lips. "And here's a kiss for your eyes. I'm sorry I didn't tell you, but I wasn't sure until I stepped out on that new path of wood chips good old Poole made for us. Yes, I can see you! My girl with the cornflower-blue eyes. And I can see those huge billowy white clouds, and the two little boats on the river-- and way to the right I see the waves breaking on the rocks, the same waves breaking on Brest and on the beaches of Viet Nam…names, Jean, places with history--my history. But our history is in this beautiful place where cornflowers think it's always summer. Let's not tell them. Look, Beasley's coming for us. He must have tea waiting. Take my hand, Jean. No, let me take yours. It's summer for all of us now."

Gerald Harnisch knew he was a ghost even though he just knicked himself shaving. All the signs pointed to the fact that although he wore a tie and taught his freshmen at 9am each MWF at Willoughby College, he was a ghost. No one saw him. Students passed him, dreaming of hamburgers and sex as he climbed the worn carpet steps to his office on the second floor of the Humanities Building. At the English desk a Departmental Assistant stared at her computer screen. "Good morning," Gerald said. " It's going to be a fine day by the look of things. The papers said rain, but…"

"What? " she said. "I was deep into Google. What did you say?" Gerald looked at her. "Nothing. I was just talking to myself. Have a nice day."

It hadn't always been thus, he mused. Time was when his voice commanded a modicum (as he put it) of respect when he read his wife sonnets from" The House of Life." He remembered long nights in bed, or early quckies, if his wife responded. That was over. Ghosts don't make love. What do they do, he wondered?

His students had some inner clock that woke them ten minuets before the end of the period so they could resume text messaging, with a glance at the board to see if there was anything that concerned them before they shuffled out: the boys with hoods over their heads, girls with short T Shirts and low-slung jeans showing a small tattoo at the pretty confluence, as he said in the coffee room.

From his window, Gerald Harnisch watched girls pull into parking spaces, bumping against other cars. In the warm spring he liked to watch them flow along the sidewalk, or through the small park in the middle of campus, skirts clinging to their legs and buttocks. He said nothing about buttocks in the coffee room. Hope had long since failed in that department, he thought. Sex was out. Gone. He did all he could. Bought movies with couples "going at it" as his friend, Malvern said. But his wife of thirty-seven years just watched, her mouth full of muffins from Java City, her hair done up in some kind of paper things for the night. Her once lithe and lovely figure was now encased in a floral "wrapper" that reminded him of a shower curtain he had seen in Miami Beach at an English convention for Victorian scholars where he delivered a paper on Clough, with the rather catchy title, "Nought is Never Enough!" Two or three of the older professors in attendance smiled knowingly. The rest looked for free donuts and coffee.

He opened his grade book, not looking up at the students to see who was there or not there. "Desirée Magellan," he said aloud, suddenly alert. "Here," came a quiet voice from the back. "Desirée Magellan?" The girl moved her head from behind a large student who was eating. "Here," she said softly. She looked at him and smiled. He knew he should continue the roll. But she was beautiful. The most beautiful student he had ever seen. Her eyes were hazel and caught motes of color in the room, as an autumn day might pick up the colors of burning leaves, or the muted greens and browns of a path in the English woods. He had discovered such a path on their last trip abroad. Since then, it had been America's National Parks for awhile, then nothing. They never went anywhere. She seemed content to watch television and read the society pages of the newspaper. If he wanted to go somewhere he went by himself, staying in cheap Bed and Breakfasts where there were no great rooms with fireplaces where guests met for drinks and discussed their day. Just a room next to someone who stayed up late playing the flute or smoking pot. No private bath. No television. No guests. No pets. No … he looked up. The class was staring at him. The girl had disappeared behind the student who carefully unwrapped a muffin to go with his coffee, making little schulcking sounds as he licked the filling oozing from the pastry.

"Sorry, didn't hear you. Thank you, uh, let's see. Miss Magellan, is it?" He continued the roll, not listening to any response, closed the grade book and passed out the syllabus and discussed the texts and required papers. He didn't remember telling them anything. He answered no questions in spite of the fact that three or four hands went up. He was thinking of the girl behind the large student. How beautiful her name: Desirée Magellan! And how exquisite she was. Like something from the Pre-Raphaelites, he thought. Rossetti, surely. He would mention her to Malvern and Brucie. They would understand.

"Miss Magellan, could you stop by my office? I'd like to discuss a possible term paper with you." He said it offhand, head down, as if he were going over a list of students to talk to. After class, she came to his desk and stood quietly, eyes wide, 'arms perfectly await,' he thought, remembering a Mark Van Doren poem he admired. "Why don't we go up to my office, Desirée, and we can go over the paper. Just go on upstairs, my office is 212. The door is open. I'll be along in a minute." She looked at him with those wonderful hazel eyes that seemed to include him with the leaves and the greens and browns of Devon.

He filled his coffee cup in the mail- room and walked down the hall to his office as Malvern was just coming out of his. "There's a student waiting for you in there, Gerry. You just might want to talk to this one." He raised his eyebrows and kept walking. Brucie was in his office across the hall, door open. "Gerry," he muttered, but did not look away from his computer.

She told him her friends called her Des. Would he call her that too? He would. He suggested they take advantage of the campus coffee house. "My office gets so crowded with students wanting things, you know, papers, grades…we could go over your topic…what was it again?"

"I was going to take your idea of writing on Rossetti. I'm intrigued by someone who would put his only copy of his poetry in a woman's casket, only to have it dug up some stormy night so he could publish them. What a ghastly thing to do!" Gerald stared at her. She was tall, perhaps five feet nine, maybe ten. She was willowy, with legs that went clear to the ground, to use Brucie's expression. She wore skirts, unlike the majority of coeds who wore jeans or sweats. Desirée, Des, wore just the right eye make-up; her hair was always combed just so, as if she were planning a day when everything depended on her appearance. Gerald liked that. At home it was wrappers and curlers and a blank stare at the TV. Des was calm, proper, yet exciting. But she was a student, he reminded himself. Keep the bloody door open. Don't make waves. Don't get anyone talking. There's nothing like a small southern college to start a rumor. Can't afford to retire just yet.

Must be careful, he told himself.

As the year wore on, he made excuses to get out of the office and walk through the campus park where the Loosahatchee River ran slowly around and through tulip trees, and one giant chinaberry tree. He bought her coffee and muffins and listened to her talk about Danté Gabrielle Rosetti. He remembered nothing she told him. He was immersed in her eyes, her smile, her long curving legs. He was falling apart, and he knew he couldn't save himself.

After supper one night, just before Thanksgiving break, his wife told him she was leaving him for someone she met at Home Depot. A man who knew what it took to make a woman feel young and wanted, she said. He drove a truck hauling vegetables out of Muscle Shoals, Alabama, so don't try to find him, because you can't. She folded her arms across her chest and waited. Gerald Harnisch stared at his mashed potatoes. They were from a box where all you had to do was add water, or if guests were coming, milk. She always used water.

"Gerald! Have you heard a word I've said? I'm leaving you. Tonight. Clean up the plates and rinse them off like I showed you, and put them in the dishwasher. And for heaven's sake, use the right soap. Last time you put the wrong soap in the dishwasher, and we had suds a foot deep all over the floor. We liked to never get it cleaned up. Can you do that right for once? Gerald?"

But Gerald wasn't listening. He was looking into beautiful hazel eyes. He was remembering what she wore on her last visit. Her long legs disappeared up into a very tight, short skirt He wondered how it would feel to lay his face against her leg. It would be warm, firm. Her hands danced in the air as she described her joy in reading the Rossettis, not just Danté Gabriel, she said, but his sister, Christina. "You must know this," she said, 'Beauty without the beloved is like a sword in the heart.' Isn't that wonderful?" Her hand was on his arm, tears forming in her eyes. He patted her hand and mumbled some nonsense about overstatement, sentiment obscuring meaning—all rubbish, he knew. Why didn't he just take her in his arms and hold her close and feel her long, lithe body melt into his own, her eyes wide in wonder as he kissed her?

"Well, Gerald, I must say you're taking this very well. I thought you would be furious and want to know all about him, so you could fight him or something. Did you understand what I said? I'm leaving. Tonight. Don't try to follow me. I'll write you when I'm settled with Raymond … oops, silly me. And don't do anything foolish like cutting your wrists or anything. I've seen that on TV where a man cut his wrists three times. But he lived, and found a new love in the doctor's nurse when they sewed him up. She does most of his writing for him because he cut some tendons or other and can't hold a pen. Isn't that heartbreaking? But you wouldn't know about life that way, would you? No, you stick your nose into your Victorian books, and pretend you live in that world. And you wonder why you don't have any friends, why no one talks like you? They think you're nuts is why! It's way past time I told you that. No, you're-using the wrong liquid again. I swear I don't know what will happen to you."

He watched her drive away in their only car. Behind him the dishwasher gurgled and chuffed its way through its appointed cycles. He waited for suds to spill out onto the floor, but he had used the right liquid. "Huzzah!" he said aloud. "Thank heaven for the right liquids! What a thing for science. A boon for mankind. A…" He didn't finish because his chest was heaving. He choked back tears he hadn't felt for years. He thought he ought to be sorry that things hadn't worked out for them after thirty-seven years. What a time to break up! But when is the right time, he wondered. He went through a checklist of couples he knew, added up their years and wondered how many were still in love.

That night, he dreamed of a tall girl lifting him up to her eye level while his feet dangled two feet off the ground. Her eyes were very large and very round with pieces of leaves imbedded in them. When she smiled, she showed a long pink tongue rolled up like a garden hose. He knew it would stretch out a foot if she wanted. He felt her breasts stick into him. He wanted to enjoy it, but it hurt. He cried out in his sleep, the pillow wet beneath his mouth.

Word got around the coffee room. Brucie and Malvern took him out for a drink. The faculty secretary brought him dinner once, and that was it. The days went by, and he heard nothing from his wife. Meanwhile, his classes were falling apart. He could not keep up with his syllabi; students skipped classes; his lectures were fractured, disjointed, and it wasn't long before the Dean sent him a note asking if there was anything he could do for him. Did he think he needed a leave-of-absence? He thought it could be worked out.

Gerald Harnisch was never a heavy drinker. Indeed, he rarely drank at all. Now he picked up wine at the market, then some vodka and whiskey. He had a couple of drinks when he got home from classes to unwind, wine during dinner, and a nightcap or two before turning in. He let himself go. His once nicely-pressed pants were baggy. Shirts had stains on the collars and cuffs. His face took on a blotchy, puffy look. Students muttered. Teachers who didn't know him wondered who the man was going in and out of buildings; one called campus security and said they might have an intruder on campus. On the last day of class, he watched her cross the street into the park. She hesitated beneath the catalpa trees and looked up at his window, then turned down the little hill and walked across the old wooden bridge.

"Des, wait. Please wait." She turned and saw him running across the bridge to her. "Where are you going? You weren't in class today, and I thought … well, I wondered if you were all right. Where are you going now?"

She stared at him. He was disheveled. His shirt was un-tucked, and he hadn't shaved. "Dr. Harnisch, I'm going to see the Dean. What did you think I would do when you put your face on my leg last week? I've been thinking what to do all week. I've got to tell someone."

Gerald stared at her "What do you mean? I put my face on your leg? When? When did I do that?" His mind raced back to their last meeting. It was about Swinburne and his obsession with what Gerald called "fragile metaphors." He remembered pacing his office while she crossed and re-crossed her long beautiful legs. Her eyes were wide and clear. Her lips were wet and open as he went on about how writing needs to be controlled, under tight control; that writers, — everyone, really, needed to be aware of who they were and what they were doing, that emotions should be kept at bay. We weren't animals, who took what they wanted … we were above all that … temptation was something one lived with and …

She turned to go. "Wait a minute, Des. I'm sorry. I don't remember doing anything." It was a lie. He did remember. She had stopped taking notes and was watching him, Suddenly, he knelt beside her and laid his head on her leg. She didn't move. His hand burned on her bare skin, and when he moved it up higher on her thigh she jumped up, dropping her notebooks on the floor, and ran down the hall. Malvern watched her go, and closed his office door. Brucie smiled.

He followed her to the Dean's office and closed the door behind him, turned the lock and pulled her close to him, wondering whose mouth forced itself on hers ... whose hands slid her skirt up and worked at her panties, pulling them down, tearing them ... someone was breathing heavily ... and there were other sounds ... sobbing ... screaming ... someone beating at his chest, slapping a face he didn't know ... couldn't feel...

"Dr. Harnisch. Dr. Harnisch, stop it. You're hurting me. Please stop. You can't do this..."

"Des, I love you. I've loved you from the first day I saw you behind that oaf I moved so I could see you ... coffee under the trees... you said you loved my sonnets ... you enjoyed my class ... no one says that ... they watch the clock and don't ask any questions ... nothing means anything to them ... you ask good questions ... you ..."

"Dr. Harnish. Stop. Think what you're doing. Let me go. Now!" She pushed him away and adjusted her skirt. "This is wrong. When you think about this later you will be ashamed. You're such a nice man—and a great teacher—you don't want to ruin your career by ..."

"Career? What career? They don't know my name around here. All those damn committees I've served on, the extra things I've done. I can't even check a book out of the library without some student helper asking who I am ... I'm sorry, Des. I am very, very sorry. Let's ..." but someone was banging on the door, shouting. "Who's in there? Open this door!"

"Here, Des, let me help you with ..."

"...Stop! don't touch me again. Just stay over there until someone comes in. I won't tell them anything. Let's just forget it ever happened. You've been under a strain for weeks, it showed in class. You don't know what you're doing."

"No, Des, I don't. I can't see myself anymore, just like everyone else: I must be invisible. My life is blank. My wife left me for vegetables. Can you believe that? My colleagues didn't vote advancement for me. After all I've done. Someone said, 'Gerry, if you were only a bit more visible around here...' Visible! Good God, do they walk through me?

Can't they see me, touch me? What do I have to do?"

"THIS IS THE OAKDALE POLICE. PLEASE GO TO THE PHONE."

Gerald looked out the window. "Well, here they are," he said. "Look, Des, a S.W.A.T. team. There, behind that willow. A sharpshooter. Guess what he's sighting on. Probably a National Guardsman turned cop. He hasn't fired his weapon since training and he can't wait to nail a man holding a girl captive. It would look good in the papers." When the phone rang he stared at it, then back at Des. "Maybe they'll hear me even if they can't see me."

"Hello. Yes, this is Gerald Harnisch. Yes, there is someone else up here. And no, she's not hurt. What? Des, they want you to say something. Take the phone and go to the window. Let them see you're ok."

"Hello? Yes, this is Desirée Magellan. Yes, I'm fine. Dr. Harnisch and I were just having a discussion and he … no he is not hurting me. No, you don't have to do that. You … He hung up! I think something is going to happen, Dr. Harnisch. What can we do?"

"I want to say good-by, Des. Last class for me!"

"You're going to be all right, Dr. Harnisch. Your classes need you and…"

" No, Des, no more. Nothing in life is ever as it should be, right? How many poems did we read about pain and loss this semester? About love not working. About people alone even in the bloody crowd. Thoreau was right. We do lead lives of quiet desperation. It's over, Des. There's no way I can explain this. I'll be fired of course. My wife is gone. They don't know me here anyway. There's no spin I can put on this. I'm only sorry I hurt you. No, don't cry. I did hurt you. I fell in love with you because you're beautiful, sexy, elegant and quiet … like a stream where one can bathe without fear, without pain…your long legs in my office...those big hazel eyes so full of nature, autumn leaves…life. I wish I had met you twenty-five years ago, Des … but it's too late, and I took advantage of our … what is it? what do we have? Nothing. You're a student, and I'm teacher … it's over … I'm truly very sorry."

"DR. HARNISH. YOU MUST LET THE GIRL GO. NOW! YOU HAVE TWO MINUTES."

"Well, isn't that wonderful. They want to see me now, do they? Well, let's give them something to look at. Des, I want you to do exactly what I say. I'm not going to hurt you … just do as I say." He sat down and took off his shoes and socks, then stood up and took off his necktie and started to unbutton his shirt.

"Dr. Harnisch, what are you doing! Please don't do that? Please don't …" He took off his shirt and undershirt, then unbuckled his belt and took his trousers off and folded them carefully over the back of a chair.

"Des, don't be alarmed. Please, just … be calm." He slipped out of his shorts and stood naked before her. " Look at me, Des. Just tell me you see me standing here. I want to know you see me … really … see me."

He looked out the window at the crowd gathered on the grass. There were a few of his colleagues, some students, and more running up the hill. They had heard about the professor who kidnapped some girl. They left their TV and beer, or had been roused out of bed to see the show.

"Des, come over here. I won't hurt you. Please, you must trust me." She brushed tears from her eyes. "Dr, Harnisch, please put your clothes back on … don't do this."

" Look down there, Des. Now they're really excited. Look at the fellow behind the tree … there, behind the man with the bullhorn. See? He's looking at us right now through his powerful scope. He can see everything just fine. His trigger finger is itching to move, just a little pressure … and … "

"DR. HARNISH, WE HAVE YOUR WIFE HERE. SHE WANTS TO TALK TO YOU."

" Gerald. Can you hear me? Gerald? What do you think you're doing up there. Is there a woman in there with you? Come down. Now!"

Gerald made a cutting motion across his throat and they dropped the bullhorn. Her mouth was still moving, hands waving in the air. It was almost funny, he thought. All that sound and fury. "At last I understand Faulkner, Des. What incredible timing."

"DR HARNISH, WE ARE GOING TO HAVE TO END THIS STANDOFF ONE WAY OR ANOTHER. I WANT YOU TO COME TO THE WINDOW."

"He's not very subtle, is he? He wants me to make a good target for his friend behind the tree. All right, let's give them what they want. It's a good show so far, but it's not what they really want. Come here, Des. Don't be afraid. I won't hurt you. I promise." She hesitated, then took a deep breath and walked to him.

"Dr. Harnisch, don't touch me, please. Just do what they want and let's get out of here."

"Des, stand in front of me. That's right. Look down at all of them. They're waiting for something to happen." He looked around the office. "This will do nicely, I think." He picked up a large black stapler and put it against her temple.

" Dr. Harnisch, what are you doing! They'll think you have a gun. Stop this now, and let me go. I promise I'll never tell anyone what happened … what you did … just let me go … please."

"Don't worry, Des. You'll be able to go down there and tell them all about it shortly. Just do what I tell you, exactly *when* I tell you. Understand?" She nodded and closed her eyes.

"He's got a gun, sir," said the sharpshooter. "He's naked with a girl up there and he's got a gun to her head. We got ourselves a real looney, Captain. What do I do?"

"Do you have a clean shot, Sergeant—?"

"—Affirmative, Captain. Target is good." The Captain picked up his bullhorn, then put it down again. "All right. We can't risk her life any longer. Take him out if he moves away from the girl. But wait until he moves away from her."

"All right, Des, this is the moment they all want. They want to see something really spectacular. Oh, they'll say they didn't want it to happen-- but just look at them, staring, mouths open. When I count three I want you to drop to the floor and roll away. Quickly! Understand? Don't hesitate, just drop and roll away. Roll away fast, Des. Do you understand!"

"They might shoot you, Dr. Harnisch, if I do. Won't they? Won't they shoot you then?"

"Just do what I tell you. Ready?" He waved the stapler around, then put it close to her beautiful ear. He could smell her hair. "Remember, Des? 'Beauty without the beloved…' Remember? Now, Des. Drop and roll. DO IT!"

The first shot caught him in the stomach. He dropped the stapler, stumbled back a step, then lurched forward against the window. The second shot shattered the glass and exploded in his chest. He fell out with shards of glass splintering the soft autumn air, made a small arc over the first-floor overhang and landed on the lawn below. The sharpshooter ran to him and pointed his weapon at his head and waited. " Ok, Sergeant," the Captain said, put it away. This guy's gone. You got him ... "

" ... I got him twice, Captain," he grinned. "Both rounds. Look at those holes ... geeze ... "

" He was my friend," Brucie told the reporters. "Mine too," said Malvern. "Of course, he kept pretty much to himself."

"We all liked him," said the Dean. "But we really never saw much of him. We would liked to have seen him more often ... "

A Journalism student looking out at the changing trees in the park, wrote: *'According to NASA, there was an Event in deep space last week. Well, there was one here in our space as well, in space just as deep, surely no less dark, when a naked man flew through a window in a shower of exploding stars, each piece reflecting the colors of autumn as his body, dark and bleeding against the sun, swooped out and over them and disappeared in the leaves. Apparently no one knew him, and so the crowd walked back down the hill to classes, talking about the rare weather, and how such a thing could happen here, leaving the place quiet and empty,-- save a girl crying in an office, and two boys riding bikes who stopped to look at feet sticking out from a blue tarp a man said he needed back.*

When the man climbed the concrete barrier and dropped into the pen of the Great Apes, the crowd cheered. One young mother pulled her toddler away, while another ran for the guard who was smoking behind a paper- mache palm tree.

Two dark eyes peeped out from a cave. A nurse said it was an ape and this was not a good thing here. A thin man wearing boots said, "From Las Cruces to Nogales we got your odd critters … we just run 'em down in our pickups then blast 'em with our 357s …"

The guard ambled up in time to see the man inside the pen crawling on all fours toward the great ape, who had pushed his massive head and shoulders outside his cave. Somewhere a whistle blew. A woman shouted something she claimed was Hezikiah 3:12 … something about ape and man and what could only be sin and pain for both. Inside the pen the man stood up and started to remove his clothes. First his shoes and socks, then his shirt, then pants and finally underwear. Small children were held on shoulders of parents. The guard pointed a can of pepper spray at the ape watching the man crawl into his cave. Guards threw rope ladders over the side of the enclosure, but no one went down.

The man in the suit came up with a clipboard and went away. A flashbulb popped, and there was a scream from inside the cave. When reporters arrived it was all over, but they asked for particulars: "Color!"

"At first we thought he was just loving him," a woman said.

"My god, he's crushing that man," another screamed, looking and not looking. The suit with the clipboard wrote something down and left. Someone said he looked like FBI.

"The ape beat his chest then threw the body over the moat, scattering the crowd. I saw it all," said a man from Missouri," sucking on a snow cone. "The man with the big hat shot him five times … "

"Ape eats man," a reporter said.

"Dumb-ass Texan shoots ape," said another.

"What happened?" asked a man wearing a GO HUSKERS sweatshirt.

The Texan sighted down the barrel of his gun, and sucked on a cinnamon toothpick from the El Paso Burrito Grande. "I've heard of Nebraska," he said. "But I never believed it …"

That night, a boy hosed out the enclosure, pocketing the change thrown at the apes. When he was finished he turned out the lights, looked at the moon over the big cats' compound, and threw his head back and beat his chest with his hands, afraid, but thrilled at the sudden flapping of wings of the exotic birds rising from their nests, and he held his breath there in the dark as tigers snuffed along their fence, growling warning—then the sudden jungle quiet—and the soft lapping at the cold moon floating in their water.

BOB FROM ACCOUNTING

He's new, they say, and watch him squirm in his chair in the cubicle Lorraine from Parts sat in for twenty years before she murdered a man she called the Mister.

Bob resists asking about it as he adds up dogs without licenses, and puts red plastic paper-clips on the lists, and walks down the quiet aisle to put them into Mr. Ian-Smith's inbox, never once asking how a Welshman came to be in California, or why he uses one of those clip-on ties. Bob waits, knowing that in the fullness of time the talk at the water cooler will enfold him into the gossamer web that floats unseen over the department, carrying the news of the cubicles.

Bob from Accounting ponders these things, and makes a neat red mark on the calendar. I will wait, says Bob, and little by little know the history of the place and feel the fears and dreams overflowing the cubicles, flowing like a tide over the silent carpets, washing against me, feeding me with the rich news of its waters.

When the jungle drums brought the news (the water thing having developed a leak, ruining the gossamer web) of his firing, he cleared out his cubicle and headed for Spokane where he was told a cubicle with his name on it had been newly painted and fumigated after forcibly evicting the NightingaleTwins, Trill and Chirp, who insisted on singing songs from the Gonzaga Song Book and questionable selections from their great- aunt's Northwest Songbook: "Guts, Guns and Idaho Back Roads: Tales of Weird Romance along the Spokane River." Alas for Bob from ....

It is to be hoped that his talents will take him far in Spokane. He has bought flannel shirts and a Subaru. Bob from >>>>>>>>>> tells his mother, recently removed to Nogales, AZ, that it's a different water cooler here, no gossamer web pulsating overhead, no warm water laving me gently with news of the department. I have gotten lost in the Palouse. His mother advises bright clothes.

Bob from ************ has taken to reading The Beats and has pierced his ear. Badly. The infection will subside, maybe, says his doctor who says this is the year for the CUBS! The Rotarians invited him to a meeting and fined him for wearing an ugly shirt. The girl he met at River Front Park cooked him dinner and showed slides of her uni -cycling nude on the 405 in Southern California.

Bob from ()()()()()() has disappeared from his cubicle and from Desiree, the unicyclist, and from Spokane. After a comfortable amount of time his mother received a single postcard from the **Queen of Golconda Pleasure Palace,** "Just a few happy miles north of Paducah!" showing him in a tuxedo and tall black hat with a red feather boa across his shoulders.

Bob from &&&&&&& has dropped out, or tuned in to other news, other gossamer webs, other warm music. His mother would not recognize him as he stands at the portal of the Palace. Except for the postcard.

He greets people. Shakes their hands. Pats their backs, and introduces them to girls sitting in elegant poses in the red salon. It suits him. He has his own room with a view of a small chapel resembling the Taj Mahal where a lawyer sits at a card table, shelling peanuts and handling divorces. He is happy. He flosses daily. He has little cards that read **BOB FROM NOW ON!**

His mother has neighbors over for coffee in her new double-wide and shows them his picture. What kind of place is it, one asks. A kind of resort, she answers. He's working, praise God. My Harold would never wear a red feather boa over his shoulders, the neighbor says. It was always in him, his mother says. His father came home from a business trip with panties in his suitcase. I never asked. He wore them on warm summer days. It was our secret. The neighbors looked at her in the fading light, their lips pursed, twitching and pursing. This is what comes from the *nouveau riche,* said one who reads books.

There is more to this than is easily accessible due to laws even in Nogales. His mother goes to bed happy. The neighbors have leaked the story and have formed a committee to buy her out. Someone painted komunist on her mail box. She is not disturbed. She too flosses daily.

It's a family thing.

Bob from A Good Place Lives On. He has decorated his room to resemble a cubicle. A satisfied customer donated a water cooler.

The girl moved in and out of his field of vision, slowly, as in a dream. He wondered if she wore a slip. He watched for her in the sudden swarm of people heading for the couch and chair on sale. Where was she? He stood aside to let a little boy pass, but he didn't pass. He stood in front of the mirror, sucking his thumb. He watched the boy closely, hoping his mother would find him. He pretended to like the desk next to the mirror, its roll-top, little brass pulls, and woodworking. How long could he look at a desk, he wondered.

The little boy was snatched away by a long arm, his mother he presumed, though he did not particularly care. No one asked him. Yes, it was his mother. He could see them now as she marched him to the bathroom. But there was the sales girl again: moving dream-like through the narrow window of his life. Does she know she's being watched, waited for? No. She's writing an order for the ugly couch and chair for some people who look as if they like chintz. He could only see half the bed, but he knew it was ugly.

The store was closing. A few laggards made their way to the big doors and into the night. Someone who might be a manager watched him watch him. He's coming over to see why I've been looking through this mirror for so long. What can I tell him? That I like looking in and through mirrors? That the real world—his world—seems blurry, too fast. People rush from one thing to another. When they're caught in mirrors, I only see parts of them, briefly. Upper torsos, usually; sometimes legs. Buttocks, most of the time, breasts, all the parts that are truly interesting. No, that's not true: the face, profiles! Yes, profiles. They are the most beautiful. You can't imagine the trickiness of trying to match a face with a swaying rump or long swishing hair. The temptation to turn around and look is overwhelming. It takes great concentration and desire to live in the narrow window of the mirror. Most people would never believe it.

His wife didn't believe it. She found him looking at himself in the long hall mirror for hours, and finally she broached the subject, gently, tenderly asking if he would like to see the Pastor, or maybe the psychiatrist that lived down the street, the one who drove that little hybrid thing. Green. He shook his head at her in the mirror and watched her back disappear down the hall, tidying up with the dust cloth, straightening pictures.

The people he worked with took rather a long time to notice he stood in front of the one mirror next to the washrooms. At first, they teased him about his vanity. "Hey, Alfred, got a new do?" Or, wittily, "Mirror, mirror, on the wall, is Alfred the fairest one of all?" Then great peals of laughter from the cubicles down the line, like chickens, he thought, clucking warning sounds from hidden nest to hidden nest until the joke and laughter turned the corner and came back the other side of the long room and he heard it in his other ear. But he stared and cared not.

How did it happen, he asked himself. Or rather, his wife asked him as he stood before the bathroom mirror, half of his face shaved, the razor poised in the air, its mission forgotten. "How did this happen, Alfred? Why won't you tell me? What in the world do you see in mirrors anyway? The children are beginning to talk about it. Little John brought his pals in last week to see you going from mirror to mirror. You didn't see them laughing behind your back, did you?" He had seen them, fleeing shadows of little bodies following him from mirror to mirror, arms and knobby legs and tousled heads. He recognized his own, of course, what he saw of him. How did it happen anyway?

The news was ghastly that Friday afternoon. Worse than usual. He was watching a special on the greenhouse effect, and saw glaciers drawing back in fast-forward. He switched to the evening news just in time to see teenagers fighting in a schoolyard. One had rings in every orifice—the ones he could see. Tattoos covered most of his upper body. The teacher he shot lay under a sheet someone threw over him. The next channel featured a man and woman staring at each other, angst-ridden, brows furrowed. They didn't talk, just looked at each other as if the world could read their private thoughts. As indeed it could, he mused. Who couldn't? Who needs it? I got angst. Everybody has angst. I have it for breakfast! My boss has angst up the wazoo, and passes it on to the rest of us in our chicken coops. My daughter with the pierced navel and tongue has it. My wife must have it, though she masks it in silence. That's lots of fun too, silence. But it's a silence that kills. It says worlds. Who needs it?

That evening, as he brushed his teeth, he was aware, for the first time, of the wall behind him. He stared into the mirror at it, noticed the striations of paint, the way the color blended or did not, and the fresh green towels that hung against it. How beautiful, he thought. Wall. Green Towels. No angst. He stood quietly until his wife came in, then quickly brushed the other side of his mouth, kissed her, sort of kissed her, brushed against her, actually, and curled up with his Patrick O' Brian book. But in the night, he rose from the bed very quietly and went into the kitchen and looked in the mirror on the back door. The room behind him was in shadow. The gibbous moon woke corners of the kitchen he had never seen before. The refrigerator loomed tall and white against the muted mustard wall. His own body was elongated and his eyes were dark holes in his white body. Fascinating.

After that, it was mirrors all the time: at home, at work, in the car that almost cost him his life, as he found the world squeezed into a point behind him more interesting than the one opening up before him as he drove 75 on the freeway. A trucker passed him and honked him back to the present just in time, and motioned to him to roll his window down, held up three fingers, and shouted, "Read between the lines!"

Somewhere he went over the edge. That's what the psychiatrist told him. "Can you remember just when it was? Try to go back to it. Find that epiphanic moment when you decided your world was the mirror's world. Can you do that, Alfred?" Alfred looked at him and wondered how much this series of visits was costing him. He wasn't a bad sort, this psychiatrist, but he fidgeted with his pencils, put his papers in neat stacks, sometimes measuring the lines with a ruler as a carpenter might measure a piece of wood to saw it. Alfred wondered about the way he swayed his coffee cup back and forth three times before putting it down. He doodled something on a yellow pad but he couldn't see what it was. He thought of asking, but that would take more time and more money.

"Take your time, Alfred. Relax, and take us back to the day, the very minute you lost yourself in mirrors. For that is what you've done, you know. Lost yourself. Let's just find yourself today, shall we? That's a good fellow." The psychiatrist leaned back in his beautiful leather chair and closed his eyes. Alfred waited. The psychiatrist's eyes popped open like a doll's, and he sat straight. "Alfred, you're not taking us back to the good place. The warm place. The comfortable place. Perhaps an uncomfortable place? Hmmnnn? Could it be uncomfortable, Alfred? Can you go there again, now, and let me see the place? Can you do that, Alfred?"

Alfred Sully was a patient man, but the TV jargon was a bit much. The psychiatrist sounded so much like the other TV people who solved problems in fifty minutes. And those they couldn't solve, they watched, as their "clients" threw insults or chairs at each other. Alfred couldn't stand those shows either. Or the news. Football was boorish. College football never talked about how many players actually graduated. Farm clubs for the pros, he yelled at the television. His wife peeped her head into the room and chided him for yelling at the television set. Once her book club was meeting in the next room when he screamed, "FOUL! You Blockhead. FOUL! Who's calling this game anyway? Blockheads." The ladies hushed in the next room while his wife tiptoed into the kitchen for dessert. "Alfred, you are embarrassing me. Please don't yell at the television, dear. Remember what Dr. Maul said. 'Breathe deeply. Relax. Sleep.'"

Alfred Sully watched the parakeet through the window of the pet shop. Kids were pestering it; parents flicked their fingers against the cage. Dogs barked from their cages, driving the parakeet into a frenzy of pecking itself, pulling out feathers, and skittering about the bottom of the cage, shredding the paper and forcing it out between the little bars until the floor was littered with paper and feathers. The sales girl scolded it with, "Now that's a naughty parrot, isn't it. Naughty parrot!" and walked off carrying a small dog by the scruff of the neck. He watched the parrot go round and round the cage, squawking and shredding paper, and pulling out its feathers, until suddenly it jumped onto its swing and pecked on its little bell again and again, pecking harder. Then it stared at the small mirror fastened on the cage. It swung back and forth, back and forth, squawking less. It stopped pulling out its feathers, and swung easier, slower, until it stopped, just looking at itself and making tiny noises in its beautiful throat.

Dr. Maul reflected on this, eyes closed, then: "Ah, Alfred, Alfred. You have gone back to it, haven't you. Good man, Alfred. Good man, indeed. We have made progress today. Yes we have. We have made progress. See my girl on the way out, and let's just see if we can't find a good time next week. We must make more of this good progress, Alfred. It's very good progress. You can see that, surely." Alfred looked at him and wondered who "we" were, and what progress, exactly, did "we" make?

The house was quiet. The kiddos must be farmed out, he reasoned, otherwise there would be blood somewhere—the walls, floor, in the sink. Where were they? Where, for that matter, was the little woman—a phrase she despised. He poked his head into the fridge to see if there might just be the remains of a TV dinner left. But no. He opened a cupboard at random, never remembering if they held food or pans or whatever. Without thinking, he turned to one of the mirrors hanging by the door, and saw her coming toward him, naked, as far as he could make out. He didn't turn, but moved his head up and down and from side to side to reacquaint himself with his wife. Yes, it was she. Her. He never could remember which. Or is it that? His years of reading had not found purchase where grammar was concerned. He looked into the mirror as she put her hands on his shoulders and pushed herself against him. He felt her breasts in his back. What would Dr. Maul suggest? Turn, no doubt. But he could not turn, and when she ran her hands around the front and unzipped his trousers, he stiffened, but kept his eyes on the mirror, watching his eyes grow larger and small beads of perspiration break out on his forehead. No doubt he should turn now and take hold of her like a real man, he thought. But he could not.

He looked at her, past his shoulder, as his trousers fell to the floor, and her hands sought him out, as they say in novels. How long he could stand this sweet but terrible ecstasy he didn't know. Her body was warm against his back as her hands rose and fell on his body like swallows, he thought, swallows, —or maybe parakeets—skipping and skittering about their cage, wanting out, wanting the swing where the tiny mirror glittered in the shadows of the ugly neon sign outside the pet store where people gawked and tapped on the window. He wanted his mirror. Into the mirror. Now!

When Dr. Maul retired to Miami, where he opened a small but lucrative practice of psycho-analysis with very wealthy people as clients, Alfred Sully's case was given to a series of people, psychologists, psychiatrists, faith-healers, and finally a pygmy from an island off some coast or other who, the medical journals wrote, achieved unlooked for success using a combination of pig's urine and smoking a native root twice daily. Alfred Sully, now fitted with a custom mirror attached to his person, walked little in the squeaky-clean clinic, and then only to peer out the long window at the other clients rolling on the green lawn that sloped down to a man-made lake. And then only briefly, watching the birds who flew madly against his window. Mrs. Sully and the children left in the middle of the night when Alfred began pulling out his hair and banging his head against the bell he hung from a cord in the kitchen, letting up only when he fastened his eyes on one of the mirrors.

He felt he had tried to tell her. He did actually talk, over his shoulder, looking in the mirror as she led the crying children down the hall to the car. He told her his world was safer this way, prettier, not ugly, rude or savage. What he saw in the mirror was enough, he said, more than sufficient for one whose tastes and needs were as simple as his. He was tired of violence on television, sordid news in the papers, gangs, bad music, rude children in restaurants, failing classrooms, tired teachers, bad psychiatrists—democrats and republicans lying, never admitting a mistake! His world was what little he saw in mirrors: bits of bodies, colorful scarves just passing, dresses or hats, shadows of people on the street outside his window, the family dog— as he remembered him—running after something, back and forth, here an ear, a wagging tail, long tongue slavering over the cat. Whatever swam into his view, he said, was what he wanted. Needed. No more. No less. He was, dare he say it, a happy man.

Whether he noticed the felled-ox look on his wife's face, no one knows. He never talks about the family, his job, his former life. He is silent. Watching the mirrors. The nurses at the clinic change the angle of the mirrors now and then just to tease him. Some talk to him. The night orderly in his stiff white coat offers him birdseed and bangs a bedpan against his mirror then waddles down the hall, white coat growing smaller, a hand on the white porcelain doorknob, a fingernail on the light switch-- and the mirrors are clear, no longer bits and pieces, but whole, silent. His breathing slows, his eyes open, drawing in the darkness, seeing nothing, reflecting nothing, waiting for nothing, wanting nothing.

"There is a time in life when, overcome by chance or circumstances, a person may find he cannot cope with what is daily before him, and slips into a self-induced hypnotic state where he sees only himself in other's eyes, until finally he finds the means to live completely in his image of himself until complete mental collapse occurs, or death. In the case of Alfred Sully, we find a death-substitute in mirrors. As you can see, no matter which way I turn him on this wheel, or rotate his room, he sees only himself,-- all other faculties, such as hearing, speech, smell are, as far as we know, gone. He is a world, a universe by and of himself. He is fed through these tubes, and constantly monitored. He lives-- and here I wish I had a better word-- in this room of mirrors. The walls, the ceiling, even the floors are mirrors. He has a chair and a bed. He sees himself at all times, twenty-four hours a day, seven days a week, twelve months a year. We don't know if he sees through a glass darkly, or clearly. He is truly sui generis: a mirror man."

Lecture given by Dr. Edison Gage to Psychiatric Residents and Scholars at an undisclosed clinic.

It was the Fourth of July, and we were having a barbecue in our back yard when the deranged man climbed over the fence, and announced he was Michael the Archangel, and he wanted a hamburger. My aunt Suzie said, "Certainly, with cheese or not?" and slapped a burger on the grill while Michael the Archangel downed a large glass of lemonade beneath the green umbrella on the patio.

No one moved. No one spoke to him. The dog sniffed him once, but went about her snuffing under chairs for party droppings. The cat eyed him from her perch on the kitchen shelf, her eyes green slits, her tail swishing nervously.

I watched my father, who was a retired deputy, back slowly up to the table where coats and hats were stacked, all the time smiling and picking his teeth from the last hamburger. When his butt hit the table, he put his hand behind him to steady himself, like he was afraid he might fall, and snaked his hand under the stack of coats until he felt his police 38 revolver, which he pushed down the back of his pants.

The strange man eating his hamburger with cheese looked around him as he ate. Now and then he stopped and combed his straggly hair with a broken comb he kept in his shirt pocket. After two hamburgers with cheese and another glass of lemonade he got up from the table and walked the length of the yard and climbed the fence. Whatever it was, was gone.

The next day the paper said a man who called himself Michael the Archangel took off all his clothes and began running up and down the Mall, and when he came out of a women's clothing store, wearing a red chiffon with a yellow feather boa across his shoulders, a guard, new and mostly untrained, shot him dead.

The paper carried a picture of him lying in a pool of blood in front of Tres Chic, the guard standing over him with his mouth open, the gun still in his hand. "I shot him," said Murphy Munn. "I caught him about to do somebody harm and I shot him." The manager of the Mall told him to go home and rest and quietly fired him. The store clerk suffered mightily from shock and hired a lawyer to sue for everything he could get. The lawyer did and won and took 35% percent, (for quick action) five more than the norm.

My father looked at the man in the picture, and said "I could have shot him on the 4th as he sat eating his second hamburger, but I didn't. And now I'm glad because I recognize him. He was in a Light Infantry Battalion in Vietnam, and won the Silver Star for bravery. I know because I was there before I did the police thing. His name was Charley Olson, and he came from a farm in Moorhead, Minnesota. He had a wife but no children. I know all this because he told me in the field hospital where he was fixed up from shrapnel when the tank he was behind blew up taking some of him with it. He was a good soldier until then."

When Thanksgiving was gone, and Christmas lights were on sale with decorations unboxed and in place since Halloween, the Tres Chic store must have run out of chic because it was gone too. My aunt Suzi said that she could get the same things from Penny's. My father suffered a heart attack and died, leaving me his police .38 special, and a box with his ribbons and medals which included two purple hearts and a bronze star.

Nobody in the family talks about the 4th of July. I think they don't believe it, that it was some kind of strange thing they pretend they didn't see and live through. There are such things. I've seen a few already and I'm still young as people are reckoned today. But I still see this fellow clambering over our fence, hair standing up, his eyes wide and falling into my mother's peonies. My aunt, who asked him if he wanted a hamburger (with cheese, or not), remembers him, too, and tells me she was scared shitless, and would have run him through with her long-handled barbecue toad stabber if he had taken one step toward her. She's gone to Oregon now where she operates a little cottage set well-off the highway, where people who would rather die than lay around suffering with tubes in their mouth and nose can listen to some good music while they drink their orange juice. She tells me some ask for diet coke. My siblings are scattered and living life as best they can what with recession and taxes, bad weather and their own children. My mother is living and rocks the day away watching the soaps and a little news. She hates all the democrats and most of the republicans and says what Congress needs is some grown-ups. I don't argue that one. She says she misses the holidays when the family was together and anything might happen. I don't argue that one either.

Time Was
(Washington)

The man shuffled past the people waiting to see the doctor, pausing at each chair as if he had been there before. He assumed he had, but the chairs had people in them he did not know. A lady with a Bible on her lap said, "Excuse me, did you lose something here? Around this chair?" The man stared at her then looked at his wife. She shook her head and smiled, moving him along the rows of chairs, the other hand gripping the back of his trousers, lifting, moving him along.

When the doctor came in, he noticed the man looking at the skeleton in the corner."Interesting, isn't it. We all look like that, one way or another." Claire Heston turned him by his elbow. "This is Dr. Hunter, Sam. He's our doctor, and he wants to see how you're doing." Sam Heston continued to watch the skeleton as he moved his body in little sliding steps to face the doctor. "Say hello to Dr. Hunter, Sam. Give him your hand. The other hand. Say hello, Dr Hunter." Sam watched his arm lift, then the other arm. He wondered how that worked, his arms raising and lowering like that. He had seen things on television do that. "Maybe I'm a thing," he said aloud. "Am I?"

Dr. Hunter laughed softly and helped him sit on the table. "Let's see how we're doing. Do you feel well today?" Sam stared at his white coat and remembered snow on the farm when everything was white, the house, the corn, the barns, even the old horse who leaned against the silo, one knee bent. He liked that. "Beautiful," he said. "Yes, Sam, it is beautiful. Tell me about it." But he was watching the moon breaking free of the far line of trees, and he knew it would find the deep spot in the pond, and would wait until he went to bed before it rose up through the cold water, turning the ice even whiter before it sailed into the sky. Once, she saw him walking close to the pond, and rushed out to turn him."Pretty," was all he said, and put his weight on his foot still on the ice, watching it crack, sending dark lines running just beneath the ice. "Beautiful, " he said.

"Sam, let the doctor check your legs. Here, let me help you lift them like I do at home." She watched the doctor's face as he tapped his knees, and felt along his legs for muscle and tendon, pressing the spot by his kneecaps to see if he would jump. But he did not jump. He was looking at the skeleton, his mouth working and rowing. She wondered if he remembered the words, or if he had words or thoughts. She couldn't tell anymore. Time was, she knew what he was thinking almost before he did.

She drove the old way home, past their son's place on the rim so he could see the lights in Hangman Valley. She rolled the windows down, letting in the cool earth smells of the bottoms. "That's Hangman Creek, Sam. You always liked that smell. You said it reminded you of your farm in Southern Illinois when you and your dad mowed the field bordering Shoal Creek, remember? You used to tell how you and your cousins would skinny-dip after work, and how you'd lie back in the water, and listen to it burble along through the overhanging alders. Remember skinny-dipping Sam? Your cousins teased you, and said they would leave you alone in the creek all night and let the water roll you along until it reached the Mississippi, where you and dead cows and boxes and chicken pens and whisky casks would bob around in the shallows before being swept far out in the deep channels with the tugs and barges, all heading south, clear to New Orleans. Remember, Sam? You said you only half believed them." She pulled at his jacket, but he was leaning out the window, taking in great gulps of air, like a dog. She pulled off the road and waited. "Sam, I don't know where you are. Are you here? Do you understand what I'm saying to you?" He stared at the moonlight on the creek, pointing, his mouth opening and closing,

That night, she tucked him in bed in the spare room beneath the eaves, then went down into the cold kitchen and made a cup of tea. She knew the snows would come very soon now. Sam's voice came back to her: "Never mind what those silly weather men say. Let 'em open a window, and stick their heads out if they want to predict the weather!" One night, after watching the news and weather, he dipped his tea bag into the hot water she handed him, and said, "What do they say about the weather tonight?" The first time he asked, she laughed, and said something appropriately silly, and confessed how she lost her car keys and her glasses case in the same day, finally putting her name and phone number on the inside of the case. And when they hosted the Fix Our Creek committee, the Neunabers talked about forgetting their daughter's birthday or, said Mrs. Neunaber, which way to turn at a familiar intersection. "See?" his wife told him in bed that night. "We all forget. Life just has so much to remember, Sam."

The day of the big weiner roast, they elected Sam as Chair of the committee and gave him a thick book entitled "Secrets To Remembering What You Don't Remember Forgetting," with much laughter and back-slapping and toasts all around. And when he opened it to blank pages, they laughed louder and raised their glasses and laughed some more, not noticing his wan smile as he drank his toast, or his furrowed brow as they pumped his hand. Later, his wife pulled him aside and said, "It's meant as a joke, Sam. It's just joking in saying that the writer forgot the Secrets."

Their days passed with walking the Creek in the spring, watching new flowers pushing up out of the black earth. And the summer bar-b-ques near the bridge on Valley Chapel Road where deer nosed among the sweet roots and berries along the Creek. Their son said "Dad's in a fog a lot lately" after she told him how he pulled the car over and sat quietly as she came around and got behind the wheel. Still they all laughed and went to great lengths to point out each other's foibles and forgetfulness, and they laughed louder and more often.

But they didn't laugh at his birthday celebration when he asked what was for supper an hour after he had eaten; nor was it funny when he forgot to put on his jacket when he went out to milk the one cow when it was 20 degrees. She did all the things she knew to do, called the doctor for an appointment, let the kids know that Dad was not himself, and made sure she knew where he was at all times. It was not so bad at first. They had been married so long it seemed natural to watch out for him, just as he had watched out for her when she was ill. It's what people do, she thought. I'm just doing more of it.

In late November they woke to a white farm, with lacy ice on the edges of the pond where the geese flapped and cried before lifting into the cold thin air, honking, finding their winter flyways over the Palouse, already white, rolling southeast to the horizon.

She could not remember just when she knew he was not in the house. She was putting the winter sheets over the furniture in the parlor, when she stopped, letting the sheet settle over the couch. She knew he was not there.

Duck hunters found him in Hangman Creek, bumped up against some trees and brush near the spillway. The one with the flashlight said, "That's Sam Heston! I know his Claire. I'll be damned if it isn't Sam Heston."

She toweled him off before the fire and gave him hot cider to drink. He touched her head as she knelt on the floor, drying his legs. "I forgot how to get home." She put her head against him. "I know, Sam. I know."

That night she watched him sleep and thought, "This time it almost killed you, Sam. Another hour and it would have. You're scaring us all to death. I can't lock you in or put a leash on you." She parted the heavy curtains, and watched the snow fill the tracks of boots and tires, until there was no yard, no barn lot or pond, just white and silence; and when an owl boomed from the timber, she pulled up his covers and laid down beside him. She did not sleep or worry God, or cry for the children. She just lay there, waiting for it all to make sense, whatever that might be, already doubting she would like it or understand it, maybe not even need it. He said he counted on her to understand things. That night he half-turned toward her: "What's happening to me, Claire? Time was I knew how to get home. Didn't I?" She felt one of his stocking feet touch hers. "Yes," she whispered in the dark, "time was …"

After that, time passed without him. They lived together, and passed each other in the halls, and went to bed. But he did not speak again. Seasons came and went, until winter locked them away in that strange farm silence that sometimes drives people into themselves, making speech impossible; and she listened to the house creak and moan and watched him disappear.

One night, late in winter, when his deep breathing began, she went to the window and looked out at the farm, white from the storm that swept off the Cascades and flowed over the Palouse to Couer d'Alene where they went boating in the summertime. She watched the barn door flap open and close. She knew the old horse had found her stall and was nosing her feed bag. Eggs had to be gathered and laid out on the strips of clean white cloth in the cellar. But all that would wait until morning, after she fixed his oatmeal and held the spoon for him. Her daughter helped him eat until she broke down and cried beside him. After that she went back to college early and worked away from home in the summer. She lied to her son in Iraq, sending old pictures of the four of them swinging beneath the clematis vine he'd planted for shade.

Days were spent replaying events, episodes, trying to pin point a day, the first time he left tools in the yard to rust, or going to the barn to milk only after she heard the two cows bellowing and moving nervously against their stanchions, their bags heavy and tight with milk; but, the times were too many, and had taken on a flat sameness of expectation and reaction. The doctors nodded and prescribed. Their friends stayed away or shouted in the few gatherings they attended, standing close to his ear or patting him gently on his shoulder before sidling away to freshen a drink in the kitchen, joining a knot of them talking low, their eyes lifted to heaven in that exhalation of the spirit when gripped by the fear that they, too, might have slipped into something other,—recalling the lost car keys, or mock horror at forgetting to pick up the children after their sleepover.

When he called, she eased herself down onto the bed, and turned to the wall, but at the touch of his hand on her back, she turned and sat up, sliding the nightgown off her shoulders and lifting her hips to push it down her legs onto the floor. She pulled him close, his breath against her neck. She pulled him even closer and rocked back and forth, feeling the length of him against her. She stopped and listened to his deep breathing. Then: "Sam? Do you know I'm here, close to you. Naked? Do you feel my hands touching you, caressing your body the way you loved? Oh, Sam...Sam... can you feel anything? I can feel you, rocking here with me, together, back and forth, back and forth, your breath against my face and neck. Feel me, Sam, please feel me here, close, like we used to be. Please, Sam..." A thin moon broke through the snow clouds and came weakly through their heavy curtains, moving up the bed until she saw him, his eyes wide, his arms at his side as she rocked him against her.

Later, she rose and went down the stairs to the kitchen. The old dog behind the stove thumped her tail on the floor and startled the pups tight against her body. "Keep them close, Tess. Keep them tight against you, and let them nuzzle and bite until it hurts." She watched them pull at the teats in their sleep, the warm milk running out of their mouths, and felt the chill coming through the cracks of the old house. She looked back to the stairs, then opened the back door and went out onto the porch, catching her breath at the sudden sting of cold on her breasts as she ran across the frozen grass toward the pond, the wind howling around her, forcing itself between her legs its loud insistent pain.

At the end of Poplar Street sits a small white house. Wild roses and morning glories climb the arbor where a woman rocks in a porch swing. "Lent always comes early," she says to herself. She does not see the child, about five, running barefoot down the block to the river.

Her husband is under his old Dodge. He turns a wrench and says, "It'll hold awhile … " He hopes it will hold awhile, not being sure, since he has no talent for mechanics. He studied astrology at a storefront university until he married.

In the barber shop, a man lay dying. The Volunteer Fire Department has been called, but the doctor is eating a sandwich at home. He does not answer the phone. The siren broke at the 4th of July Parade last year and does not work.

The river is running full this year, says a woman watching a child, maybe four or five, run past her house. The man under his Dodge sees white legs flash by. Oil is dripping from the nut he broke so he does not know whose white legs.

Uptown, civilized people are meeting to discuss the Blacks moving in. They talk while eating fried chicken and beans provided by the Daughters of the First Settlers. They wear long white dresses with wide blue sashes diagonally over their shoulders. In Dewey & Sons Mortuary the new man watches the embalming tubes change color as blood drains out and chemicals go in. He is sweating. Tomorrow he will get on a bus for Chicago to try for the Cubs. He will not make the team. Nor the White Socks. He will be shot by a woman from Vandalia who takes him for her husband who left her ten years ago with four children.

The above paragraph is "packed" as deconstructionists like to say at parties where they drink white wine, huddling together like parakeets, bobbing their heads to whatever's playing on the stereo. They do not listen to the lyrics. The other guests are happy about that.

The Daughters of the First Settlers are regulars at everything, swaying and bending and tottering around in their flowing robes and wide blue sashes. Their husbands sit in a knot in another room, looking at an old National Geographic magazine that has pictures of African women.

The new man at Dewey & Sons Mortuary watches the tubes flow, and wonders how it feels to be deceased. The Director gave up wondering early on and went about his task in a workmanlike manner, not unnoticed by the local Chamber of Commerce who invited him to a meeting where they sang patriotic songs and fined the Director of the Mortuary for wearing an ugly tie. When they asked him what it was like to work in a mortuary, he said, "It's a living," and they fined him again for a bad joke.

"Lent always comes early," she says and hopes she will remember to call Mrs. Neunaber to tell her a little boy that looked like her Bobby was heading for the river, but she is already falling asleep, her Gideon Bible on her lap, —the Bible she kept from the Song Bird Motel on the Ohio River after agreeing with her lover that they would not take anything as a souvenir of their meetings there. Her Harold wondered but never asked, but Mrs. Neunaber knew and said it was her bounden duty to let him know. He has paid $250.00 down to have someone kill the "other man." He watches her sleep until it gets too dark to see, then he goes upstairs to bed. He takes off his W.W.J.D. bracelet and lies down.

The paper carried a photo of Bobby Neunaber being carried out of the river at Cottage Grove, fifteen miles away. His mother is sedated by the doctor who showed the driver of the Volunteer Fire Department's fire truck how to tell if a person is dead. Like the stranger in the barber shop, the driver says. Yes, the doctor says, like him. Too bad he's not still there in the barber shop, the driver says. I could practice on him until he, you know ... yes, the doctor said. It doesn't take long.

No one knows who the stranger was in the barber shop. The fact that he was a stranger and, thus, "not from around here," set their minds at ease.

Little Bobby Neunaber was not stopped as he went running down Poplar Street toward the river running fast and full. There were things, moments, ideas, actions that might have, should have prevented his drowning in that river, but you can see how nothing was done. There were extenuating circumstances some said. Underlying premises said others. How things might have turned out for Mrs. Neunaber or Harold or the lady from Vandalia or the mortician-baseball player or the doctor chewing his sandwich—or any of the others on or near or aware of Poplar Street is moot. Or mute, as the barber said, snipping ear hair out of the Mayor's ear. So be it.

Bluebells and mayflowers are fading along the river and in the woods beyond. The woman takes up her Bible, and turns to the Book of Job. Her husband looks at her through the window, trying to remember when they last made love, and if the $250.00 would have bought a good used snow plow. Winter means shoveling snow off his driveway and sidewalk, and the cold makes his bursitis worse. His fate is in shadow. Other fates are in other shadows. So be that too.

Harold stepped out onto the porch, and tasted snow in the weather. He looked up and down Poplar Street, glanced at his wife's peonies hanging in their strings as if they had been crucified, and went upstairs and laid down. He did not sleep, but turned this way and that, searching for answers. Finding none, he went to the window and opened it, watching a cold winter moon come out of the river; and when it filled his window he jumped into it.

Where summation is called for, answers to be answered, deeds praised or called to account, there is this: life is not tidy, not always celebrated, rarely understood. It's often just mute. Or moot, as the paper boy throwing today's paper under the sprinklers on Poplar Street says. And after the news has been dried out and pieced together on family rugs, and people return to their own private dreams and terrors, there is left but to listen once again to the last conversation of the couple on Poplar Street, and make of it what you will.

"Lent comes early," she says. "There's so much misery."

"Yes," he says. "And it just keeps coming."

"Yes," she says, "but look at us now. It missed us, Harold."

In the Deep Blue of Early Morning
(The dreams of Sister White of
Mt. Hope Church)
-The Palouse

Velvet against her face wakes her suddenly, and rain on her nightgown startles her. Dust on the walk outside her window holds a footprint she recognizes. She sleeps again, and dreams of the imprint of his hand.

Her mother and sisters watch from the orchard. They will sing hymns, and throw her into the river and watch her flow under the bridge, her hair streaming out behind her in the swift current, her mouth a dark hole of sound. In the church, candles gutter in the wind from a door opening and closing. Saints standing in their windows glow briefly, then go out.

Waking, she presses herself against the cold window, touching the memory of touch as the moon shivers away into the deep blue of early morning. Tomorrow she will teach Sunday School and sing in the choir. She wonders if others dream such dreams and wake up singing or crying. The footprint belongs to the man in the brown suit in the second row. The minister watches him closely. If the burning from his touch is felt by the choir, they will hit the high B flat, and wake the babies in the cry room. From her pew in the last row, she thinks of the sin she has brought to this holy place and plans to move to Sandpoint where strangers all look like Jesus with signs saying Free Eats.

People stand up for the blessing, and turn as she faints dead away, her Bible open to the map of Israel. The man in the brown suit knows first aid but hesitates to give her mouth-to-mouth lest her eyes open. But Sister White's eyes will not open this side of Paradise. She has crossed the great river where the Saints gather to drink and dance and shout while sunshine falls like gold. Sister White cannot tell the man in the brown suit his touch was wonderful, nor can she let the preacher know she knows where he goes when he goes ice fishing on the Red River.

The choir hits the high B flat and God his ownself floats down to join the Saints as they circle Sister White and embrace her, singing and laughing and showing her their burns from memory and hurting and longing and love.

Sister White is remembered as the person who sat in the back pew. The man in the brown suit has gone to California. The preacher preaches on sin, death and destruction. There are fewer left to listen. His wife needs therapy because he makes her wear a gunny sack under her dress to remind her of sin. Sister White knows none of this. She is showing where the burn touch was or is, much to the delight and wonderment of everybody, including God and Jesus and the Holy Spirit. Amen.

"We had cockroaches in the dressin' room when I worked the sewers in those days—millions of them crawlin' into our lunch sacks. It got so bad, we brought in a sack of frogs, and they bugged their eyes, and flipped out those long tongues, and snatched cockroaches off the ground and back into their mouths for days." Jurl looked at me and waited. "After awhile, the frogs got so fat they couldn't jump, so we threw 'em into the river." He looked at me over his Moon Pie and big orange. "Just chucked them right back," he said. "Did you ever see a mess of frogs swimmin'? Lots of neat stuff in a river."

Chicago's got rats. My sister-in-law found two in her baby's crib, and swung at 'em with a duster but hit the baby. Alfred, her husband, came home and got out his father's 16 gauge, and blew a hole in the wall then beat the rats to death with a Louisville Slugger." I watched the big clock on the wall, waiting for the whistle. It had been a long hot day in the sewers.

"I knew a man once over to Hillsboro, no, Litchfield, who had a Red-Bone Hound who could track Moses his ownself over the desert wastes, as they say in the soaps. That dog had a nose! Have you seen a Red-Bone Hound?" A large shadow like spilled ink slid under the door of our locker room. Jurl drained the last of his big orange and spat at the door. "It's the Foreman," he whispered, "seein' if we're leavin' early." He watched me to see if I was still listening. "That dog tracked a possum as high in the tree as that possum could climb, then grabbed him at the neck just as the possum jumped, and they both went flyin out of that tree, and when they hit the ground, the hound gave one swing and broke the possum's neck and that was all she wrote."

The ink spot retreated from under the door, so we took off our coveralls and called it a day. Jurl walked in silence, then stopped.

"That Red-Bone Hound was my dog. I raised him from a pup, and trained him to hunt. I used to make a little fire in the woods, and wait 'til I heard his voice—like a deep iron bell, and I knew from the sound whether he was on the trail or had treed somethin." I watched his mouth twitch, and his jaw drop open. "When I didn't hear him anymore, I went off lookin', and you know where I found my dog? He had chased a big old raccoon into Shoal Creek, and the Coon had turned on him, grabbed him with those claws they got, and pushed him under until he drowned. Big raccoons will do that to a dog, even a big one like Red. Red was his name. I buried him next to the creek and never got another dog up to and including today. I could not bear to raise another."

I had no words for him as we walked along. I don't think his grief would have stood it. When we reached the bridge over the river he said, "Are you baptized?" I stopped, sighed, then set down my lunch pail, and leaned against the railing, watching the green river flow over some stars just coming out. I could tell he was watching me, waiting.

"Yes, as a baby," I said. "I think it was in Greenville, just after I was born, one winter night in the big front room that was only opened when somebody was born or died." Jurl picked his teeth with his pocket knife, flipping out chunks of apple."Wuz you born again of the spirit? And did your folks lift you up, naked and cryin' unto the Lord of Hosts? And did the choir sing the next Sunday, and join hands, and dance around you there on the floor, muling and puking, your mom and dad raisin' their hands and clappin, tryin not to step on you. Do you remember 'ery thing about that night?"

I watched a boat filled with party goers chug under the bridge, their laughter coming back to us after it was gone. A sliver of a moon came out of a dark cloud and fell into the river and sank, but you could still make it out, rippling under the water. I hoped he would let it go and not ask any more questions. I had no answers he would like. "I got to get home, Jurl," I said. "Supper's waiting." But when I turned, he was gone, or almost gone. Half of him was kneeling on the bridge, his hands upraised. He was outlined in black but I could see the green river and the sliver of moon in his eyes. Then I heard him singing or praying: "Oh, Lord, this here's Jurl, frog catcher, rat killer and lover of good dogs. I am down on my knees over this here river to ask your blessin' on my friend, Jake, here. He was baptized in the snow of '34, and held up to you as an offerin' when he was barely out of his mother's womb. I wasn't there, but I know you wuz and took him then and there for one of your own, and I just thank you and praise you for holding him close to you all through these years. I thank Thee and praise Thee and ... and, Amen."

When the phone rang late in the night, I knew it was Jurl or about Jurl. I just knew. They found him floating in the river two miles south or east as the river goes. There were no details in the small notice in the Sun-Times, and even less in the scribbled notice in the locker room the next day. People read it and looked down or at me, patted me on the shoulder and went out to the sewers, so I picked up my long pole with the net he had given me and stood on the ledge, the water rushing over my shoes and waited for whatever the sewers sent my way. It was a dirty business, a stinking business, and I knew it was ending, had ended up on the bridge over that St. Patrick's Day river. A change was coming. What kind of change I didn't know, nor particularly care. But change. And I also knew I would go by a church when my shift was over. And if I could bend my stiff neck and stiffer knees, I would get down on them at the altar rail and speak whatever words Jurl or the Lord put there. And I would stop at the pet store on the way home, and if I could find a Red Bone Hound puppy I would surprise my wife and kids with it. I'll look until I do find one, I said aloud. Hallelujah! I said louder. And I kept on saying it.

WHEN SOMETHING IMPORTANT HAPPENS

The big room was opened for birth or death. It was cold and stale until the windows were thrown open, and the drop cloths removed from the sofas and chairs. The old photographs were dusted, the vases filled with fresh flowers from the garden. The rest of the house was quiet as she moved among the old furniture, moving a doily or arranging a pillow.

Today, he will have a clean room, she thought. I will make it as nice as I can, and he will be happy when the family comes in, quietly, and walks around him, some stooping to kiss his face. His mother will cry in the corner, and the men will hurry out to milk or bring in the horses from the upper pasture. I will stand by his head and shake hands with them, she thought, though they will not see me as family anymore than the dog who will lie beneath the casket. You have to be here for a long time, an aunt told her when they came back from St. Louis on their honeymoon. You will cook and clean and eat with them, but you will not be family. But do not be discouraged. You will become family when something important happens. You will see.

She straightened her dress, and arranged the veil so it covered her forehead, leaving her eyes clear. She wanted to see it all, and she wanted them to see her, to acknowledge her as his wife. She waited by the door, and when she heard the cars pull around and stop she went to her place at his head and stood straight and still. They were coming, she thought, to see how I look, then they will tell others in Flat River I was skinny or fat or nervous. They will be wrong. I am none of those. I am, was, his wife. That is all they will remember. And when they put him in the ground tomorrow, they will turn away, some staying for dinner, the rest home to Missouri, and cousin Margaret to Albuquerque where she lives with her friend. The family will not speak to her. They know she is that kind and so no kin of theirs. What she does is her business, whispered Arthur, but his wife looked at him; he closed his mouth tight and ground his teeth. He was part of the family but not of the family, he said to his friend at the feed store. They are a tight bunch, he said, and do not take much from anyone not blood.

The room smelled of strong perfume, and sounded like wind in wheat as the women walked around the casket. She looked straight ahead, and took their hand if they offered it. Some did, holding it like a piece of meat they meant to save in the fridge for their man's supper. Someone she didn't know said she looked nice in her black dress, but needed something bright, so she took a small white pin off her coat and put it in her hand and moved on.

That night, when the room was locked and dark, she stood just outside the door with her hand on the white porcelain doorknob. She liked the cold, roundness of it, and wondered if he had ever thought of those old doorknobs as something elegant, to be touched, felt, while he turned it. He never talked much about such things, and she soon became part of the strange farm silence. What she thought or felt was not important. She was not pigs or cows or horse weeds or broken fences or silos leaning against the barn or new calves born dead or wild hot winds killing the wheat. She was a woman in the house, eating second table with the other women and children, watching the men hunker down over their biscuits and gravy. She moved in the kitchen with pots and pans and scraped plates and washed in the sink and laid the cups upside down on the clean towels and waited until it was done then retired to her room.

Now that it's over, she thought, now that it's all done and over, I can pack and leave what won't fit into the one suitcase, and write the note I started our first night when he left me to get undressed in the cold spare room while he helped the men plow the section they rented by moonlight. When he came to bed in the early morning, she watched him start to undress, then fall on the bed beside her. Her life with him, she thought, was pressed into an album, like leaves from Autumn, and closed.

The stir in the old farm house began early because the men had to take the milk to town. The women bustled about the kitchen, talking, wrapping and unwrapping their hands in their aprons. No one asked where she was, though the note had been found and read. Hot biscuits were taken out of the oven, and the fried ham and eggs scraped out of skillets into plates as the men held their forks and knives. After breakfast, some of them took the milk to town while the others carried him up the path and buried him in the family plot. There were no prayers or songs as two men shoveled the hard Illinois dirt into the hole. A younger cousin cried at the first sounds of dirt hitting the casket, but she was shushed by aunts who stood on either side of her, each holding an elbow. When it was over, they walked down the path to the house, and put aprons on and lit the fire in the big stove and let out sighs and began to work.

Jaspe Twill was dying. He was ready to die because he was listening to Mahler's Fourth Symphony as he lay in the narrow cot provided for people who were ready to die. It was a stunning performance. "One," he said, "that I could die by."

It was sometime in the first movement that Jaspe Twill rang the little bell on his meager med stand and called for a lawyer to witness his last will and testament. It was late, and the lawyer wore a Lakers jersey and sneakers. He started to talk but Jaspe fluttered a hand toward the chair, the other to his lips. Jaspe Twill was entering Mahler's "Paradise Theme" and wanted no talk, no movement, and as little breathing as was possible. Mahler was introducing the flutes and Jaspe Twill saw the "uniform blue of the skies" as Mahler had predicted a listener might. It was beginning.

His friends were used to the ascetic look when he talked about music. At his retirement party, speeches were made, and toasts drunk in his honor, and when he was called upon to say a few words, he turned up the music, and, hand in the air, listened in silence until the music faded away. The room quiet. His soul away. Few knew he was dying, but they all knew he loved music, Mahler most of all, and all knew of his intense love of the violin. "He will go with the angels into heaven, provided they have traded their harps for violins," said one, "and God help us if a viola sneaks in!"

Jaspe Twill had a wife who stood by him through thick and thin and in between. His children were active, loveable, and called frequently to see how life was with him. When he became ill, they called more often, visited, and asked about details of life and death. "I am an average person who lived an average life, and death will find me unchanged." But, since Jaspe Twill loved music to an extraordinary degree, and the sound of the violin most of all, his dying was consumed by hearing all the good music he could. "Mahler's Fourth Symphony beyond this life and into the next or I might not go."

The books he read and taught in the English Department were underlined, marked with colored ink and bore his remarks about the poem, story or play. Or essay. Or creative nonfiction. He loved all genres, taught them and wrote them, and he imagined his favorites were close to his bed, and would turn his head to see Frost, Dickinson, Shakespeare, Yeats, Van Doren, Lawrence, Keats, Wordsworth, — and when he could no longer turn his head, he touched them, sliding his fingers over their leather bindings.

All was now ready, he opined to the wife of his bosom, a phrase she suffered now with the usual pout. The glass of cranberry juice glowed in the morning sun. His wife plumped his pillows, four for reading, three when not, two to think, and his flat "disreputable" pillow for sleeping .

Ready for what? he mused. His wife sat in the one chair, the window framing her lovely face like an almost perfect painting—the best paintings being almost perfect, he reminded her. The doctor came and came again, and this time stayed away. "Call me," he whispered to his wife. The halls were quiet, though he learned there were others in little beds with meager med stands and single chairs. He wondered what juice they would drink to carry them to Nirvanna or Heaven, or beyond the stellar systems into the face of God. Then he wondered no more because he lifted one hand towards the CD player, and one to his pillows. His wife removed three. He sighed as she bent to his face and laid her cheek against his, then closed his eyes as the third movement began.

He listened to the macabre tension, inspired, as he told his wife, by Mahler's vision of "a tombstone on which was carved an image of the departed, with folded arms, eternal sleep." He always smiled when he said that. This morning, he did not smile, but moved his eyes to her and held her. They both knew the music well, and waited for the fifth section of the third movement to travel through many variations in both sudden and surprising tempo changes. Nothing else moved in the little Private Care House; no bustling in the halls, no phones or knocks on the door. She stood by the window, her long hair burning in the sudden sun through the blinds, waiting with him for the strings, harp and winds to charge forth into the booming triple forte climax. "...the horns, the horns..." he whispered, hand in air, his eyes closed as the music died away into silence.

Jaspe Twill liked a ceremony, any ceremony, often quoting Yeats' "A Prayer for My Daughter." Decorum is next to Godliness, he said, and so it was, as he received the cranberry juice from the little glass held to his lips by his wife, the sun having left the window, leaving the small clean room with the narrow bed and the one chair half in shadow as the theme, sounded in the choral styled phrase he loved, led in to the fifth and final verse which 'praises the music of heaven,' played by flute and muted violin, his lips moving at the final word sung by the soprano: *Erwacht,* "awaken," and silence.

Whether he heard the finale, no one knew. He certainly loved the clarinet in the fourth movement, and the gentle phrases of the winds—and, JOY, the plucking of strings as the theme is restated. And then, the single voice. The soprano singing the Bulgarian folk song entitled, *das himmel hangt voll geigen*--and here, he raised his hands off the coverlet to include the others he felt were in the room, his children, friends, the minister, nurse and doctor as he translated Mahler: "Heaven is Full of Violins."

Did his lips move at the final notes of harp? Was a hand lifted, a finger, leading the orchestra in the final notes, the hand, finger, lowering slowly, fingertip the last to fall? We don't know. As Jaspe Twill, turning to his Keats, was fond of saying: "What do we really know anyway? What do we really need to know?"

A telephone rang and a dog barked once from far away as someone opened the door of the little room. His wife listened to the long held note of the violin fade away, and still she waited, not knowing when it ended, or if it did.

somehow the wrong box got opened and the delivery boy was fired but the young girl who found the flute on her doorstep looked up and down the street but figured it was a surprise from her father working in Bombay

on a tea plantation and had just parachuted into a jungle to put down a fight between one faction or another who didn't drink tea anyway so her father hiked the five hundred miles back to base camp then by mule to the plantation

where he fixed things up pretty good and sent her a telegram telling her a surprise was coming and to be sure she learned how to use it before he came home next year just as soon as the rains stopped and then the government stepped in and took him

to some secret spot and trained him to be a spy and so she didn't hear from him anymore but knew he was doing big things and that this flute was from him and she learned to play it without any help from a teacher and joined the junior high

school band and was given a standing ovation at the big concert and offered a big job playing the flute with the city orchestra and maybe a screen test for the movies if someone sees her playing center stage under the spotlight picked out to match her

new dress her mother stayed up for nights sewing while her brothers and sisters watched and hoped she would fall off the stage but she didn't but she took her flute home after one concert after playing the wrong notes at the wrong time

and buried the flute in the back yard and prayed to the stars that if her father parachuted into her back yard this very night she would dig it up again and learn to play it right but he didn't come and her mother took her to the special home for children with imagination and put her in a white room with a white bed bolted to the white walls and closed the door after the doctor gave her a shot and comforted her mother who cried and left the state and never returned to listen to her daughter

playing a flute no one saw but somehow liked each hearing a different music when she stood on their little stage and played to people rocking back and fort hand talking and some looking out the window listening to music that told them to jump or sing with her which they did and the nurses too bustling back and forth and...

giving meds and cheer while she played and cried lifting her eyes to the ceiling in the dramatic parts when the music rose and broke overhead like thunder rolling away then quiet as breath and soft rain falling

When I first saw her in high school, I thought maybe I had gone over the edge and was seeing things, I mean she was beautiful. Beautiful! I told my buddy Aaron about her, and he said, "What's she look like?" "Beautiful," I said.

"Ask her out," he said, unwrapping a sandwich.

"Are you crazy?" She would not go out with me. I'm a slug. Nobody. She's Suzie Cream-cheese, and I'm nobody. I write articles for the school paper. Big deal! That makes me a side step from Nerdness. Not even a step up. Just over. She goes out with Bolt Upright types, guys who peel bananas with their toes. I write stuff for the paper. No chance, Lance, no way, Jose. I'm out of it."

Aaron finished his sandwich and wiped his face with a napkin his mother had stuck in the sack. It had initials on one corner, with little silver bells. A wedding, I figured. Aaron had a sister. "When did she get married?"

"When did who get married?"

"Your sister."

"How did you know she got married? I never told you. Just happened. In Las Vegas; at some hotel. They were the thirteenth couple that day. In and out. The minister looked like he had a hangover. He mumbled something about being kind, and doing the dishes once in a while, and that was it. His wife stood at the door and chucked little bags of rice at them as they left. In the bag! Hit him in the head with a bag. A very moving service."

I watched Phyllis walk into the cafeteria, and into a gaggle of girls, their skirts flaring out like upside-down umbrellas. Three guys, in Letterman jackets, crowded around the girls, hitting each other, and combing their hair. One jock tossed a wadded-up napkin at her to get her attention, but she flashed that toothy smile that just about destroyed the jocks.

The cafeteria was also the school library—where they kept books. My Sophomore English teacher, Mr. Laferla, sent me there to check out THE RAPE OF THE LOCK. It was the first and only time I "used" the library. I was disappointed to find there were no good parts, just some stuff about fairies and nymphs horsing around with Belinda's hair, which some guy wanted to cut off. It had been checked out a lot.

I told Aaron I was going to write her an article, but he said that was a dumb idea. "Write her a song, you boob!" I looked at him, waiting to see if he was laughing. But he wasn't. One thing about Aaron, he was always serious about things. A song? I thought about it, and decided I might be able to do it, given my eight months of piano lessons from Mrs. Olson when I was in the eighth grade. I never appreciated the time Mrs. Olson took with me, teaching me to read music and letting me play in her recitals. Playing SWANS ON THE LAKE was easy, then I discovered the little kids were playing it.

The piano room was in the music building. (No one else saw the irony there. Maybe Aaron did, but he didn't say.) I snuck in through a window and began thumping away on the pianos with something like SWANS ON THE LAKE, changing a note here and there and throwing in a few runs up and down. I thought it was going pretty good until I looked over at the door where a face was plastered against the little window. One eye roved left and right and up and down, searching for the person playing the piano in a locked room. It was Mr. Metcalf, the music teacher. He had one good eye and it was busy. I don't know where his other eye was, but his good eye was roaming the room, searching. He didn't see me under the piano bench, holding my breath, hoping I wouldn't wet my pants.

Phyllis liked the song, but she felt nervous about listening outside the music room. I told her if she heard a big racket she should take off because that would mean that Mr. Metcalf was on to me. But he wasn't, and Phyllis liked the song. I snuck into that music room every day for the next two years. Old Cyclops never found me.

Swimming naked in the pool was something I took for granted at Inglewood High School in the '50s. Whether I was trying to beat Bud Kremer in the distance, or practicing water polo, we went as is.

I don't remember anyone asking why. Each day we swam we had to climb a ladder up to the rafters and jump off, holding our breath and the family jewels. The coach wanted us boys to be prepared to jump off the fantails of ships in case we were torpedoed in war. We never questioned that either, though exactly which war they had in mind was not specified. Just in case, they said.

Phyllis knew I played water polo, and when I asked her to come watch a game, she said she would. We wore white Speedos for the games, with little green Indians on the sides. We were the Sentinels. Few of us were sure what that meant, but we knew an Indian when we saw one. As luck would have it, I got my nose broken in that game when a guy took me out with his elbow as he turned to fire the ball. We lost the game, and from underwater I watched legs pumping up and down through the blood, wondering if Phyllis was watching.

When I graduated from high school, my father let me drive the old '38 Dodge over the pass to the San Fernando Valley where Phyllis was a senior in another high school. When she moved from Inglewood, I thought I would never see her again, but my father came through. I never understood why he let me take the car. I don't think I ever thanked him. I would now. If he were still alive I think that would be the first thing I would say.

Johnny and his girlfriend, whose name I've forgotten, could really dance. Backwards! She went backwards. At the Friday night dances at the Rec.—the 13-20 club— Johnny and ? danced backwards. The other dancers, draped all over each other, saw nothing. Sammy Bono and Dave Price were great at those dances. They were always squirreling around, making noise. Everybody loved them. Their specialty came at the end of the dance when the band was packing up. Sammy would get at one end of the floor, Dave at the other, and at a signal (sometimes from the drummer), Sammy would run like crazy towards Dave, and when Sammy was about ten feet from him, he would jump and turn over, his body facing the ceiling, and at the last possible moment Dave would catch him just before he slammed into the floor. It never failed to stir up the crowd. After that, it was everyman for himself as we looked for girls to take home. I didn't drive, but Aaron did. Jim Killackey had a little MG later, but not soon enough. I never thought "Sonny" would go on to TV fame and political fortune like he did.

But here we were in the Valley, with Phyllis looking stunning in a blue skirt that spread out like a big flower. Her teeth sparkled, and her red lips were curved just right. She had some teeth all right.

Johnny and Marilyn (I just remembered) were there for the weekend too, so Phyllis' mother said she would teach us to tango. I still remember "Blue Tango" playing from her record player as we dipped and swayed back and forth. Johnny and Marilyn never got the hang of it, and continued to dance backward across the room while Phyllis and I looked seriously at each other as we did the steps her mother taught us. It was a great night. It was the second to the last time I ever saw Phyllis.

Johnny and Marilyn left the next morning, and Phyllis' father, seeing we had nothing to do, flipped me his car keys and said, "Here, kid, have a good time." I thought that was something right out of a Bogart movie, like where he takes his cigarette out of his mouth and says, '*Here, kid, have a good time…*' What trust, I thought. His shiny, new Oldsmobile purred down the hill and around the hilly streets to Ventura Boulevard to the movies. I made a mental note to buy one someday.

I don't remember the movie. I only remembered that a goddess was sitting next to me in the dark theatre. I could barely breathe. Once I looked over and she smiled, lifting those tulip lips from her shiny white teeth. But I said nothing! Did nothing! Thought less than nothing. I've often wondered, since, what I would say or do if I had the chance. No, that's not true. I know what I would do. I think I would.

When we drove up to her house, the moon was hovering over the hills behind her house, framing her in its light, her face in shadow. I waited. "Jack," she said in that velvet voice. "We won't be seeing each other anymore." I wanted to ask her to repeat the words I heard too clearly, but I just sat there, stunned. Then: "Why?" I still remember that as the worst question I ever asked anybody anytime anywhere. "Why" is all right for an opener, something to fill a gap. But that was all. I had nothing to say but "Why?" And in the silence that followed, I knew my question would, could, never be answered. It was a life-moment thing. One of those too late to turn back times, so I gripped that beautiful bumpy steering wheel of that immaculate Oldsmobile and waited. Here it came.

"You've put me on a pedestal, Jack."

Many years have passed since that one-line answer to my one-word question. People have come and gone in my life; in hers as well, I have no doubt. I don't know that, because I never saw her again. Not once.

Wait! I take that back. Years later, I was watching television, and a commercial came on showing a woman with her head in a sink, washing her hair. When I saw that beautiful face come up, dripping water, her hair like whipped-cream, I almost had a heart attack. There was my—no, not *my*—there was Phyllis, blinking in the water and suds, smiling that devastating smile, her tulip mouth pulled away from those white, white teeth. Phyllis always wanted to act. Sometimes we would "do scenes" at her house. I would read my part, staring into her blue eyes, never knowing what I read. It could have been "I'll kill the son-of-a bitch!" or "What's for supper?" The lines were just lines. I couldn't breathe, much less concentrate on my lines when her face absolutely sucked all the air out of the room and out of my brain. She would pout a little (which almost did me in), and suggest we not "do scenes" anymore. We never did.

"Why?" There's the question. From this distance of time and miles, (I assume miles divide us, though I have no idea), my simple or simple-minded question has become a kind of mantra for so much of the world I cannot understand: wars, poverty, bad TV, really stupid wars and my own ignorance. The core of her reply was something very simple, but at that moment it was completely hidden from me. Much later, it began to dawn on me that the lovely Phyllis was saying, "Jack, I'm a young woman. We go out on dates, play miniature golf, drink those thick malts in Morningside Park, take drives in the hills… and you bring me home and say goodnight. I wanted, needed more. I could not tell you, and you could not ask for anything more. You put me on a pedestal I didn't want to be on. Good-by, Jack. I hope you'll be happy."

I am happy. I still ask "Why?" a lot, but my kids are used to that. My students are used to it, too. I still play a little piano, my own, with no eyeball searching left and right for the player. Memories come and go, some forgotten altogether. Maybe the mind holds onto the important ones, forgetting things it thinks it doesn't need, letting the heart remember things that appear and disappear like mist in the morning, or two kids bending and swaying to "Blue Tango" with moonlight framing a face half in shadow, a tulip mouth opening, now.

194

"Where were you when I needed you?" she asked. "I went to the war!"

"No, you went to Cleveland."

"I started for the war. How did I wind up in Cleveland?"

"It's a story for the ages," she said.

Oatmeal and conversation over, Henry Mott and the Missis, as he liked to call her, readied up the table, her washing, him drying. The family dog was let in to take her place on her pad in the family room so she could attend to morning ablutions, starting with her front paws, licking, nibbling between the claws, licking and smoothing, then her ears, rubbing them forward until they were wet and glistening. Henry watched in wonder.

"Can't you just watch her do that?" he asked. Minnie Mott blew a strand of hair out of her eyes, then swiped at it with her wash rag, spraying the window where hummingbirds attacked each other at the feeder."You know what's coming next, don't you?"

She turned her head away as the schulcking sounds began. Henry guffawed. "I can do without the cleaning of the parts," she said. "Why can't she do that outside?"

"You don't," he answered. "Yes, but I do it quietly," she said. "I don't make those great sucking and sloshing sounds either."

Minnie Mott brought in the morning paper and pulled it into sections before her husband dismembered it looking for the sports section. She knew him and understood him, two mutually disagreeable things, she thought, and said so to Rev. Nobs at the weenie roast and fund raiser for the "Fix our Town" celebration. "Knowing and doing are twins who don't look alike," she continued, wondering if what she heard about the Reverend and Shirley Bleak were true.

"There's Shirley Bleak," Henry said, pointing with a wiener.

A tall and leggy woman dressed in shorts and tank top climbed the nearest ladder and stretched herself up and up to pin a banner, one leg raised for balance. Minnie Mott sniffed. "Balance my Aunt Suzie. She knows exactly what she's doing. In my day we wouldn't wear those shorts at a civic function."

"What exactly is or was 'your day?'" He watched Shirley Bleak bend down to take a hammer from Rev. Nobs who had climbed a few steps behind her. Banners fell and wieners burned as people watched her take another step, stop, then laugh gaily as Rev. Nobs gave her a boost.

That night they settled themselves in bed, he with his stack of four pillows on top of his favorite pillow—flat, smelly and useless, his wife said; she with her latest Book Club novel. Then: "Henry, are we happy?" The question hung on the air, as her novel said, begging for space to land and be heard. He wondered who wrote stuff like that. He knew who read it.

"I think we are, Old Sock," he replied, knowing she hated the expression, endearing or not. He mused on the question as he threw each pillow in turn off onto the floor, thus letting his head get used to the flat, smelly and useless one she threatened to throw out. Somewhere between half-dreams and forgetfulness, he turned to her and said: "I thought we were happy fifty years ago, didn't you? Lots of water under the old bridge, and all of that, but still, our little boat is afloat and goes in and out with all tides."

He looked at the large crack running like a jagged scar across the ceiling, and noticed small pieces of plaster were beginning to flake off. She had asked the question before, wanting to know what could happen to spoil it all,-- and even if you knew, what then? "If you mean by happy, are we content, then I would say yes, but if you mean by happy, will we suddenly start ripping each other's clothes off and make love on the kitchen table, then I think not that happy. Besides, you set great store by that tea service from your grandmother, so sweeping it off like they do in the movies would not make a good start for sexual pleasure."

Henry Mott knew she was asleep, the book open to the page she started with. He also knew her question was rhetorical, and that the boys down at the feed store would not care about their nightly Q&A.

But the question hung in the air like those things do, he mused. He had answered it with a bit of wit and common sense, so he was satisfied. He had his flat pillow bullyragged into just the right position under his left jaw, his right leg raised as if he were pedaling a bicycle, his left arm half off the bed. What needed to be asked? What answers would serve after fifty years? Shirley Bleak and Rev. Nobs ... now's there's an item, he thought, bringing into focus her short shorts and Rev. Nobs' feverish eyes following her every move. And he wondered how many men or women, listening to the night sounds in their walls as the Autumn moon filled their windows, will turn their faces to the wall rather than ask the question, 'Are we happy?' What will be, will be, he thought, and inched his right leg higher into the power stroke position before closing his eyes. Outside, an owl boomed from somewhere close and he imagined the head pivoting full circle, its bright eyes fierce in the dark, knowing the mouse was just under the leaves at the foot of the tree, and he opened his eyes in the dark at the lift of wings and silent drop. And as sleep took him there in the bosom of his flat-pillowed world, he wondered if the mouse had lived completely, and was content as the sudden air convulsed, stirring the fine hair on its back,-- and did he know, then, it was too late to be happy or sad or full of questions. And if he did know, what then?

When their Washington farm sold at auction, they bundled her into a train to Peoria, Illinois, where they had paid a driver to take her up to Galena, to a sister living in an old quarry who said she would take her in if she didn't bring any animals and used some of the sale money to go halves on fuel. "She won't like Galena," one said. "It's colder than the Palouse. She may not find company soon. Rev. Nobs says Lutherans in that part of Illinois are a tight bunch." "She was always quiet," said another. "You know she wasn't from around here. I wonder, now, what Eldon saw in her."

She watched the fields along the Illinois roads, trying to see his face in the barren trees frozen on the window. A thin ribbon of water ran beside the road, and she thought of Hangman Creek behind their farm, and how they watched the ducks lift into their flyways, going south over the white Palouse hills. "I used to drive for Caterpillar," the driver said, turning his head. He hummed and hunched his shoulders. "What'd your husband look like?"

"I don't know," she said. He looked at her in the mirror as she pressed her face against the moon on the cold glass.

"Did I say I drove for Caterpillar?"

She stood on the brink of the quarry, trying to make out her sister's place on one of the dirt roads that wound around to the bottom where yesterday's rain dropped into a deeper blackness. She moved her suitcase to her other hand and started down as the last of Galena's lights vanished behind the rim. "I wish you hadn't died, Eldon. Or I'd died first. Oh, how I wish I'd died first."

She went down and down, stumbling toward the cluster of lights wedged between slag heaps. "You're the lucky one, Eldon," she whispered. "I'm not from around here! I'm not from anywhere anymore." When she could make out a line of small houses, she brought out the note she had scribbled and held it up to catch the light of the first house. Number 4. No street name. Just 4.

Four houses down, she found it, dark except for the light above the door. The shades were drawn. There was no sound from the house, or from the heavy machines that had eaten away at the hills until the quarry had created its own darkness. She set the suitcase down, and tucked some stray hair under her hat. She wondered why she bothered with the hat. "You have a pumpkin face," he told her, laughing, "and that hat keeps your face going higher." She never understood why that was a good thing, but she wore it for him; and when he died she wore it to the funeral, and to the reception at Mt. Hope church where two sisters from Rockford sang a patriotic song before she spoke a few words while women carried fried chicken and lemonade. Now, she fussed with it, reseating it on her head, wondering if she really did have a pumpkin face.

"Yes, who is it?" came a voice behind the door. "It's your sister, Lura. I've come from Spokane to live with you." She waited for a reply, but there was only the sound of a pump somewhere past the last house of the row. She knew the sound because Eldon had used a sump pump the year of the big rain when their basement flooded. "Comes from living out here in the Palouse," he said, "instead of in town like civilized people." She could still see him on his hands and knees in two feet of water in their basement, turning, tightening things under the water. "My hands are like a duck's feet feeling for crayfish in Hangman Creek," he said, laughing.

"So it's you, sis." The voice was tired, flat. "I thought you were coming next week, but come on in. Scrape your feet there on the iron thing. It's hard to keep the slag dust and mud out of everything. Come in and sit down. I was going to make a cup of tea. You still drink tea, don't you? My land, Lura, you look like you lost your husband and your best dog. You need to buck up if you're going to live down here. We call it a street, but it's just years' worth of packed sludge from the quarry. There's seven houses built for foremen and plant managers. Now each house has a woman who lost their man to the piles of slag or machinery, or the weather. That's what we are here: widows of the quarry. Do you take sugar or cream? I have milk."

Lura Mayfield woke in the night and listened to the rain run down the window, thinking it was just like home in the Palouse when storms rolled in from Canada and shook their little house with heavy rain. This rain was weak, though, intermittent, running out of the down spouts into the muddy stream pouring off the edge of their level into the darkness of the latest scouring. Four weeks had not been long enough to have good sleep, she thought, and four months or years will not do it either. She remembered too much. How many years did she have with Eldon out there on the edge of the world where geese offered the last and best sounds before snow filled the gullies and piled against their house and barn, muffling the days and nights, until they stopped talking, not wanting to break the farm silence as they looked at each other in passing, or caught at a hand over the table when the wind howled and the house shook. Now her days were spent walking from one end of the road to the other and back again, surrounded by tall slag heaps reaching to the lip of the quarry where she knew people lived and talked and grew flowers. Here it was run-off water from the powerful impact hoses that ate the earth away, and the sump pumps working all night to keep the water from seeping into the basements.

She wondered how her sister Emma had stood it. Otto Riggins took her away at sixteen to a life he painted of big cities and forests and flowing rivers somewhere northwest of Chicago, he said. Just the life for a young girl who wanted more than the monthly trip to Spokane where she rode the merry-go-round in Riverfront Park, he told her. When Otto Riggins saw her on the prancing pony, he said he knew she was the one, and he ran around and around, faster and faster, until he grabbed a pole and heaved himself onto a horse straining at the bit, its painted mouth open wide, gasping for air. Six months later, they were gone. Tears and curses did nothing to stop them. The last night in their bed in the loft, the sisters held each other close, promising to write and never to forget. The next morning she was already gone when Lura went to the large porcelain bowl to wash her face in the cold water, watching the drops fall through her fingers, creating little circles that spread out and out until they vanished against the side of the bowl. As she dressed and combed out her long hair, she wondered if her life was a little circle going out and out until it hit the edge of something and stopped.

When the first winter in Galena was over, she gathered her things together and told her sister she was leaving. "Where?" was all her sister said, and bustled about the kitchen making up a lunch for her and wrapping it into a red and black checkered towel to put into the backpack she had in her closet.

"I don't know where, Emma, but I can't stay here. I'm lonely and I'll stay lonely if I don't climb that muddy, rutted road to the top of this quarry and see what's up there. You've been kind, but it's not kindness I need. I don't know what it is either. But I've got to see if I can find it. If it's there."

Emma stared at her, then took her hands and sat her down beside her on the couch. "When I came to Chicago with Otto, I thought there was no such thing as loneliness. He was good to me and showed me the sights. We even talked about a family when he got settled; then he heard about this quarry and thought he'd try it, so off we went to Galena. It wasn't hard to find, even then, this great black hole with levels running around on the inside of it where huge trucks travelled all day and sometimes all night under lights that kept you from sleeping--if you could sleep-- waiting for the blasting of big rock, hoping the hill would not collapse and bury everything. I don't remember when I knew, or we knew, that this was not the life we wanted. I began to miss the solitude of the Palouse with its mysterious hills rolling away southeast out of Spokane. Isn't it strange that I would miss the very sights and smells I couldn't wait to leave behind?"

Lura stared at the picture of General Ulysses S. Grant on the table. "Otto bought that at a fair in Galena when we first came, Emma said. "He thought a lot of General Grant, but not President Grant. But he thought if Grant could live in Galena, he could. It wasn't long before he stopped talking about him, or anything very much. I still see him as he left the house, carrying his black lunch box. Something about a break in some line or other while he was working on the lowest level. The manager brought me his bucket and a week's worth of groceries.

I've come to know the other women in the houses. We sit like black birds on a branch, talking about how it was and where it was and when it was. All in the past. Everything we talked about was past. We never talked about tomorrow or next week or next year. Our men, dead one at a time from machines or illness, inhaling slag dust or falling under a four-ton truck, until it was just seven of us, huddled up against this tallest of the heaps, so tall it blots out the stars we used to wish on. One by one, the women have died or gone off until it's just three of us left. We stopped gathering of an evening to talk and remember. It got to be more painful than the deaths, so we stopped. We nod as we pass, bonneted and bent like women too used to the hard work and bad weather that have left us useless and old. But it's the memories, Lura. The memories that have consumed us, with their insidious sounds and smells and sights of other homes and times, until we're just memories, not living people, just memories walking up and down this dirty road."

She handed the backpack to her sister and kissed her on both cheeks. Then: "Don't *want* to do. Be! Live! Go back to those hills we both said we hated when we had to walk a mile to the school bus and sit in the front seat, knowing the town girls were sitting in their clean starched dresses, their hair in pigtails, with bright shining little black shoes. We hated that, remember? But we lived it, Lura, we lived through it and in it and out of it and helped our mother feed the sheep and helped dad mend the fences against the wolves at night. Remember, sis, those warm summer nights when we couldn't sleep? We'd wait until mom and dad were asleep, then go down the ladder, and out the door. We'd stand awhile, letting the warm wind run up our nightgowns before we started across the barn lot and past the sheepfold where the lead ram came up to the fence, tinkling his bell. Then up the hill, up and up until we stood on top, our arms outstretched, eyes closed, turning around and around,-- until you lifted your nightgown up over your head and danced naked in the hissing grass. I was mortified! But only for a second. Then I ripped mine off too, and we held hands, turning and turning under those thousands and millions of stars rolling across that great black sea of night. Remember?"

She had kept the name of the driver who brought her to Galena. He remembered her, he said, and asked her if he ever told her he used to drive for Caterpillar. She remembered that, she told him, and a great many other things, how he never married, his recurrent gout and his love of driving, and if he had no other plans for a few days, would he drive her back to Spokane, and then southeast into the hills of the Palouse? She could show him how the sunset looks on Hangman Creek where foxes watch the Poor Clares, singing hymns on their evening walks, and how the road winds down Valley Chapel Hill, and over the bridge past farms, smelling of cut hay and manure. And would he take her as far as Mt. Hope Church out in the country where she and her sister sat every Sunday, holding their plastic crosses that glowed in the dark? If he would do that, then let her out at Rockford where she could get her supper at the Harvest Moon Cafe? Could he do all that?

"What'd your husband look like?" he asked, as they drove west through silent fields, the moon rising up on the highway in front of them. "I'm going home to remember," she said, opening her lunch on her lap. "Carl, if you'll tell me how it was, driving for Caterpillar, I'll share this Braunschweiger sandwich with you." She leaned back against the seat and rolled down the window, taking in the rich, heavy smells, listening to him tell how it was, the boys and men he grew up with, and the loves he had known or almost known, pausing to look at her in the mirror.

"There's a big old moon sitting right on the highway," he said. "Must be the same moon they're watching in Galena and in Washington. Isn't that something?"

"Yes, that is something. That really is something," she said, and leaned her head against the cold window, her face looking back from the barns and dead fields. "That is really something." Then they were quiet, watching the moon grow larger on the road in front of them, until it seemed they must stop or hit it, already knowing they would hit it and keep going.

"I'll fix the tea, while you stoke the fire, then we'll let the dog out to sleep in the barn where he'll be just as warm and comfortable as on his pad behind the stove." He looked at her, wondering she could be so organized, compartmentalized, even now. But, why not now, he thought. Why should she be any different on this day. The media neither knows nor cares; the old dog will follow Neunaber back to his place after he has found what he is not going to want to find. Children and grand-children—great-grandchildren—all of them will learn in bits and pieces depending on who phones who first, or which neighbor tells about it. And the world will spin on, fast or slow in all weathers, and Neunaber will say what he always says: "It is what it is."

"Did you tell him goodnight?" she asked him when he banged the screen door for the thousandanth time.

"I did, and I checked on the new calf, and its mother to make sure the oat trough was full to overflowing. Water too. I left the barn door open, that way it will attract attention to any and all on the highway better than a smoke fire or sign saying FREE EATS!" He fumbled with two logs until a red ember caught the outside fuzz on the logs, sending up bright spirals of sparks into the chimney and out over the farm.

"The sparks will die outside, you know," she said. "Either in the cold air or when they hit the snow—if they're lucky enough to last to the ground." He watched her at the stove, her long hair pulled back against the sides of her face like the Indian in the painting he kept in the attic.

"Is that what we are, sparks?" She turned, and in her place on the window, was part of the moon. "I suppose we aren't much better, or last any longer. And when we die out the great galactic furnace, God's fireplace in heaven, will go dark and cold until he stokes it up again and new embers spiral up and up into some night sky for awhile. Is that too much thinking?"

"Not too much," he said, easing back into his rocker by the fire. "Not too much. Too little, if anything. Too little. Surely we are more fire than embers, no matter the age or kind of wood. We certainly aren't green wood that takes up space and won't catch until older, dryer stuff is underneath it, catching fire and heating up the new wood. We aren't that, exactly, but I guess we're something like a wood fire. Ours is getting hot now and you'll be moving your rocker back from it before lon-- like you do, you know, in spite of the many times I've told you to start back and stay there. You like that dance, soaking up the heat until your face burns before you move five feet back; then when your sock feet feel cold, in you come again, scooting that old rocker closer by fits and starts. There's runners worn on the carpet from your winter evenings by the fire."

"Maybe that's my embers," she said softly. "A path on this old carpet right where the smoke from their fire drifts out over the farmhouse. You notice the two dogs don't move though. That old farmhouse will still be sitting in that copse of woods until hell freezes over—if one of our grandkids doesn't take it for his garage. I doubt anyone will take this carpet for their house."

She got up and went into the kitchen at the first sound of the kettle. All the other pots and pans had been boxed up, with tags telling who to take what. "Do you want anything in your tea tonight?" He stopped rocking and watched a log break, sending up a flurry of sparks. He thought he might ask for milk, or a little sugar. "Well? Do you? Or will you take it anyway I bring it to you?"

"There was a time when I would have laughed at that. Doesn't sound right tonight, does it." He got up and tapped the top log with the iron tool he used for anything that needed prodding. The log settled into the fire but did not catch.

She stood in the doorway with the tray. "I'm using the blue service you brought back from St. Louis that time you tried to swim in the river and nearly drowned. When they called me, I thought you had jumped off the Arch! What in the world possessed you to go swimming in the Mississippi at any time, let alone in the fall with the leaves changing and falling is and has always been a mystery to me. Do you even now know what in thunder you were doing in that water?"

"Neunaber said he would buy me dinner if I would take a dip, as I've told you many times. I think you see a different thing in your mind, some devious reason why I would throw myself, clothes and all, into that cold dark river."

"It's true I did wonder if you were trying to drown yourself." She set the tray down on the table between them."I couldn't think that for very long, but I never came up with a suitable explanation. Dorothy Smalls down the road said I should be on the lookout for another woman, and that was why you did it, to drown your guilt or shame or whatever it is you have when you decide you've had enough—or it has had enough. I say *it* because the thing that drives you into and then all the way out of yourself is an eater, and it doesn't stop eating until there's nothing left to eat, and the shell throws itself into eternity."

"That's pretty heavy, that is," he said, stirring the sugar in his tea. "I take your meaning, though you know that wasn't the case with me that frosty afternoon with cheers and boos coming from Busch Stadium where the Cardinals were losing again. I had no such romantic reason, nor was I suffering from lack of love. I just looked at Neunaber, and he had that prissy cat look on his face he gets; you know the look cats have that says, "I know what you're thinking. I don't give a damn, but I know." Anyway, in I went and out I came, fast, but not fast enough to escape that eerie feeling that something in that river was waiting for someone to hop into it, and it rushed more waves, fast and heavy to snatch me away from the bank. I often wonder I could get out so quick. I had the strangest thoughts then that I should or could just give in to that roiling water that was over me and around me and threatened to drag me along with it under the bridge and down past St. Joe and clear to Memphis and on down to the gulf where I would be remade, refashioned. But then what? And it was in that instant I fought it. I floundered around until I grabbed what was left of the old wooden bridge and hauled myself up on the rocks. I never said all that, have I? I was afraid to say it for fear it was true, that something in that river wanted me, and that the next time I wouldn't have the old bridge to grab onto."

They rocked, and watched the fire flame out, then draw back into wood as if the flames needed more strength to blow up into the chimney." "I'm scooting in closer now. And you'll also notice the two dogs sleeping by the silo in this carpet have not moved a stitch."

"But I can imagine them suddenly running down that slope of hill, telling her he's coming through the woods, following the curl of smoke from their fire through the ruined corn to supper."

"But that smoke curling out over that old farm is still, false smoke that can't rise or fall. That's exactly what it is, false smoke coming out of a painted chimney and moving over a farm where animals never move, never die, and the two dogs sleep unconcerned about it all. I wonder if the man and wife inside are sitting by their fire, and if she has brought the old man his evening tea just as I have you all these years. We can't hear their thoughts, though I wish we could."

The snow proved too much for the slender birches outside their parlor window, and sluffed off with a soundlessness that made them look. "There we are," he said, "there in the window, looking back at ourselves, just like the couple in that house on the rug must be seeing themselves even now as their fire wears itself out. That couple in our window will follow our every move until we stop looking at the window. And then what? Does the reflection go somewhere else? Or is it gone for good, and the window just waiting for other faces to mirror back. I think I could use that other cup now."

She rose and went to him and kissed him on his head. "You're not gone all bald, after all, though I thought sure you would, just like your father did. It's odd what you wonder at or fear when you're young. I worried myself sick that you wouldn't love me if I got heavy, though the Lord knows that's hard to do on a farm. There's always milking and cutting horse weeds, not to mention the cooking and washing, and..." He took her hand and brought it to his mouth.

"There's those finger tips I loved to kiss," he said. "I still love kissing them. We called them knuckle-nibblers, remember? I wanted to kiss the worries from you, though I caused many of them myself. I have never told you how sorry I've been all these years for the heartaches I brought you. I was senseless. I know that doesn't explain anything. I've tried to understand it these last happy years, but I can't. I can't."

"Hush. And take that toad-stabber you call an poker and stoke up the fire."

"I'll hush now. It's been said."

"It's coming on night early now. Are you sure the old dog's where's there's some hay she can curl up in? She's not a pup anymore with her puppy fat."

"He's as warm as we are. Here, let me kiss those fingers. Both hands. There. Now, you try to stay put, and let that farm under our feet slumber on. All the animals are sleeping in their shadows, and the pigeons are finally roosting on the smooth rafters. You can almost hear the thrumming of their wings against the tin roof. No, sit still. I'll pour the tea. See, I didn't spill a drop. No, don't say anything. We'll watch the fire until we get drowzy and put our cups down. I'm there now ... I see you in a haze ... you're walking across the fields in that carpet, looking for me to come through the corn with rabbits I've shot ... shhhh ... you mustn't bother with my hand ... I'm here ... the fire will burn itself out ... and when our smoke's gone ..."

"Did I say it's getting dark earlier ... are you there ... the room is getting colder and it's snowing again ... the branches are heavy with it and may break ... but we won't hear it fall, will we ... why don't you answer me ... Neunaber will come around... won't he.... good old Neunaber ... good old ... but look ... the dogs are moving ... the smoke is rising ... "

Betty Jo Mukowski and the Hidden Chapters of Scripture

I

When her mother told her to sit down, cross your legs and uncross them slowly, but keep your knees together, the very prissy Betty Jo Mukowski was four years old. She kept her knees tight together as her mother taught her, and when she was fourteen, and Elroy Mather slid his hand up her legs, she snapped them shut so hard she broke two of his fingers. She was, as her mother said, a marvel of mechanics. At nineteen, and interviewing for a job in a sausage factory as apprentice to Moe Bobka, she sat down in front of his desk, crossed her long legs, then when she had his attention, she uncrossed them very slowly and brought her knees together, slowly. She had the job.

It wasn't that she didn't know how to count and add, but her legs, as Moe Bobka told Marty Burns at the local bar, were not just long, "they go clear to the ground, and when she puts her knees together there's just the slightest hesitation, as if she's not sure how to do it, or why, and in the micro-second of silky space, I've given her a raise five times."

"Wow," said Marty Burns. "Wow. And did you get a peek?"

"No peeking, Marty. I had to restrain every bit of male Id hidden since I married Bernice. But I knew it was there, nestled deep inside the no-fly zone. I knew and I looked her straight in her eyes as she brought those bronzed knees together like the lid of the Ark. So help me god, it was a moment."

Betty Jo, now twenty-four and weary of small-town life was ready, as she put it, to see, feel and know the world, but when her mother ran off with the TV repairman, she moved in with her saintly grandmother who gave her supper and showed her the flyer announcing a revival at THE TRUE LIGHT ROSE OF SHARON BIBLE THUMPING

OLD TIME RELIGION TABERNACLE (The Rev. Connie Wrench, Minister, and Hoss Marucci, Rector), Betty Jo Mukowski was in the front row, knees together, hands folded, an odd little hat like a box on her head, ready to be revived. Or something.

It was a warm southern Illinois night, with thunder a long way off. Humid, but nice, Betty Jo thought as she sat with her Bible open on her lap. She smiled at her neighbors and powdered her nose just the way June Alyson did in a movie she saw three times because she liked the way Peter Lawford sang to her and kissed her on her nose. She would purely like to have a nice man like Peter Lawford kiss her on the nose, she thought.

Children scuffed in the back rows or fell asleep on their mother's laps. Then a hush fell. Betty Jo Mukowski looked up from her powdering as The Rev. Connie Wrench rushed in from a secret flap in the back of the tent, and she saw Mr. Nice for the first time.

"Good Evening, all you sinners!" he bellowed. "Yes, I'm talkin' to you out there gettin comfortable in those new plastic chairs we bought after we left Peoria when their new sheriff saw fit to take away the privilege of people hearin the gospel…now you good folks of Greenville get to hear it. We gonner bring you the word tonight! Hallelujah! Give me a Amen, somebody!"

"Amen," they shouted. "Bring us the good news, Brother Wrench. We not from Peoria!" More laughter. Viola smiled and straightened the pleats on her new skirt that was catching in the hinge of her plastic chair.

"Folkses," he cried, "this here meetin's goin' to bring salvation and good feelin' to all of you here tonight. If you go away unhappy, or disgruntled in any way shape or form, you get your money back. How's that for a deal tonight? Give me a Amen!"

"Amen," they shouted. "What money, Reverend?" Laughter. The women in the back row laid their children on the grass behind them and noticed the words, Grace Baptist Church of Peoria on the backs of the chairs in front of them.

The music suddenly blared "Bringing in the Sheaves," and a heavy-set man with hair that grew black and heavy almost to his eyes bustled in from the secret flap and commenced to pass the plate. Some looked nervous since they had not heard any of the good news yet. Betty Jo smiled up at the Rev. Connie Wrench and cooed, "Mr. Reverend, aren't you going to preach to us? I'm ready to hear what you got for us tonight."

"Now honey," he crooned, "don't you worry 'bout that. The gospel's comin' just as soon as my Associate, Rector Hoss Marucci takes up a little collection to offset the expenses of movin' this here huge tent and all those new plastic chairs you all restin' in … give me just a minute and you'll hear the darndest gospel you ever heard in your sweet life. How old are you anyway, sweet cheeks? How'd you like to help me up here tonight? I could use somebody as pretty as you to turn the knobs of this beautiful music machine. Come on up here. Give her a hand, everyone."

People clapped, and men whistled as Betty Jo rose demurely from her chair and minced her way to the front of the tent where The Rev. Connie Wrench took her hand, bent close to her and whispered, "Honey, you come to the right place tonight. Yassuh … you come to the right place tonight."

"Folkses, I'm goin' to preach on Hezikiah 3:12 tonight, and I want everlast one of you to listen careful. No, don't go rummagin' around in your Bible, 'cuz you won't find that particular chapter, and I'll tell you why you won't find it—because it's one of the lost chapters of the holy scriptures you don't know nothin' about."

Betty Jo stood beside the music machine, and at a wink from Rev. Wrench, she flipped a switch and music burst loud and gravelly from the huge speakers on either side of the stage. "Turn it down a little, honey," he said. "Don't have to drown 'em all in noise, ha-ha. You doin' fine, honey. You just stand beside me and clap when I do and say Amen! when I ask for one. Can you do that tonight?" He passed his arm around her waist, and gave her a little hug, which caused the women to gasp and fan themselves. Betty Jo Mukowski smiled and gave herself a little twitch to settle her bosom in her new bra with the gay deceivers she got from the Montgomery Ward catalog.

"There we were, hacking our way through the underbrush near the Ufrates River which runs out of Turkey into the Casberg Sea, when all of a sudden a swarm of natives of that part of the mideast came shoutin and wavin their swords and such until we thought we wuz goners. But Rector Marucci here, man of God that he is, held his Bible in the air and I be dogged if the crowd didn't come to a stop right in front of us, mumblin and moanin. 'The Book … The Book,' they cried. And they fell down in front of us with their heads in the mud and their behinds stickin up in back like pinch bugs on a hot rock." The crowd tittered. Some shut their Bibles and leaned back in their plastic chairs that read Return to Peoria Rest Home.

Betty Jo thought the people were getting a mite nervous with The Revrend's message, since he didn't seem to have any message. Two women in the back picked up their limp children and were heading for the back flap, when heat lightning licked at the tops of the tall thorn trees across Shoal Creek and thunder boomed in the bottoms. Still the music blared and the preachers preached, and Betty Jo Mukowski began to prance around the little stage with the Rev. and The Rector in a three way two-step that delighted the young people and offended most of the older women. When it started to rain, people watched the dark ring at the top of the tent spread wider and wider until thunder roared above them and water poured in through the top, scattering the faithful to their cars. Betty Jo watched the tent sag until the poles bent and more water poured down on those still in their Peoria Masonic Lodge plastic chairs. The Revrend sang at the top of his voice, and The Rector danced a jig while Betty Jo thumped her Bible against her leg like a tambourine.

When the lights failed, the tent collapsed and the music stopped. Men laughed and threw their song books at the Rev. and Rector who fought through the women and children to the flap at the back, scooping up the offering plates as they ran.

Later, when the storm moved on toward Indiana, Betty Jo took stock of herself and the camp meeting. She wondered just how she got so brave as to dance in front of so many people. Her makeup was smeared from kissing the Rev. Connie Wrench in the dark, an act made somehow proper when he told her she reminded him of the temple priestess in the southern part of the mid east where he was initiated into the mysteries of Hezikiah 3:12, so she surrendered herself to his amorous kisses and touches and his promise to buy her a new dress after he ripped it when he moved his rough hand up her warm thigh and tried to pull her panties down. Betty Jo thought of stopping him by snapping her knees together, but he sang a strange song in her ear about corn dances seen and danced with the Apaches deep in the forests of New York when he was a scout for the government. Such secrets shared by this man, she thought, were given but once to mortal woman, and if he went a little beyond what she thought right for the first encounter, then so much the better that it was she who endured the caresses and torn skirt and ripped panties and bra with the gay deceivers than some poor farm girl who would have cried and carried on and called the authorities and maybe even tried to drown herself in shame in Shoal Creek behind the tent. All this she thought out. And she was satisfied.

The next Monday the girls in Lud's Drugstore giggled behind their hands as Betty Jo went about her business of convincing women that Voluptuous Fushia was just the shade of pink for them and their particular curve of lips. But her boss got the word from the Sisters of the Copper Skillet that "that kind of woman" was not needed in their town.

It is time to move on, she opined to her grandmother. "I am bound for something better," she said. "I am still young and mostly unsullied, and my body yearns for the touch of mankind." Her grandfather, sitting on the porch swing, put his hand to his bad ear, wondering what her body was yearning for, but she had already picked up her suitcase and was half-way down the white-rock road to the highway.

II

Betty Jo Mukowski's grandmother kept the postcard she received from Betty Jo in her Bible that had no hidden secret chapters. She showed the card to her husband rocking under the clematis vine on the porch. He looked at the picture of a young girl dressed in a red dress with a long red feather-boa wrapped around her shoulders, but he didn't understand who she was, and gave it back to his wife backing out through the screen door with a tray of cold fried chicken and lemonade. She grabbed the postcard with her teeth and set the tray down so she could sit awhile, watching the fireflies flicker on and off in the horse weeds beside the milk house where the bull roared and butted his head bloody half the night.

The grandmother sighed, and drank her lemonade, and thought of telling THE GAZETTE about her granddaughter's new life as the sun went down over the Illinois River that ran, as she liked to say, to the mighty Mississippi where sins and sinners alike were washed down to the great gulf of forgiveness and rest. She stood up to go in, then turned and looked down the lane to the highway, listening to a truck gearing down for Mill Hill.

That night, she combed out her long grey hair, and took out the postcard. Everything was close and still, save the cicadas' whine rising and falling in the trees as she read aloud the part that said Betty Jo would be sending them some money now that she had found employment, thanks to her mentor and friend, The Reverend Connie Wrench. Such monies as she could spare, she said, would come in the form of a check drawn on the Bank of Golconda, Illinois, a nice little place on the Ohio River where she found friends and employment both. Her Grandmother turned it over and looked at the picture of a big house set off the highway, with the words, THE QUEEN OF GOLCONDA PLEASURE PALACE, Just a few Happy Miles North of Paducah. Surrounding Betty Jo were several women all dressed in red, and behind them a line of men going up the wide-board porch and into the big white house.

She heard it raining, and remembered the tray on the porch, so she went down the creaking steps and out the screen door, still holding the post card which curled at the edges just where Betty Jo's red feather boa went around her shoulders. I hope she's happy down there in Golconda in that Pleasure Palace, she said aloud, and went inside, past the old dog sleeping on her gunny sack behind the stove, and climbed the stairs to their room, pausing on the landing to listen to the rain sluicing through the rain gutters. She got into bed and turned to the wall and closed her eyes. Tomorrow I will look up Hezikiah 3:12, she thought. It may give me comfort. I will send this postcard to Cousin Rose in Cincinnati. She always said there's nothing like a woman in red to get attention.

(Authorial intrusion) The nights along the Ohio River are warm and pleasant. Betty Jo Mukowski has "worked" her way up the social ladder and now has a room to herself. The clientele favors her with flowers and candy before heading north to riches or south to chiggers

in their socks, all satisfied that they have experienced love in ways
hitherto unknown in places like Cairo or Memphis or Tupelo. For her
part, the very prissy Betty Jo Mukowski, (now called 'The Scarlet
Flower') enjoys an active life. On her days off she practices yoga in
the garden; on Saturday nights she plays the tambourine while the Rev.
Connie Wrench and Rector Hoss Marucci rouse up the folks in their
new tent by the river. On Sundays she reads her Bible in the window
niche in the parlor where all might, and do, see her in her best see-
through scarlet dressing gown. Life is good, she tells her grandmother.
Her Grandmother tells the Ladies at Lud's Drug Store. The Sisters of
the Copper Skillet enjoy their outrage. Life is good.